DIASPORIC
VIETNAMESE
ARTISTS
NETWORK

ISABELLE THUY PELAUD AND VIET THANH NGUYEN
DVAN FOUNDERS

ALSO IN THE SERIES:

LONGINGS

CONTEMPORARY FICTION BY VIETNAMESE WOMEN WRITERS

TRANSLATED BY
QUAN MANH HA AND QUYNH H. VO

TEXAS TECH UNIVERSITY PRESS

This book is typeset in EB Garamond. The paper used in this book meets the minimum requirements of ANSI/NISO Z39.48-1992 (R1997). ⊗

Designed by Hannah Gaskamp
Cover designed by Hannah Gaskamp

Library of Congress Cataloging-in-Publication Data

Names: Ha, Quan Manh translator. | Vo, Quynh H., translator. Title: Longings: Contemporary Fiction by Vietnamese Women Writers / translated by Quan Manh Ha and Quynh H. Vo.
Description: Lubbock: Texas Tech University Press, 2024. | Series: Diasporic Vietnamese Artists Network (DVAN) | Summary: "Collected fiction by contemporary Vietnamese women writers, showcasing both established and emerging voices"—Provided by publisher.
Identifiers: LCCN 2023048066 (print) | LCCN 2023048067 (ebook) | ISBN 978-1-68283-206-6 (paperback) | ISBN 978-1-68283-207-3 (ebook)
Subjects: LCSH: Short stories, Vietnamese—Translations into English. | Short stories, Vietnamese—Women authors. | LCGFT: Short stories. Classification: LCC PL4378.82.E5 L66 2024 (print) | LCC PL4378.82.E5 (ebook) | DDC 895.92/230108—dc23/eng/20231213
LC record available at https://lccn.loc.gov/2023048066
LC ebook record available at https://lccn.loc.gov/2023048067

24 25 26 27 28 29 30 31 32 / 9 8 7 6 5 4 3 2 1
Printed in the United States of America

Texas Tech University Press
Box 41037
Lubbock, Texas 79409-1037 USA
800.832.4042
ttup@ttu.edu
www.ttupress.org

CONTENTS

v

INTRODUCTION

Forty-five years have passed since the American War ended, and Vietnamese women in contemporary society no longer face life and death situations due to bombs and bullets, yet they continue to grapple with economic and political upheavals, as well as societal changes and moral degradations. Especially after the normalization of United States-Việt Nam diplomatic relations in 1995, Việt Nam has integrated itself forcefully into the global community, bringing about an influx of new commodities, knowledge, and values. More Vietnamese have been exposed to new ideas and concepts of globalism, Third-World feminism, gender politics, and intercultural interactions, thanks to the internet, an increase in the diversity and accessibility of translated literature, and international travel, which has helped them to analyze, question, and even challenge dominant cultural values, norms, mores, and expectations.

This increase in critical examination of Vietnamese society and women's place in it has had a significant impact on the country's literature. However, in many of the works written by women, female characters still hold conventional values that perpetuate a heteropatriarchal mentality that is at odds with newly emerging views. For example, women's fidelity and submission, long considered noble elements of Vietnamese femininity deeply rooted in Confucianism, remain a prominent theme in works of fiction. Nguyễn Ngọc Tư, a highly acclaimed female writer living and writing in Cà Mau, the southernmost province of Việt Nam, lamented this reality while judging submissions for the 2019 Vietnamese literary contest, "The Other Half of the World," sponsored by the Liberatupreis-Frankfurt Award:

... the majority of women characters in this collection, *The Other Half of the World*, is submissive, vulnerable, and acquiescent. ... They are naïve, altruistic, and gullible in the face of sins, and always sacrifice themselves for others if a tragedy otherwise would strike their family. Compassion and empathy compel female writers to use their pens to celebrate miserable, submissive women while leaving women who dare to confront injustice and who know how to love themselves as much as they love others to remain in the shadows. Writing about sacrifice, resilience, and the endless love of women is a double-edged sword. It can result in locking them behind walls. Even if those walls are made of gold, existing in such a space is not freedom at all. (12; my translation)

In Việt Nam's heteropatriarchal society, where Confucian doctrines of hierarchy and masculinity are still dominant, feminism is deemed a luxury. A Vietnamese proverb says, "A worm that wiggles will eventually shrivel." Feminist sentiments in Vietnamese literature have "wiggled" since the 1930s. Female authors like Nguyễn Thị Kiêm (a.k.a. Manh Manh), Huỳnh Thị Bảo Hòa, Phan Thị Bạch Vân, Đạm Phương nữ sử, and Sương Nguyệt Anh, as well as male authors such as Nhất Linh, Nguyễn An Ninh, Phan Khôi, and Đặng Văn Bảy appeared, blazingly for a time and then ceased to "wiggle." Between 1955 and 1975 in the former South Việt Nam, Trùng Dương, Nhã Ca, Túy Hồng, Nguyễn Thị Hoàng, and Nguyễn Thị Thụy Vũ were often known as writers of existentialism. It was not until the end of the twentieth century and the beginning of the next that female characters more consistently exhibited more self-consciousness and resistance, making female literature more enchanting. Some of the female writers that have gained reputation outside Việt Nam are Dương Thu Hương, Phạm Thị Hoài, Đoàn Ánh Thuận, and Nguyễn Phan Quế Mai.

In regard to writing style, narrative techniques, and perspectives, these newer works share many traits. They tend to focus on one specific moment in the quotidian life of a character as opposed to chronicling their entire lives. They also prefer to dwell on the common as opposed to the fantastic so as not to romanticize life, thus expressing the author's true feelings about the evil or grotesque aspects of traditional humankind and society. Finally, the fiction articulates the author's aspirations for freedom, social recognition, compassion, and love, while promoting individuality and examining private life via a first-person narrator to reveal multifaceted, complex human psychological states.

Longings: Contemporary Fiction by Vietnamese Women Writers reflects these trends while also presenting examples of stories that break conventions. The anthology brings together twenty-two literary works from both prominent, well-established female authors and younger, emerging voices. *Longings* introduces English readers to the diverse styles, themes, and subjects that are contributing to a burgeoning body of contemporary Vietnamese short fiction. The authors come from various regions, backgrounds, and ethnic groups. Their narratives reveal the aspirations, struggles, sorrows, and joys of Vietnamese women as they navigate uncharted landscapes in the new millennium.

The majority of these selected stories were written after the year 2000, and many have been published in major Vietnamese literary magazines, newspapers, or short-story collections. Some of them have won national or regional awards. While many of the stories are set in contemporary times, a few look to the past and instill wartime situations with post-liberation views. For example, among the many famous writers in *Longings* is Dạ Ngân, a former soldier who fought against the Americans. Her story, "White Pillows," celebrates the extraordinary traits of a woman whose marital bed becomes a psychological battlefield. The character must endure her husband's impotence caused by a battle injury. The couple lives together and shares the same bed, but the wife constantly feels empty and must resign herself to seeking solace in the white pillows that represent her suppressed emotions and desires. On the one hand, the story depicts the cruelty of war and its aftermath; on the other hand, it condemns outdated notions of female dignity, as the main character seeks sexual gratification outside of her marriage.

Another story that is related to the war is Trịnh Thị Phương Trà's "On the Rạng Riverbank," which depicts a woman named Mịch who remains single for decades after her husband is killed in battle. The couple had been able to spend only a single night together before the husband left, ultimately never to return. For the remainder of her life, Mịch does nothing but long for her husband and reflect upon their brief time together. Such a depiction serves as a reminder of the monstrosity of war that left many Vietnamese women living in solitude, haunted by nostalgia.

The stories involving war in this anthology do not describe the sound of gunfire and explosions or offer gruesome images of bloody battles. Trần Thanh Hà's "Desolate Grassy Hill," for example, takes place in a mountainous region in central Việt Nam, where a man's flute playing conveys the hidden sorrow he experiences after discovering his lover had married someone else, after he himself was believed to have died in combat. He ultimately builds a life with a schoolteacher who had been made an outcast due to her bearing children out of wedlock. The story thus articulates the need to overcome or ignore prejudices and social stigmas. Human efforts to reconcile one's post-1975 life with the war are found in "Boozing with a Khmer Rouge" by Võ Diệu Thanh. Set in the years directly after the Sino-Vietnamese War (1979), a bloody period generally unknown to many international readers, Võ's story focuses on a female veteran whose strength is tested when confronted with the need to forgive.

"The Smoke Cloud" by Nguyễn Thị Kim Hòa conjures up a pre-1975 Sài Gòn where people rummaged through airport trash for items to sell and where nearby bars served soldiers' sexual interactions. The love triangle between Diễm Thuý, Bình, and Phillips reflects less a political tension than a love-versus-gratitude dilemma. The war's legacy is presented even more traumatically in "Mother and Son" by Phạm Thị Phong Điệp, in which the female protagonist marries a victim of Agent Orange, and the couple is thus unable to have normal, healthy children. Their adoption of a child abandoned by his real mother demonstrates the unconditional sacrifice and love Vietnamese parents typically have for their children—qualities that are challenged as the boy grows into a wicked adolescent character.

The legacies of war, as well as natural disasters and ineffective political leadership, resulted in poverty, tribulations, and social injustice even as the country enjoyed relative peace in the 1980s and 1990s. The majority of the population was victim to a stagnant economy and food shortages. Although author Trần Thị Thắng crossed the Trường Sơn Mountains and went South with thousands of other NVA soldiers to fight, her story "After the Storm" is not about the war. Rather, it is a realistic depiction of contemporary life. Việt Nam's long coast is hit by several typhoons annually, and each storm wreaks havoc, ravaging property and taking lives. In major cities, thousands of people, like the story's female protagonist who has lost everything, must attempt to eke out a living by leaving their hometowns and working as maids, caregivers, and bricklayers.

Fragile and impetuous women often face tragedy in Vietnamese literature. The heroine Thúy Kiều in Nguyễn Du's national epic *The Tale of Kiều* (1820) sells herself into marriage with a middle-aged man who turns out to be a pimp; the female peasant Dậu in Ngô Tất Tố's classic novel *Light Out* (1937) vehemently resists the arrest of her husband for failing to pay exorbitant taxes. Similar themes are explored in this anthology, including the unjustified suffering of the daughter in Tịnh Bảo's "Under the Blooming *Gạo* Tree," who loses self-control and accidentally murders a thug to defend her mother, which results in her wasting her youth in prison. Võ Thị Xuân Hà's "At the Border" depicts how many women have become the victims of human trafficking at the Việt Nam-China border.

The story ends with an optimistic message of moral redemption, while "Green Plum" by Trần Thùy Mai, involves similar themes but concludes on a more pessimistic note. Trần writes about some women's degradation with compassion, while revealing the all-too-common fate of those young women who must trade their bodies for survival as the free market careens along.

In the introduction to an anthology of Vietnamese short fiction by women writers since 1986, critic Đoàn Ánh Dương observes that Vietnamese women writers do not often attempt to subvert the patriarchy completely, but instead attempt to find equilibrium within the centuries-long reality of Vietnamese culture (11). The domestic sphere poses a challenge to many women, as men are still regarded as the head of the family, and feudal concepts of gender inequality remain rampant in society. External circumstances need to be taken into consideration as well: poverty, the expected role of the male breadwinner, and the pressures of socio-economic conditions often lead men to take their anger and frustration out on their loved ones or rely on alcohol to cope with their stress. In response, Vietnamese women turn to marriage brokers to find them a Korean or Taiwanese husband in the hopes of assisting their relatives back home financially, while also attempting to escape domestic violence, even if it is just as likely to occur abroad.

The Vietnamese patriarchy dictates how a person should act, think, and live, and often women grapple with how to balance the expected role of a nurturing mother and a caring wife with their aspirations for freedom and gender equality. Such aspirations are becoming more commonplace with each passing decade. Trịnh Bích Ngân's story "The Eternal Forest" can be read as a Freudian-influenced text that depicts how Vietnamese women indulge or suppress their true emotions and hidden desires.

Both Nguyễn Hương Duyên's "Longing in Vain" and Phạm Thị Ngọc Liên's "Innermost" address the issue of adultery. In "Longing in Vain," the wife commits adultery, while in "Innermost" the husband does. Although their motivations for adultery are different, both stories emphasize karma and seem to show sympathy for the male characters, thus revealing how concepts of patriarchal dominance remain in literature that ostensibly seeks to include more progressive principles.

For centuries, Vietnamese people have shared the belief that one's failure to produce a male offspring represents bad karma for immoral behavior. The wife in An Thư's "The Red Cushion" is forced to practice an antiquated custom in order to give birth to a son to continue her husband's family's lineage, because her pertinacious husband and superstitious parents-in-law refuse to believe in medical science.

While some of the stories in this anthology are content to poke lightly at social norms, or simply to shine a realistic light on them, others approach the issues more boldly. The aunt in Nguyễn Thị Châu Giang's "Late Moon" defies every traditional value that her older, conservative sister holds regarding gender expectations. Similarly, when the character Aunt Sửu in Trần Thanh Hà's "Desolate Grassy Hill" leaves her impotent husband and has a child out of wedlock, she defends her taboo behavior simply by offering: "I don't give a damn about what people say." In Trầm Hương's "The Haunted Garden," the character Hằng refuses to be affected by toxic rumors when she invites her brother-in-law and his children to live with her after her sister dies in a fire.

Việt Nam's urbanization in the past decades, and its increased global connectivity, have created a clear hiatus between city and rural experiences, which is reflected in many of the stories in *Longings*. Cosmopolitan views are offered in "Selecting a Husband," an erotic story by Kiều Bích Hậu. Leaving a traumatizing marriage, the character An ventures away from her agonizing fate, like a water hyacinth drifting to distant shores, following the current's whims. She resists the traditional mindset that a woman needs a husband, and she pursues physical fulfillment with numerous partners. She even aims to mold a man into an individual who is beholden to her own emotional and sexual needs. Meanwhile, during a trip abroad, the character Lan, in Nguyễn Phan Quế Mai's "Spring Buds," must decide between reuniting with a former Australian lover or dutifully returning to her husband and children in Việt Nam.

Unbeknownst to many foreigners, the Vietnamese are not a single ethnicity, as the majority Kinh people constitute just one of fifty-four different ethnic groups. *Longings* thus includes three stories about ethnic Vietnamese women, one of which was written by a member of one of those groups. Đỗ Bích Thúy's "The Sound of the Lip Lute behind the Stone Fence" focuses on a Hmong family in which the husband has decided to take a second wife. The story wrestles with how women in such situations can either resign themselves to a marginalized life or take active steps to secure their own happiness. Meanwhile, limited education and patriarchal assumptions make it difficult for the Dao women, Mắn and her sister Mẩy, in Tống Ngọc Hân's "Raindrops on His Shoulders" to take control of their fates. Niê Thanh Mai's "The Bitter Honey" is a heartbreaking narrative focusing on three women from the Êđê ethnic minority community who reside in the central highlands. While a matriarchal social structure allows Êđê women to choose their husbands and live with them in their own houses, the invisible ropes of ethics and commitments bind them to a traditional niche in their culture. The story seems to argue that even outside of the patriarchal system, bitterness and loneliness continue to lurk.

During wartime, women longed painfully for the return of their husbands and sons while managing to carry out all domestic duties. In peace, they continued to wait agonizingly for husbands confined to reeducation camps, and they had to risk perilous journeys when fleeing in rickety boats just for the opportunity to toil in a foreign place far from their beloved homeland. During these times, longing became a virtue of Vietnamese women which persists to this day.

This anthology contains stories that depict past longings as well as ways in which their longing expresses itself in many contemporary women's outlooks. But rather than connect longing to unwavering concepts of patriarchy, the stories reveal how new ideas and emerging notions of feminism and equality can add a new dimension to the virtues that today's Vietnamese women aspire to uphold. A woman's longing can be a source of power, a means by which to expose society's problems and even rectify them. While *Longings* aims to present an introduction to the vibrancy of contemporary female writers, it also seeks to instill in readers an appreciation of and hope for Vietnamese women whose stories reveal their inner aspirations.

HUỲNH NHƯ PHƯƠNG

PROFESSOR OF LITERATURE, HỒ CHÍ MINH CITY

NATIONAL UNIVERSITY OF SOCIAL SCIENCES & HUMANITIES

WORKS CITED

Đoàn, Dương Ánh. "Những khúc quoành của văn học nữ Việt Nam đương đại" ["Twists and Turns in Contemporary Short Fiction by Vietnamese Women Writers"]. *Truyện ngắn nữ đặc sắc Việt Nam từ 1986 đến nay* [*Selected Short Fiction by Vietnamese Women Writers since 1986*]. 2nd ed. Phụ Nữ, 2015, 5–12.

Nguyễn, Tư Ngọc. "Dát vàng nước mắt" ["Gilded Tears"]. *Một nửa làm đầy thế giới* [*The Other Half of the World*.] NXB Văn Hoá-Văn Nghệ, 2019, 10–13.

A NOTE ON THE TRANSLATION

Translating Vietnamese literature into English is like walking a tight rope, especially because the two cultures and languages differ vastly from each other. During the process of translation, we served as both translators and editors. While we attempted to remain as faithful as possible to the original Vietnamese, we sometimes had to add a few phrases or even an occasional sentence to a scene to make the meaning or intent more understandable to English-speaking readers. Our translations prioritize the story's context and content as well as the natural flow of the narrative and the voice(s) in the storytelling. Vietnamese literature does not undergo the same rigorous review process before publication as American literature does; therefore, we occasionally have accepted this role, as well. For the sake of conciseness, we removed redundancies, repetitions, and wordiness; we also rearranged passages when necessary for clarity. When making the changes, we were careful not to distort or alter the meaning that the authors have revealed in their stories.

Việt Nam is a tropical country, and in many of the stories, certain regional trees, flowers, or food might be unfamiliar to Western readers. In some cases, we preferred to use the original Vietnamese word, as in the title of Tịnh Bảo's story, "Under the Blooming *Gạo* Tree," because the *gạo* tree in this story is not significant as a species or as a symbol or image. However, in the opening of Dạ Ngân's story, "White Pillows," the author describes many regional trees in the Mekong Delta, and none of the Vietnamese names will be recognizable to Western readers. We thus used their English names so that readers easily can look them up and visualize the story's setting.

A few stories in this collection are a bit longer than their original Vietnamese versions. We selected many of the stories from Vietnamese newspapers or magazines, which often impose strict word limitations. Free of these constraints, we contacted the authors and asked them if they might prefer to include additions that elaborated on descriptions or plots. Võ Thị Xuân Hà added nearly two pages to the beginning of her story, "At the Border," for example, which affords the story a socio-economic angle. Tịnh Bảo also elaborated on the abusive male character in "Under the Blooming *Gạo* Tree." We also consulted with the authors when we made some minor changes to make their stories more readable and accessible to English-speaking audiences. For instance, in the original Vietnamese version of Trịnh Bích Ngân's "The Eternal Forest," the female protagonist's roommate does not have a name, and in order to distinguish them, we named the roommate Hạnh, and it by no means affects the story's plot.

Communication between characters was an issue in translation, because English and Vietnamese do not mirror one-another in casual speech. For instance, it is typical for a Vietnamese to ask, "Have you eaten yet?" or "Where're you going?" as a greeting, while an American might typically ask, "Hey! How's it going?" In some cases, we had the Vietnamese characters speak in a way that would be familiar to English readers so as to preserve intent, if not the literal wording.

Another conundrum of translation involves personal pronouns. The Vietnamese address each other with a variety of pronouns dependent on age and gender, rather than by first names, as is common in the West. A man, for example, can be addressed as *em, anh, con,* ông, *bác,* or *chú,* depending on age and relationship with the speaker. Thus, in Vietnamese literature, a character may be treated with various honorifics or titles based on the speaker or point of view, while their given name remains unknown. In our translations, we avoided confusion by adhering to Western notions of referring to individuals by a single name and adding necessary relationship indicators accordingly.

The significance of regional dialects and ethnic attributes are also impossible to capture from Vietnamese to English. More so than English in America or in other Western countries, Vietnamese differs greatly by region. Accents and terms vary between the North, South and central areas, to say nothing of terms specific to ethnic minority groups. Vietnamese readers will pick up on an author's background based on the use of language when reading a story in their native language, but it is impossible to engender such differences in English. The translations thus make no attempt to translate local slang literally, for which English has no appropriate analogy.

Another decision we were forced to make involves the use of diacritics (the accent marks above letters that inform how a word is pronounced and thus what it means). These markings give words drastically different meanings in Vietnamese (for example: áo means "shirt," *ao* means "pond," and *ảo* means "illusive"). We chose to keep the diacritics as they appear in Vietnamese to maintain the beautiful musicality of the Vietnamese language and to help those who are interested in learning the language look up certain Vietnamese words easily.

The most fascinating but also the most grueling task we wrestled with was in remaining true to the narrative point of view. In a typical English story, the point of view is normally clearly indicated, whether it be first-person limited, third-person omniscient, or third-person limited. For a variety of historic and linguistic reasons, this is not the case in Vietnamese fiction. Perspectives often shift, and details are presented from the perspective of varying characters who may not logically be privy to the alternate perspectives. In our translations, we attempted to alter the narrative perspectives to conform to Western conventions of storytelling, which provide the narrator with the necessary omniscient knowledge or perspective. This means that we occasionally had to change the point of view for various sections of the stories.

Translation is an imperfect act; thus, some nuances are inevitably lost. However, these minor flaws do not negate the value of the process. If one is unable to read the stories in their original language, translation is vital for unlocking the pleasure and knowledge they contain. We hope these translations do justice to the original authors' intents and talents, while also standing alone as powerful stories in English.

QUAN MANH HA AND QUYNH H. VO

LONGINGS

WHITE PILLOWS

DẠ NGÂN

In this region, kapok is a residential rather than a commercial tree. Some other popular, residential trees here include banyan trees, which are planted near river piers to prevent erosion; pink shower trees, which have beautiful blossoms; tamanu trees, which are used to make chopping boards; and sakae trees, which are used to make monkey bridges. Only those who have sophisticated taste plant a kapok and even then only one in a corner of their garden. During sunny months, kapok pods look like bats' wings dangling in the wind. They gradually drop off the trees and land on the ground. People dry them in the sun and then keep them in bamboo baskets or sacks. When they are not too busy with farming, they peel the kapok pods, remove the seeds, and put the fibers into a sack again to dry further. The fibers are used to make pillows and mattresses. In this rural region, local beds not only have regular pillows but also bolster pillows.

In fact, this story has nothing to do with kapoks. I briefly mention them so that you can imagine the scene further. Let's imagine that there is a woman who, as a habit, always refreshes her pillows before Tết. She lives in the city, so there is no land for a garden, and thus no kapok. But that doesn't stop her habit. She tells the pillow shops in the market to save some sacks of the fresh, cotton-like kapok fibers for her. She doesn't know how to drive a motorbike, so she carries the puffy sacks home on a bicycle. She washes the pillowcases, opens the pillow protectors, and throws away the old fibers or dries them in the sun to make them soft and fluffy again. She stuffs new fibers inside, which smell fresh and natural. Her pillows are like children who wear new clothing for Tết. The pillows lie all over her bed. She stuffs them with a half-a-century of emotions and suffering. If Heaven blessed her with beauty and dignity, Heaven also challenged her.

"If I don't hug a pillow, what will I hug?" This is what she says when I glance at the white pillows that occupy her tidy bed. She doesn't punch me in the chest or do anything violent, but it feels as if I had been punched in the chest, making it hard to breathe. *What if her husband had been cautious when crawling in like everyone else . . . by sliding on his back into the bomb shelter. . . . What if . . . ?*

My dear friends, she used to be very beautiful, undoubtedly. She was a Phong Điền countryside woman with ivory skin and elegant manners. Her face was slightly angular; not a meek oval face. Her youthful years carried her down the river's currents, like hyacinths floating on the water with newly blooming purple flowers. And he was waiting for her somewhere; people call it fate. They were compatible. He was a stalwart and caring gentleman. He was also from the countryside, the same district but from a different commune. Back then, I was a clumsy rural Southern adolescent while they were already a perfect golden couple, although back in those days nobody would describe them with such flowery words.

"You know, it would be weird if my hair hadn't turned gray," she's cried out many times. Her hair turned gray remarkably, right after 1975, when she was only thirty. She doesn't dye it because that would be time-consuming and useless. I feel like someone punched me in the chest again and I can't breathe. *What if he had been cautious when crawling in like everyone else . . . by sliding on his back into the bomb shelter. What if . . . ?*

I had heard about them before I met them in person. They were in the same subcommittee, a perfect couple, no other could be more perfect than them, people said. But . . . *What if he had been cautious when crawling in like everyone else . . . by sliding on his back into the bomb shelter. What if . . . ?*

During the war, she used to go to a farmer's house located on a dike embankment where her twin daughters were being cared for. That day she was with her daughters. Her husband's injury, caused by bomb shrapnel, was not life-threatening, but it was severe. She was beautiful and he was a wonderful husband. I didn't witness the injury and by the time I joined the military, she had already sent her children to her family in Phong Điền so that she could devote all her time to taking care of him in the hospital. Then, she returned to her subcommittee, and he was transferred to the subcommittee that I had just joined. It was said that he had requested the transfer because they needed some time away from each other. Everybody was concerned about it although they understood the situation very well: he could no longer fulfill his role as a husband, so there was no need for him to be by her side.

After spending a day with him, I immediately recognized that he was the kind of man that any woman in search of happiness would want. He was mature, the shape of his mouth looked cheerful, his eyes were calm, he talked politely, he was hardworking. No wonder it was said that they were compatible. But his skin started to grow pallid and dull. He looked reserved, and his laughter was no longer jovial. This is unusual for a person possessing such positive traits. A few days later, I saw him whittle a bunch of short bamboo sticks, wrap cotton balls around one end, and tie the sticks in small bundles. I asked, and he replied without hesitation, "I have constipation; I need to eat more fiber, like sweet potatoes or papayas, but I can't find them here. Whenever I defecate, I need to use these sticks." I shuddered but couldn't imagine how the bomb shrapnel must have wounded his intestines. I saw his wife wrestle with her plight and misery every night. *What if . . .*

It is impossible for a bolster pillow to replace a man who joins the revolution. Women like us rested our heads on diaries and a few notebooks, and held an ammo box, or a memento from the war, tightly in our arms. A strap attached to the ammo box allowed us to carry it across our bodies while marching. We coiled it behind us in the mud before worming our way down a secret trench, keeping all necessary personal items in that ammo box, including an olive mosquito net, a plastic hammock, some clothes, a mirror, a comb, toothpaste, and a toothbrush. You might want to know where we kept our towels or scarves. Well, we carried a large piece of parachute fabric on our backs, also seized in battle, for camouflage, and we wore checkered scarves around our necks, which functioned as towels, or as something to keep us warm, or to drive mosquitoes away. I held the hard, cold ammo box while lying on my side, imagining how she, my pitiful friend, was also holding an ammo box whenever she missed her husband and couldn't sleep. Nobody separated them; they had confronted their dilemma: they couldn't leave each other, and they couldn't be together, either.

He often rowed a boat to visit his wife. He departed in the early evening so that he could go to work in the morning. However, after each trip, he would no longer be the same person as before. He was losing confidence, his skin became more pallid, his face more gloomy. The men in his company were polite and said nothing. They asked no questions, and what could they have asked anyway? Of course they couldn't ask something like, "Did you and your wife have a good time?"

Behind his back, they talked about his situation hesitantly: "When they meet, they only hold each other and cry." I couldn't imagine him crying or holding her tightly against his chest and listening to her sob. If she cried too much, her tears eventually would dry up. Every day I looked at him from different angles and saw that the muscles around his mouth rarely moved, causing a depressing atmosphere to surround him.

She didn't visit him often, and when she did, she always stayed with him for two or three days. A young man named Liền helped

her row a small boat to reach him. She sat at the bow and held a
paddle. She made her own broad-brimmed hat and blouses. The
dark color of her blouse highlighted her beautiful skin; her long
hair flowed down her back, reaching her tiny waist. Her husband
would hurry toward her, smile genially, touch the bow of the boat,
and anchor it with a rope to a Y-shaped tree branch. Then he would
look at me mischievously. He wanted to be a matchmaker for me
and Liền, who, according to him, was a tall and robust man, with
wavy hair. Liền was around my age—and so compatible. I realized
that he was fond of Liền simply because he gave him and his wife
something interesting to talk about whenever she visited him. I had
no special feelings for Liền, but I admit that I liked his youthfulness
and strength. Liền often stayed and hung out for a while with them,
and he always asked her before leaving when she wanted to return to
her subcommittee so that he could come and fetch her.

On unofficial days off, she turned me into her younger sister. She
offered me tips for when I would be married. How to add spices to
a pot of sweet and sour soup. How to cut herbs properly and how
to throw them into the pot once the fire was turned off so that
the herbs' color remained green. How to make caramel sauce when
cooking *kho* dishes. How to make chili and garlic fish sauce for a
fried fish dish. How to properly cook white cowpeas with coconut
milk sweet soup. Her voice was clear, her heels soft, her eyes had nice
edges, her mouth was charming, and most importantly, she knew
how to manage a family budget efficiently. All men wanted a wife
like her. When visiting her husband, wherever she sat, he sat behind
her and wrapped his arms around her to help her with whatever she
was doing. At night, on the bamboo bed, beneath mosquito nets,
I heard them whisper, sniffle, turn their bodies to kill mosquitoes,
and then whisper again.

Suddenly, we heard a rumor about her and Liền. Night came. A
boat. Clumps of bushes. A creek. A small, remote riverside neighborhood abandoned by those fleeing the war. Bombed roads. Moments

of deep feelings. Liền was a young single, and although she was a married woman with two daughters, her life had been empty for years. Their affair became a great scandal ushering in judgmental opinions. The male superiors in my subcommittee were tactful and said nothing. However, her husband started to talk more, about all kinds of topics. When he talked, he looked clumsy and didn't know what he was talking about or what role he was trying to fill. There seemed to be a wall between him and his colleagues, and an invisible Buddha seemed to be whispering to us: "Don't discuss it. Don't exacerbate things. It's a normal human affair."

Of course, Liền had to transfer elsewhere. She must remain a dignified woman to maintain the respect of others, and her husband must remain a hero, despite his horrific wound, and play the role of a perfect husband of a woman whose reputation had been slightly tarnished. Her friendship with me ended abruptly, simply because she no longer came to my subcommittee to visit her husband. And he only went to visit her at dusk and came back late at night. I saw him a few times at correction training events or at year-end parties that united all the subcommittees. I was surprised to watch him from afar as she sat quietly and unnoticeably in a corner. She only left her seat when he walked at her side; he wanted her to be brave like him in front of others. Despite their efforts, they appeared more desolate—they both had salt and pepper hair, they couldn't even smile; gloomy like a water-damaged painting in a golden frame. The campaigns in the Spring of 1975 involved everyone; people ran and panted heavily, and boat trips ceased, and no happy life seemed to lie ahead.

After the war ended, each person was given a personal dwelling based on new criteria. Important bosses were offered large houses facing main streets; lower-ranking bosses were offered confiscated houses in narrow alleys. The pair moved into a townhouse in the former ARVN housing quarter for married couples. I was nobody and single, so I temporarily slept on a folding bed in my company's kitchen. When my company threw a party or welcomed a special guest, she acted as a top-notch chef. Sometimes I visited the military housing quarter, crossing the small yard full of various flowers, to see how stuck they were in their lives together. I saw that he was still very caring, but his wife's hair had turned miserably gray.

During the ten years following 1975, her twin daughters were in grade school. She shared a room with them next to the living room, which had ventilation gaps. He occupied a room at the house's interior that smelled of old food stored in the kitchen, because the odor traveled in through his room's ventilation gaps. He didn't mind it at all. After ten years, their daughters had grown up and needed to share a room of their own, so he reluctantly moved his bed into his wife's room.

She had a queen-size bed with a bunch of white pillows. She often cried out, "You see, if I don't hug a pillow, what will I hug?" In his single bed, there was a lone pillow, a small blanket, a backscratcher made from coconut wood, a few books, some mothballs, and tiger balm. In the next ten years, their daughters married and moved out. The room adjacent to the kitchen became a playroom for their grandchildren; toys were everywhere. Their shared room remained unchanged—the big bed was full of white pillows; there was a small shelf at the head of his single bed. On the shelf sat all the kinds of pills that one sees in a hospital room.

I wander through life, but I always miss them and want to see them again. Fifty years have passed since he crawled on his back into the entrance of the shelter and was hit by bomb shrapnel. There are more flowers in his garden: mums; pompons; chrysanthemums; yellow, white, and red peonies; roses; orchids, etc. He looks as calm as a Buddhist monk although he doesn't wear a brown robe. Her hair is as white as kite strings. She pulls her hair back into a charming bun and wears white silk clothes. Knowing that I am curious about her room, she gently pulls me to the entrance and turns on the light. The small bed has become a place to store pillows; the two nightstands on either side of the big bed have reading lamps, piles of books, and various other items. I immediately notice two pillows and two bolster pillows—white and fluffy. I know which side of the bed he often sleeps on because one nightstand has the bottles, tubes, and pills that he needs.

My thanks to the pillows for helping my friend become extraordinary. And my dear sister, you're so pure and shouldn't be concerned about morality. You are like a kapok pod dangling in the wind and then falling to the ground; you have offered life a marvelous white Gift.

THE RED CUSHION

AN THƯ

During Lam's first visit to Thành's house, she saw an ancient grave located in the middle of a quiet garden surrounded by verdant champak trees. The large stone grave was reminiscent of a mausoleum. Inside stood a small stupa pointing upward, engraved with a dragon holding a round, flame-covered pearl in its mouth.

"Whoever burns incense at this grave will become a member of the Hoàng family," Thành gently said to Lam at the grave.

Lam shuddered at his words. She had been in love with Thành for three years and had talked with his parents over the phone several times, but this was the first time he had introduced her to his parents in person. His words, which evaporated and merged with the gray and tranquil smoke coming from the burning incense, along with the sudden fragrance of champak leaves, sent a chill up her spine.

Thành's house looked different from the many ancient houses that Lam had seen. The main wooden house was quite long, painted red, and had green glazed roof tiles. On its sides were two separate additional houses facing each other and lanterns dangled in the verandas. Thành once told Lam that three centuries ago his eighth-great grandfather was an affluent man, and that was why he was able to build such an opulent mansion in the desolate, hilly area. Thành always talked about the house and the ancient grave with the deepest respect and utmost pride.

During Lam's first night at her fiancé's house, Thành's mother took her to the last room located on the right side of the main house. The room looked rather usual but had no furniture except for a large rectangular wooden bed that could accommodate five or six people. An old red pillow lay at the center of the bed. Despite its age, the pillow had been meticulously preserved and its striking red color immediately caught her attention.

Lam's future mother-in-law helped her hang her coat on the wall and then said, "Please sit on the red cushion."

Realizing that it was not a pillow but a cushion, Lam felt awkward but obeyed anyway, taking off her shoes and climbing onto the wooden bed. A cold air hovered over the bed that made her cower. She clumsily sat on the cushion with her legs crossed in a meditative pose. Thành's mother stood behind Lam and breathed a sigh of relief when seeing the red cushion fit her future daughter-in-law perfectly.

Lam spent the night all by herself in that empty, unfamiliar room. Thành's mother said that she often prayed to Buddha around midnight, so if they shared a bed, Lam wouldn't be able to get any sleep. She turned off the light and lay alone in the dark. The cold air rising from the wooden bed made Lam uneasy—she felt as though some distant history was rushing into the room. She stared into the darkness. Through the cracks of the door a dim light from the lanterns flickered across the floor. The ticking sound of a clock lulled her into a deep sleep.

Around midnight she was half awakened by someone praying. A layer of mist unfurled in front of her but she couldn't tell if it was a candlelight or an electric light she saw. She said to herself, So strange! I turned off the lights before going to bed. She then got startled by the shadow of a woman wearing a silk blouse with her hair tied up into a ponytail, her teeth blackened and shiny. The woman opened her eyes wide and stared at Lam as if wanting to tell her something.

Frightened, Lam was about to call out to Thành, but her lips froze, and her entire body was paralyzed. She couldn't utter a word.

A howling dog woke her. Her back was soaked with sweat although it was cold outside. She realized she had had a dream. In the adjacent room, Thành's mother was praying while striking a wooden bell at regular intervals.

A few months later Lam and Thành got married. Upon arriving at the gate of the house, the wedding procession immediately went to the ancient grave in the garden for a formal ritual. Lam heard people whispering but they were soon silenced when her oldest uncle turned his head around and glared at the crowd.

A clutch of burning incense sticks placed on the grave emitted straight spools of smoke that dissipated and permeated the entire garden. Lam recalled Thành's words when he first took her to the grave. A shiver went down her spine. But her feeling of discomfort vanished when the joyful music started to play.

That night, after the guests had left, Lam walked out of the bathroom and her mother-in-law appeared and whispered into her ear for a long time. Lam's face turned red and then pallid. The newlywed couple didn't sleep in their connubial chamber but in the room that had the large mahogany bed with the red cushion. As they opened the door, an herbal scent filled the air. Lam reluctantly thought about her mother-in-law's words earlier—she had to sit on the cushion before consummation.

The cushion was warm. Unlike other cushions it was round. Her mother-in-law had stuffed all kinds of desiccated herbs into it. Sitting atop it, Lam's seat felt warm, and the warm feeling seemed to crawl up her spine, neck, and the roots of her hair as if someone's soft hand were caressing and massaging her body to relax her muscles. Lam closed her eyes tightly and felt elevated until Thành's cold hands on her neck startled her.

"You must be exhausted. My family practices odd customs. Don't worry," Thành said affectionately. "You'll get used to them eventually."

His hands then gently unbuttoned her shirt. The night was tranquil. Plants, trees, and grass seemed to whisper to each other. Darkness. Thành breathed heavily.

That night, the shadow reappeared.

The mysterious woman looked the same and gazed at Lam neutrally. Lam wasn't sure if she was dreaming. The shadow then gradually vanished in the dim light. Lam wanted to reach out her hand to pull the shadow toward her, but she couldn't. When her feet were about to slip, she woke up. It was completely dark, Thành, lying next to her, was snoring. She felt a pain in her lower body after they had consummated their marriage and couldn't go back to sleep. Thành's mother was praying in the adjacent room. The cushion was no longer warm but the sweet scent it emitted still filled the room.

In the morning, Lam told Thành about her strange dream, to which he simply responded, "You had a weird dream because you struggled to sleep in a strange bed."

Lam wanted to share the bizzare dream with her mother-in-law. But when seeing her lost in meditation and wearing a brown Buddhist gown, Lam decided not to. Her mother-in-law was distant. She looked neither intimidating nor friendly. Her black eyes were as deep as the water at the bottom of a well.

The furniture in the main house's seven rooms was neatly arranged, unlike any house in the countryside that Lam knew. The first room contained the large wooden bed and the red cushion. Next to it was the room devoted to Buddha where her mother-in-law prayed every night. The third room was Thành's parents' bedroom. The fourth room was the living room that held the ancestors' altar at the center. The altar, with its large bowls of incense, tall flower vases, and brass incense burners, stood behind an antique, hand-carved wooden table and chairs. The fifth room was a library filled with all kinds of texts, including valuable antique Chinese books and carefully rolled-up landscape scrolls kept in wooden boxes. When Thành secretly opened a box for his wife to take a look, he said,

"These antique books and paintings are worth the cost of a house in the city."

Next to the family library was Thành and Lam's comfortable, fully furnished bedroom, but they weren't allowed to sleep in there until an opportune time.

The last room of the main house was always locked. "You may not enter that room," Thành warned Lam several times. "It's a family rule."

After the honeymoon, Thành and Lam returned to the city, but every two months they got on a train and visited his parents for a few days. During each visit, the first thing they did was go to the garden and burn incense at the ancient grave. They knelt in front of the grave a little longer. The champak garden was heavy with the smell of incense.

Even on hot days, Thành's mother, as a habit, dried herbal leaves in a frying pan and stuffed them into the red cushion. Sitting on it felt like sitting on hot coals. Drops of sweat covered her forehead and fell onto her short-sleeve silk blouse, staining it.

Lam's nuptial joy was soon replaced by the haunting image of the red cushion. After having sex on hot summer nights teeming with buzzing mosquitoes, Thành sighed as he inhaled the unpleasant odor of herbal leaves and human sweat. In the other room, his mother's chanting mingled with the repetitive sound of the wooden bell.

In Lam's exhausted sleep, she sometimes saw the shadow of the woman with a sweaty face, her hair tied into a ponytail.

More than a year had passed, but there was no sign of Lam's pregnancy. Her belly remained flat. Her mother-in-law became upset and told Lam to go to a Buddhist temple to ask for blessings. Her father-in-law always looked reticent and became more taciturn. No good news for Lam, even after she prayed to Lord Buddha at several temples. At mealtimes, the atmosphere was tense, and Thành got irritated whenever the word *pregnancy* was mentioned.

When they returned to the city after a visit to Thành's parents, Lam asked, "Why do we always have to burn incense at that ancient grave? Why do I have to sit on that disgusting cushion?"

Her questions ignited an intense argument.

"Because we must have a son. Don't you understand? For the last seven generations, each has had only one son. And I must not be the last one in the family's bloodline!" Thành replied.

"What if we can't?"

"Shut up!" Thành yelled at his wife. "That ancient grave is so sacred that it would be impossible for us not to have a son."

Looking into his furious red eyes, Lam realized that he had become a different person. But their argument gave her access to his family's secret.

The ancient grave belonged to the Hoàngs' eighth-great grandfather, Hoàng Dục Vĩ. In China, the Hoàng clan had been opulent and was known for their excellent martial arts prowess, which led them to become official border security guards who protected envoys that carried valuable items such as elephant tusks, rhino horns, and peacock feathers across the border. Three centuries ago, a member of the Hoàng family was charged with being disloyal to the King. Hoàng Dục Vĩ was afraid that three generations of the family could be wiped out in a single night, so along with his relatives, he collected his valuables and fled south. A local landlord who knew Hoàng Dục Vĩ through business dealings welcomed the escapees. The Hoàngs bribed corrupt mandarins, bought several lots of land, and seized the property of many local villagers. The local landlord was a dignified man and tried to help the peasants get their land back but was unable. Thus, Hoàng Dục Vĩ and the landlord became adversaries. During a hunting trip, the landlord was mortally wounded by an arrow. Before he took his last breath, he gave his family his last words:

"I should've been more cautious, but I know who caused this. May my adversary be cursed for the rest of his life!"

Nobody knew if the curse was real or not, but a few years later, the Hoàng clan became worried because they had no male to carry on the family's bloodline. Hoàng Dục Vĩ had three sons, but two of them died at a very young age. His third son, Dục Đạt, had several wives and mistresses but they only gave birth to girls. So Vĩ invited a soothsayer from China to help solve the problem. The soothsayer counted his fingers and suddenly the color of his face changed. Before leaving, the soothsayer said a few words to Vĩ in private. A few years later, Vĩ died, and on his deathbed, he told his family to put his corpse in a sitting position in a large clay jar—which would nullify the curse. Three years after his death, Dục Đạt married a sixteen-year-old virgin who later gave birth to a son. Since then, each generation has had only a single son.

After Thành told Lam the story, he was soaked with sweat.

"Now you understand everything," he said. "Although the Hoàngs have been cursed, the sacred spirit of my ancestor in the ancient grave will bless us. We'll definitely have a son."

Lam stared at her husband. She was an engineer and didn't believe in superstitions or the supernatural. She was skeptical about the ancient grave but realized how important it was for her to give birth to a son. She thought about the shadow of the woman who sometimes appeared in her dreams.

"What about the scented red cushion? Why do I have to sit on it every night?" she shuddered and asked.

"It's a family's secret. The cushion helps you get pregnant. It's a family tradition and you can't violate it."

Lam quietly approached her husband and hugged him from behind. Her arms reached up and held his muscular chest.

"I believe what you say, but we should see a doctor. I want to make sure there's nothing wrong with us," she said softly and affectionately.

"Of course there's nothing wrong with us. We're completely healthy," Thành huffed, and yanked her hands from his chest. Then, he turned his head back and looked at his wife furiously, saying, "My faith in my ancestors' blessing is immutable. Don't ever mention this again." He then stormed out of the room and slammed the door.

On the way to visit Thành's parents two months later, Lam's heart was heavier than ever. She was slumped in deep dejection and tears rolled down her cheeks. She watched the world race past in the train window. The rush of the wind and the clamor of the train were suffocating. Next to her, Thành's eyes were half-closed. She wasn't sure whether he was sleeping or not.

When Lam walked through the gate of the house, her mother-in-law looked down at her belly critically. Red lanterns dangled in the wind, and as she walked along the veranda, Lam felt as if the house's pillars were about to fall on her. In the afternoon, her mother-in-law dried herbal leaves in a frying pan while her father-in-law sat quietly at a tea table in the garden. As usual, Lam went to help her mother-in-law but when she got near the kitchen, she heard her talking to Thành.

"So, still no news? It has been two years! Her chest is so flat that it's difficult for her to get pregnant. Did you tell her about the red cushion?"

"She did ask about it, but I told her nothing," Thành replied.

"That's good. Our ancestors will bless us. You'll have a son soon."

Their conversation made her feel uneasy. What is so secret about that cushion? Lam asked herself.

That night, Lam couldn't sleep and instead stared at the dim lantern light seeping through the cracks of the wooden wall. She was obsessed with the image of the locked room that she was forbidden to enter. Once, she noticed that her mother-in-law kept the key to it in the room where she prayed every night.

Lam sat up while Thành continued to snore beside her. Her mother-in-law would still be sleeping too. She trembled as she entered the Buddha room clandestinely. She fumbled around searching for the key to the forbidden room. There, beneath a stack of thick Buddhist prayer books, she found it.

Lam walked back across the veranda beneath the red lanterns. When she reached the door to the forbidden room, it felt as if her heart might stop beating at any moment. She almost turned back around, but her curiosity was irresistible. She gently opened the door and used her cellphone light to look around. In the center of the room stood a table with an antique incense burner. On the table was a thick book written in classical Chinese that might be the family's genealogy book that Thành had once mentioned. Hand-painted portraits of Thành's ancestors lined the wooden walls, but there wasn't one of Thành's parents. All the figures were dressed in strange clothing and had expressions that were half somber, half confused.

Then Lam saw something that frightened her to her core: a painting of the woman who appeared in her dreams. Lam covered her mouth so that she wouldn't scream. When she was about to run away from the room, she realized her mother-in-law had been standing behind her, watching her.

"Mom . . ."

"Shut up! How dare you! If you give birth to a son, you'll have the key to this room. Why can't you wait?"

"I . . ." Lam couldn't finish her sentence. She dared not look again at the woman with a ponytail in the painting. She pointed her finger at the painting and asked, "Who is she, Mother?"

"One of our female ancestors."

"Not true. Sometimes I see her in my dreams, but I've never seen her in person."

"Are you telling me the truth? Does she really appear in your dreams? How could that be?"

Lam said nothing and nodded.

Her mother-in-law, after a long while, spoke slowly, "Well, I won't hide anything from you now because you'll eventually find out anyway. She was the first woman to give birth to a son after the Hoàng clan resettled here. She was sixteen when she married Dục Đạt and became his fifth wife. She was born into a poor family but was chosen to be his wife because her lower body fit into the cushion perfectly. You and I, the Hoàngs' daughters-in-law, have been chosen simply for the same reason."

She smirked bitterly after finishing the explanation and continued.

"You must've asked my son why you have to sit on the red cushion every night when you're here. It was made when Vĩ died, as the soothsayer had instructed. They poked his finger and the finger of his only living son, and their drops of blood fell onto the cushion. Thus it holds the cold blood of the dead mixed with the warm blood of the living. Dục Đạt's fifth wife sat on the cushion every night and that was how she became pregnant and later gave birth to a son. Although she came from a low-class family, she later became his most respected wife. Unfortunately, she didn't live long."

Lam cowered as she listened to the story. It was like listening to a dream. Her mother-in-law's voice was soft and emotionless.

"One stormy night, Dục Đạt's fifth wife was in labor. It wasn't an easy childbirth, and the midwife was late. She writhed in pain on the wooden divan but the baby would not come out, despite how hard she pushed. Dục Đạt was nervous and scared. He desperately wanted a son and lost his patience, so he used a sword to open her belly and pulled the baby out, although he had been advised not to. The baby boy survived, but his wife convulsed painfully and bled everywhere. Her eyes rolled upwards before the midwife arrived. Her blood was all over the mahogany divan and the cushion."

Lam's eyes felt greasy. Two teardrops slowly escaped her eyes and rolled down her cheeks.

"That son grew up," Lam's mother-in-law added, "and then when his wife was pregnant, she was overfed with nutritious food. The baby in her womb grew so big that they had to open her vagina up with a surgical knife to deliver it. Ten days after the birth of her son, she took her last breath. And when that boy grew up, his wife also gave birth to a single son. But when his son was young, he broke his arm while playing. The child's father blamed his wife for not keeping an eye on him and beat her so badly that she became permanently paralyzed. These stories are all written in that genealogy book over there. As for me, I gave birth to two girls during the first four years of my marriage. Just when my mother-in-law was about to get another wife for her son, Thành fortunately was born. I would've been in trouble if he hadn't been."

Lam looked at her mother-in-law and then at the portrait of the woman with a ponytail.

"Mother, what if I can't give birth to a son?"

"Impossible! The ancient grave is still there in the garden. The cushion is still in this house. How dare you say this will be the end of the Hoàngs? If you can't give birth to a son, that's your own fault."

Lam laughed sarcastically. She quietly left the forbidden room. The veranda remained lit with red lanterns.

The next morning Lam disappeared, and nobody knew why. She left a note sealed in an envelope on the red cushion. When Thành opened and read it, he fell to his knees. His wife had secretly collected his sperm and had it tested. The results came back that he was infertile.

Waiting for the train by herself at the station, Lam stopped weeping. The train's iron wheels began to inch forward on the tracks among rows of black eucalyptus trees. The blustery wind outside the window that seemed to pull the scene back sounded as if it were calling her name.

GREEN PLUM *

TRẦN THUỲ MAI

Plum's temporary home was nestled in an alley, next to a school and overlooking a temple. It was a somber neighborhood except for that flamboyant red house that the locals considered an ostentatious eyesore. Its front sign, Chastity Inn, drew attention to itself like a shameless grin.

When I stopped by, Plum was holding the hem of her dress in her hands and jumping back and forth over a charcoal stove. The inn's owner, Madam, and the other girls were not around. Her friend was squatting on the floor, throwing some plastic bottles into the fire, which produced a disturbing odor.

"Thank God, you're here!" Plum screamed gleefully, shaking the ashes from her dress and rushing toward me.

"Only a moment earlier, you were craving a customer," her friend, looking at Plum, said, enviously. "Then you took my advice and fumigated yourself. Look! He arrives."

Plum's friend then began jumping back and forth over the smoky stove like a sewing shuttle.

Slamming the door shut, Plum turned on the karaoke speakers. I flung myself onto a couch, grabbed Plum's arm, and said, "Let's

---

* "Plum" is an intentional translation of the protagonist's Vietnamese name, "Mận," which carries the connotation of something desirable in both Vietnamese and American cultures.

turn it off. I'm not here to sing, babe."

Plum turned down the volume.

"Well, we should play some music as if we are singing Karaoke."

Then Plum came near me and dropped onto my lap, throwing her arms around my neck.

Leaning her body into mine, she caressed my forehead, rubbed my shoulders, and pressed some pressure point on my neck. Plum knew what I liked: first, my tense nerves and face muscles needed to be relaxed. After hours of driving with a brain congealed and eyes throbbing, I would complain about anything.

The backs of Plum's hands were rough, but her palms and fingers soft and warm. She once told me that during her first days working at the inn, she watched her Madam soak her hands in warm water to slowly remove all their calluses. It took Plum several months to cultivate such gentle hands. She turned me around and vigorously massaged my spine, refreshing my frail body.

I stretched out on a couch that was as large and soft as a bed. Plum sat up and removed her shirt. I stared at her tender, supple breasts, feeling some uncanny warmth move into my body. My passion was like a fire that blazed intensely and then vanished as swiftly as it had arrived.

I got up and fumbled around for my shoes.

"Wait! Let me give you a massage."

I remained on the bed, letting Plum rub my neck.

"Did you stop by Cổ Kỳ? How was it? Anything new?" she asked.

"Of course! I went by that barren village filled with nothing but simple adobe houses with unplastered walls and warping planks." Every time we met, I had to make up a new story to please Plum. "Recently, people have shipped more bricks to the village to frame a new well. They just built some dams near the fork."

"Is that all?"

"I guess."

Preparing to leave, I took out my wallet, and Plum waved her hands, saying, "It's free for you."

"Business is tough, and you always exorcise my bad luck," I insisted. "Why free?"

"Please go." Plum pushed me away. "When you drop by next time, tell me again about the village."

"That's easy." I smiled, nodding.

As I buttoned up my shirt, Plum sat with her arms around her knees, staring at the wall. "Time flies. I've been away from home for six years," she said.

"Haven't you been back?"

"I told my neighbor that I was moving to the city to get a hair-styling license and during the first two years, I came home frequently. But then, my neighbor, On, happened to stop in here and saw me. I was stunned. My grandfather hasn't allowed me to return home ever since. He would kill me if he saw me again."

Plum chuckled. Her laughter sounded like a groan.

"So when you asked me to send your family money, didn't your grandfather question where it came from?" I asked.

Plum sighed, her eyes vacant.

"My grandfather might've had a vague idea about what I was doing all along. But now the neighbors know, which is a real problem."

I couldn't understand her family's logic.

Cổ Kỳ Village, Plum's hometown, was not far from the national highway. Surrounded by hills that stretched down from the mountains to the highway, the road to the village ended in a fork. The magnificent hills provided Cổ Kỳ with a spectacular view, but they also separated it from the surrounding towns. While tile houses were being built on both sides of the road's entrance, they didn't make the village look any different from fifteen years ago. Now I knew why Plum didn't take my money. If it weren't for her request, I wouldn't swing by the village. It took me only thirty minutes to rush in and out. It was nothing but a glance at something new.

Sometimes, Plum asked me to drop off money and gifts to her family. She never gave me the address though, only telling me to stop by the commune post office and deliver them to her acquaintance who would hand them to Green Plum.

"Another Plum?" I asked the first time she told me.

"I'm Ripe Plum. She's Green Plum." She nodded.

The words *Green Plum* made me drool, only because they reminded me of my childhood spent climbing trees to pick green fruits I would enjoy with salt and chili. Plum glanced at my heaving Adam's apple, her eyes narrowed in an inscrutable smirk.

"Why don't you give me the address?" I suggested. "I'll deliver the gifts to your family myself."

"Well . . ." Plum hesitated, and then evaded my question. She later said, "Green Plum is still in school. Let her be, please."

"Why did you say that?" I was furious. "Do I look like a pervert?"

"I know, but if you went to my house, the neighbors would suspect the gifts are coming from me, and my grandfather would throw them away. Also, I'm afraid that Green Plum would beg you to tell her where I live."

I nodded, emphatically.

With my jeans, necklace, and watch, I exuded an urban lifestyle. The appearance of a prosperous, city man might stir something in Green Plum's innocent heart, urging her to leave the village for the city, like Ripe Plum had done nine years ago when she hitchhiked here in my car. Back then she didn't even know how to wear perfume, high heels, or trendy clothing.

Driving long distances is harrowing. I crossed central roads bordered on both sides by dry fields. The boléro music floating out of the radio soothed my sorrows: *Long distance, I keep going . . .*

I arrived in the city after dusk and parked safely under a lagerstroemia tree. A shadow approached from afar.

"Who wants some balut?" asked a scrawny woman holding a lamp, who scurried to and fro with a basket in her hands.

The noise of selling fertilized duck eggs echoed in the rainy night, making me sad at first, but then bringing a smile to my face. Seeing the shadow hovering around without leaving, I quipped, "Is that all you are selling?"

"If you need something else, I'll go and get it," the woman hearing my voice offered right away.

"Alright. I'm exhausted and still stuck with this carful of goods. I can't go anywhere right now."

"I'll fetch whatever you need. Only fifty đồng for my service."

"Okay, please go get me someone from the Chastity Inn."

Plum came out in the rain. I slammed the car door. She coughed. I turned on the light. Plum waved her hand and said, "Please turn it off. We should be careful. Cops are fierce around here."

In the darkness her shoulders looked thinner and her breath was hot.

"Do you have a fever?" I asked.

"It's been busy recently, so I've been working hard." Plum laughed hoarsely.

"Busy?"

"My Madam is quite fortunate. She has been blessed by both the living and the dead. She just bought a new house and opened a coffee shop." Plum forced a smile and continued, "A cup of coffee costs four thousand đồng in the front, forty thousand in the back. Oh, come on, tell me about my village."

I told her that people were pulling power lines into the village, and they might have electricity by now. Her acquaintance at the commune post office informed me that Green Plum had received the money she had sent. Just as Ripe Plum guessed, Green Plum kept asking for her sister's address. I handed her letter to Ripe Plum. While resting at a station on my way south, I snuck a peek at Green Plum's scribbled words: *Sister, my school is so far, and everyone in*

27

town but me has a bicycle. So I'll move to the city and learn sewing to make money.

Without wanting me to turn on the car's interior light, Plum asked for my lighter so she could read her sister's letter.

She began reading. "No! Don't let her go to the city. She has to continue her education. If she needs more money, I'll send it," she said. "My life is blemished, but my younger sister is a fairly educated girl. Some of the other girls in the village don't have the opportunity to go to school like her," Plum muttered; her voice was weary but proud.

I slipped the money into Plum's shirt pocket, Plum moved back in the seat, but I pushed her out of my car.

"Please take it this time and eat better so you don't look so haggard."

Plum had gone to the bathroom and washed her hands before coming back to lie down beside me. I slipped my hand into her shirt. Her body was cold and soft today; only her sagging breasts were a little warm. My hands lingered on that sensitive area. As usual Plum snuggled her head against my chest and I inhaled her cheap cologne. After a moment, she pushed me away and looked at me with the most miserable expression.

"What's wrong?" I asked and got up. "I have money."

"I would have given you everything. But I'm not feeling well today." Plum frowned.

I remained quiet, somber, but not too surprised. A nomad myself, I knew this moment would happen sooner or later. Plum pulled me down, slipped her hand to my waist, smiling awkwardly.

"Don't be sad, I'll make you happy somehow."

"You don't need to. Please open the door. I want to smoke."

Plum got up and plodded across the tile floor. When she started to work at the inn, her Madam kept yelling at her for dragging her feet. "Only a rural girl tramps like such an elephant. Your footsteps sound like rocks striking the floor!" Plum had to practice very hard to shake that habit.

When I returned, Plum kept a shy distance from me. I pulled her closer.

"Why don't you go see the doctor? Do you want to die?"

"I will, but I'm waiting until next week. Is there anything new in my village?"

"Someone was electrocuted."

"Who was it? Do you know his name?"

"I heard his name was Bình. He was holding a sprinkler in his armpit while watering some plants, and unfortunately, there was an exposed wire that got wet."

Plum looked down and clicked her tongue. She said when she left the village, Bình was destitute. Things were just starting to improve for him when he died so tragically.

"The fork in the village has been paved with asphalt. From now on, Green Plum won't have to wade through mud to get to school." I switched the topic.

"Good to know," Plum mumbled to herself. "Who knows if I can take care of her forever?" Suddenly, Plum's eyes beamed. "Hey, why don't you get married? You can't keep wandering forever."

"Who would marry someone so dull as me?" I asked.

"Come on! Don't play dumb with me. If you want to marry my sister, I'll be glad to be your matchmaker."

I burst out laughing.

Plum seemed annoyed. "I know I'm the black sheep of my family and they have disowned me. They're all decent people, so becoming my brother-in-law isn't a bad idea, is it?"

"Geez. How did we get here?" I shook my head.

"So what don't you like about Green Plum?"

"Nothing. I haven't met her in person and thus know nothing about her. You have been very protective of her, and now, out of the blue, you want me to marry her. What if she doesn't like me, or slaps me, or chases me away for being rude."

"Don't be so dramatic. If you can love Green Plum truly, I'll tell you where to find her." Plum grinned, withholding her cough.

"I can't promise anything. Believe it or not, marriages are matters of fate. Who dares to promise anything like that?"

"I do believe in destiny. I think you should marry a countryside girl." Plum held my hand, her eyes glowing. "I'm a prostitute, and you've been very kind to me. You would be kind to your wife and children, wouldn't you?"

The old man's delicate fingers fumbled with the parcels I had placed in his hands. Aiming his nebulous eyes toward me, he said, "Forgive me if I'm wrong. Did Ripe Plum send these things?"

"No, she didn't," I dithered in silence and then lied. "A friend of Green Plum asked me to deliver these things to you on her behalf."

"Green Plum has lived in this town her entire life. How can she have a friend who lives so far away?"

Unwrapping the gifts with his bony hands, the old man pulled out a box of tea and a couple of bottles of herbal balm. Teardrops fell slowly from his blurry eyes.

"Please don't lie to me. I'm sure these are her gifts," the old man muttered. "If you know where she lives, tell her to come home. I want to see her again. The village is better now; she can come home and work for a living."

His words both stunned and pleased me.

"Definitely," I said. I was worried about Ripe Plum. She was sick, so how could she go home now? I then suggested, "Why don't you ask Green Plum to write Ripe Plum and tell her sister exactly what you just told me? I'm afraid that Ripe Plum wouldn't trust my words."

"My goodness! Ripe Plum has been gone so long. Please tell her that I'm getting very old and won't live much longer. She ought to come home now."

"I'll tell her, then. And I'll be back."

Bidding the old man goodbye, I felt a great burden had been lifted off me. I had no idea if Ripe Plum would dare to return home, but at least she had a home waiting for her. I was so delighted that I forgot my hunger.

This region had vastly changed since Ripe Plum had left for the city. Dozens of tile-roofed houses had been constructed. Restaurants lined the swamp. After crossing the bamboo bridge, I stopped at a place with the words *Homemade Food* handwritten on a basket dangling on the front door.

The owner, a tall and muscular man, welcomed me in. The restaurant had only a few sedge mats on the floor and bamboo tables without chairs.

"What would you like, brother? Fish porridge? It's right from the lake—super fresh."

The fish flopped around, making a soggy racket, as the man carried them into the kitchen in the back. Left alone, I gazed out the window. Delicate coils of smoke rose from tranquil shops into the sky. Several cars were parked beneath a shady tree on the pavement next to mine. Most of the sedans had license plates from other cities far away.

A steaming bowl of porridge was set in front of me. I looked up—it wasn't the shop owner, but a neat and strong-looking young girl in a silk outfit smiling innocently at me. Inhaling deeply, I felt a sweet and pristine calm embrace me.

I took a spoonful of porridge. My gut relaxed as the flavorful broth touched my tongue.

"Green Plum, did you get a fan?" asked the owner loudly.

"I did."

The name Green Plum left me flabbergasted. I put down the

spoon and turned toward the girl. She was waving a handmade fan made from a dry areca leave.

"Enjoy your meal. No rush," she said.

Green Plum continued waving the fan as she lay down next to my sedge mat. She eased up the hem of her blouse, revealing the smooth, tan skin on her taught navel. She spread her legs suggestively, her thin silk pants leaving little to the imagination. It was an awkward and crass but inviting exhibition. I understood immediately the meaning behind the words *Home Food* dangling outside the shop.

Green Plum raised her fingers to show me the price. She saw my bewildered face and must have assumed it was in response to the rate. She explained unapologetically, "You know, my dear . . . the price of gold is surging, and so is my . . ." Without finishing her sentence, she continued, "Nowadays homemade food is worth more than fancy meals in the city."

I was speechless. All I could picture was the look of longing that sparkled in Ripe Plum's gloomy eyes the last time I had seen her.

THE ISLAND

NGUYỄN NGỌC TƯ

A drizzle weaved itself into a curtain of fog, and the Trống Island seemed to sway as the boat docked to pick up "the Gift."[*] The Gift scanned the horizon but couldn't see a single thread of rising smoke. The island was serene. There wasn't a single soul in sight. Perhaps the mist rising from the water kept the smoke of the stove from drifting above the trees' canopy and the moss-covered boulders. On the way there, the boat tossed and jolted as it plowed through the waves, dizzying the Gift's empty stomach and making her feel nauseous. She hadn't had time for dinner. Oversleeping, the Gift dashed to the pier where the boat was waiting. A group of men laughed lecherously at her unevenly buttoned blouse, one lapel down, one lapel up.

The Gift looked at the lustful men, unable to remember if she had put the blouse on herself or if someone else had done it. The men brought her to tiny Trống Island by boat. They said if the Gift traveled along a range of menacing rocks, she would find Sáng's home, which was the most imposing one on the island. The Gift couldn't miss it. The men then maneuvered their boat back into

---

[*] "The Gift" is an intentional translation of the main character's Vietnamese name, "Quà," which holds the meaning of "gift" in English. Furthermore, it serves as a metaphor highlighting the commodification of women as "gifts" within the context of men's business affairs.

the ocean, not forgetting to tell the Gift that Chín Ái passed along his greeting.

But the man on the island didn't remember who Chín Ái was, or what gratitude had made him send such a bizarre gift. He usually received things like beef, warm clothes, a radio, and so forth, but nothing that promised sweat and moans. Every month, dozens of boats swung by to ask about storms. Even when the weather forecast didn't warn of any imminent tempests, the ocean was only peaceful if Sáng said it was. People trusted him the way they believed that underneath placid waves unfathomable perils were concealed. Sáng said he could predict the weather via simple "intuition." More than once he frantically warned boats from unfurling their sails: "It's not a joke! A fierce wind!" It was one of the people who survived a storm because of Sáng's warning who had sent him the sultry gift.

She, the Gift, shook her pants to dry them and looked across the small island, lamenting how dreary it was. Why didn't humans come here? The house she arrived at was even weirder. Wind permeated every corner of it, leaving it without a cozy nook. Was there something edible in the kitchen? Even burnt rice would be fine. Since early that morning, the Gift had had only one bowl of noodles at the Đông estuary. She waved her hands in front of her host's eyes and confirmed what she had been told. Blind. It was incredible that a blind man could live in this place.

The Gift said that she had been paid to come stay on the Trống Island and play the role of a wife for a day. They said her husband would be a blind man named Sáng, which means light. The Gift smirked and calculated her price, not offering a discount on account of his disability. All men were men, after all. The Gift didn't care about her journey to an island twelve miles from shore, to partner with a lonely man living on water and beneath the sky. It was like being marooned, the Gift thought when she first gazed upon Sáng's "mansion" nestled amid rocky ridges of vegetation and wildflowers. The rocks were just specs of dust on the surface of the ocean.

When the Gift got off the boat, she sensed that she had forgotten something—her bulletproof clothing. But she didn't care because her blind husband looked gentle. Curling herself up in a torn blanket, the Gift thought she would sleep a bit. Who said that a wife shouldn't sleep? As she thought about it, she could already feel herself slumbering. Lying straight on her back would help the Gift forget her life—the sound of someone knocking over a frying pan or ripe mangos falling to the ground in the front yard.

The Gift got up when the chickens had returned to their perch on the back roof of the house, after wandering around all day in search of food. Sáng was groping around and stumbling.

"Stay still, honey, don't panic. Your wife won't eat you," the Gift flirted while looking for food.

He sat down and leaned his back against the door like some neglected beggar. He knew the darkness that sheltered him would eventually be penetrated.

While rare, it was not the first time he received a woman. There was once a lady who came to stay for only a week before leaving, because she couldn't endure the suffocating solitude. "I would wait for you if you came to the mainland," she said as she left. Sáng could only smile. The ocean breeze soon whisked in salty air to replace her scent. It was like waking up after a six-day dream to the sound of splashing waves. The eternity of the ocean was a magic balm that healed all wounds.

A brisk wind roared in and the Gift groaned at the pain of the cold air striking her body. How could she bathe in such temperatures! Pulling Sáng closer to her body on the wooden board, the Gift unwrapped herself as the wind slid up her skin, making all her delicate body hair stand on end. The Gift nudged her husband to make love to her and warm her up. After clumsily groping the Gift's skin for a while, Sáng sensed a flame burning in every cell of his body. Even so, he left her skin cold whenever their bodies melted into each other. "Because of the wind," the Gift said.

When Sáng's hand touched the scar on her wrist, she said, "Oh, this was when I tried to kill myself."

The scar resembled a worm lying across her wrist right above the veins, and the Gift had numerous different stories for its origin. She said her name was Đào and her old house was located next to a small temple where a grove of cedars rustled beneath rain all year round. Đào's mother was a vocalist for a group of traditional singers in the Gò Tây neighborhood. They performed at funerals, and thus often got drunk. One time at midnight, the straw heap in the middle of the neighborhood caught on fire. The blaze rose to the sky and gave off a repugnant burning smell. The villagers soon learned that Đào's mother was still sleeping inside. Half a month later, her father remarried. On his wedding day Đào had joined some other children in the neighborhood to catch mice. As she put her hand in a burrow, a mouse dashed out and one of the boys quickly sliced it, injuring Đào's hand at the same time. Blood streamed down her wrist, mixing with the mouse's blood.

After unlocking from one another, the Gift's hair lingered on Sáng's neck and she flirted, "Call me Phượng, dear. I didn't have a father until I turned twelve. One day, my mom brought home a man with prominent facial bones and hollow cheeks; his eyes were mostly white. My mom introduced him, saying, 'Phượng, this is your father.'"

The Gift explained that her stepfather usually helped Phượng bathe when her mother was collecting money in the neighborhood. Half a year later, her mother found out about his inappropriate behavior and they had a terrible fight. The father was enraged and attacked Phượng's mother with a cleaver. Phượng stretched out her arms to protect her mother and was slashed. The father was so frightened that he ran away. Phượng's mother didn't call the bastard back. His name became a curse word.

"Hey, I just made up those girls to entertain you. This island is so desolate; it needs a human voice. At Đông estuary, they called me Mỹ Châu. My grandmother loved *cải lương** so she baptized us with the names of the artists. My grandmother was the owner of a rice mill, the wealthiest in Bàu Dừa. There, only us Châu sisters could afford to wear dresses that billowed like butterflies. When I was sixteen I heard that a buyer would stop by the mill to get rice. I had been sitting by the pier reading a novel when someone called out, 'Hey, dear.' Looking around, I only saw a blackbird turning its head, listening, and hopping around in its cage. 'Hey, dear, follow me, an impoverished life is joyful.'"

"I stealthily slid down into the boat, rolled up my blouse, and unveiled my body. As the boat drifted away, I burst into laughter along with the silver-haired boat owner. Bidding farewell to dresses, I became the thirteenth wife of the grocery-trading boat owner. That is, until the fourteenth wife showed up. I left and took the blackbird with me. The bird sang to me, 'Don't cry. What the hell are you crying for?' then it flew away, leaving me desperate. That's why I cut my wrist."

"Are you still listening?" the Gift asked before turning over on her side. Her heavy thigh was stretched over Sáng's lower belly. Her cracked heel rubbed against his thigh. Her body reeked, probably because she hadn't taken a bath since her arrival. Those who came to Sáng never knew that he used his imagination to trace their bodies in the dark. Using their voices, the sound of their smiles, the way they breathed, he sketched their portraits, knowing that they were only smoke when exposed to light. Raising his fingers to the lips of the woman to ascertain her colors, Sáng wondered how old she was, and what her name was, Châu, Phượng, or Đào. The Gift was exuberant, not living just one life that lasted only three sentences, like him.

Light stopped dancing across his eyes when he was seven and got chicken pox. At the age of ten, his mother had pulled him close and said, "If only I had birthed an egg, I would've put it in my bag and carried it with me."

---

* A form of modern folk opera, particularly popular in the southern region.

He had an unknown disease and became blind. Three years later, he woke up and could sense in the darkness that there was no one around him. He was the only one left after the boat, in which he and twelve other people were fleeing the country, went missing. In his first days on the Trống Island, he hoped that in those waves that kept rushing onto the shores, there remained his beloveds.

As the morning neared, after warming each other up, the Gift turned Sáng onto his back and asked, "Why did you run all the way here?"

He wanted to offer up some gripping story, but couldn't, so he joked, "I peeped on someone's wife while she was taking a shower."

The Gift laughed uproariously. Her left breast was pressed against Sáng's body, sagging and cold. Sáng heard that question time and again. Nobody believed that he lived on the island because he preferred it. Whenever he had offered, "Because I like it," other questions always followed. Anyone else who drifted to the island was always caught up in some crime or debt. Or they were misanthropes. They said that on the Sếu Bạc Island, there was a gang of wanted thieves. Everyone knew where they lived, but nobody bothered to go after them. Surrounded by water and sky, listening to the sound of rushing waves every day, humans become docile. After observing how they dug for water, planted vegetables, and raised chickens to eat, the officers acquitted them. If bumping into one another on the ocean, they treated the past as insignificant.

While fabricating her life story, the Gift kept asking Sáng about nothing. The part about drifting across the estuary and becoming someone's mistress was true, but the rest was only fabrication she added to give her life some glamour.

When she woke up on the island the next morning, she washed her face, which recalled the pubescent beauty that used to harvest rice stalks at Ngã Hai. One time, a sickle cut deep into her wrist. At the time it made her angry to think about how such a beauty had to labor under the roasting sun all day, her blood mixing with sweat.

So she became a prostitute. It may have been a shadier profession, but it was also more lucrative.

"Since yesterday, I haven't received any wounds and I've enjoyed free meals," the Gift said with gratitude.

This woman was so blunt, worlds apart from one Út Hên who had turned twenty-six the previous afternoon. The girl from the Rơm Market followed her boyfriend to a film studio, where they were making the movie *Billowing Grass* at an ancient temple. Someone asked her if she would like to act in the movie. The role was simple: a character riding a motorbike that turns her head to tell the main actress, "The enemies are after us." After shooting, the film crew left abruptly, as did Út Hên. For three years she worked with the film crew, never playing any role but someone riding a motorbike. She never even had any more lines. Film producers, after looking at her breasts and thighs, concluded that she couldn't land any other roles. But just the other day, she was assigned the part of a prostitute who cut her own wrist. Út Hên thought she would play the role with all her heart. She made a real cut, bleeding so much that it poured through the band aid and the antiseptic cotton ball. Thinking about the role made her dizzy.

"More dramatic than the lives of those who came before me, right?" asked the Gift, her mouth smelling like ripe mangos. Mangos were dropping onto the muddy ground all around them and the Gift tore into one while asking for more to take home. "If I get pregnant this time, I'll quit my job, go back to my hometown and deliver our baby and name him Mango."

Suddenly, Sáng trembled, enraged. He had expected the Gift to use the mangos to scrub her cracked heels. He tried to withhold his anger. He wasn't the one who had invited her here, so he didn't mind seeing her off at the dock as the men on the boat cheered her arrival. During the twenty-seven hours she was with him, the Gift never once even approached the kitchen. Who said being a wife meant cooking rice? The Gift only idled around, offering up different stories of dramatic young women.

The boat's engine eased into the crashing waves. The ocean would be rough for the next few days. Sáng could feel the colossal waves cover his body. She said she might have a baby. Was that true or something she said just for fun? If it was true, what could he do? He didn't even know her name.

RAINDROPS ON HIS SHOULDERS

TỐNG NGỌC HÂN

I t is the last Tết that Mắn will celebrate with her family. Afterward, Mắn, a Hmong woman will marry Chá, a Dao man from Hồng Ngài, a remote mountainous village in Ý Tý, where there are Dao people, old forests, and cardamom plants. Chá's family has grown wealthy thanks to the annual harvest of cardamom.

Nobody knows why Dao women never marry Hmong men even though their villages stand next to each other. When asked, Mắn's mother explains, "Probably because our cultures are too different, or because at one time, our communities had feuds and prejudices."

None of Mắn's friends or relatives marry Hmong men, and Mắn does not know why she has chosen Chá from the several men who proposed to her, especially when Chá had been married once before. Their engagement took place last week, and the shaman picked the most auspicious date for the Phàns to marry their daughter off to the Thàos. Mắn's family is by no means poor, earning a few hundred million đồng each cardamom season, which helps them achieve a respected position in the village. The Phans are a big clan, and Mắn is as beautiful as any other girl in Chu Lìn, and soon she will become Chá's wife.

"Do you love Chá?" asks Chanh, Mắn's younger sister, during lunch.

"No. Not yet." Mắn shakes her head.

"Then why are you marrying him?" Chanh inquires. "You know you don't have to, right?"

"I don't know."

"You must want to please someone in our family. Is it Dad?"

Mắn does not answer Chanh's question, instead urging her sister to go to bed.

In the morning, the two sisters go into the forest to chop two big bundles of wood to bring back to the village. Chanh is eighteen, and Mắn has just turned twenty. Both of them dropped out of school after the ninth grade. In Chu Lìn, they are considered to have received more than enough education, compared to most girls. Her mother once said to her, "If I add up the number of school days that your grandparents, your Dad, and I had, it's still less than the number of days you spent in school." In their family, only Mẩy, Mắn's older sister, finished high school. She then got married and had children. Mẩy married a man in Pa Cheo, but he is a drug addict and the government committed him to a treatment camp a few months ago.

During the Tết holiday, lots of wood is needed to cook holiday specialties for the people and their livestock, as well as to keep guests and elderly family members warm. Thus, when preparing for Tết, the ethnic minority villagers are more concerned about having enough wood than about having enough wine or meat. This is Chanh and Mắn's last wood-collecting trip and they need to give their machetes a break.

When they return home, Mắn notices a strange scene: a large cauldron of water boiling above a roaring fire and a slaughtered pig strung over a basin of pig blood. Why did Dad slaughter the pig so early this year? Mắn says to herself. Today is only the twenty-sixth!

Mắn's mother sees her two daughters returning from the woods and rushes out. She looks cheerful and speaks in a whisper, "Your sister Mẩy just gave birth to a baby. It's a boy, and she'll move back here to live with us."

"Why does she want to come back here? Where's she now, Mom?" asks Mắn, thinking it unusual.

"She's on her way here. She called early this morning and told us to get ready to welcome her newborn. Hurry up! Give me a hand."

"Let me take a shower first. I stink," Mắn says and rushes off to get her clothes.

The best wood is found deep in the forest, and the wood collected for Tết must be of the highest quality. The government permits Mắn's family to harvest from the forest and also allows them to trim the dry cardamom branches to use as kindling after the plants are picked. Mắn and Chanh had to leave at dawn, and they took along large balls of rice to keep them nourished. They chopped wood all afternoon, slept in a tent at night, and returned early that morning.

Mắn emerges from her shower and sees her father striking the wooden boards directly outside Mắn and Chanh's bedroom with a machete. He seems very aware of the noise he is making and uses a piece of charcoal to mark three consecutive planks. Mắn has no idea how he is able to remove the three marked pieces of wood so quickly and then lean them up against a langsat tree. Her father has taken them off to make a new door for Mẩy and her newborn to enter the house through. Mắn and Chanh must give their older sister Mẩy their bedroom and sleep in the kitchen.

Nobody knows when the Dao people in this region started the practice of not allowing women to enter a house's main entrance after giving birth. If there is no side door, a new entrance to the nursery chamber will be made by removing a few wooden planks from the wall. The new mother will use the new entrance for an entire month. Many families leave the new entrance open to the elements from the time a woman goes into labor until she gives birth, and then they cover it with a new door. Thus, when building a house, carpenters often leave a few planks loose and mark them so they can be removed easily when needed. If the marks fade over time, the owner of the house needs only to knock on the wall and listen, as Mắn's father has just done. The planks are like humans—they can talk.

Mắn grows introspective. If she gets married right after Tết, she will have her first child at this same time next year, just like her sister. But she doesn't know where she will be when she gives birth to her son or daughter—at her husband's home or her parents'. Will her parents-in-law be kind to her? If she gives birth at her parents', her mother will boil water with medicinal leaves for her to bathe in, as she is doing now for Mấy. This will put more of a burden on her mother, and the villagers will surely offer their judgmental opinions. She hopes that her parents-in-law will love her as much as her own parents do. Dao mothers are often like that: they prepare leaves for their daughter-in-law right after she gives birth. Leaves for bathing. Leaves for drinking. Leaves for eating. In her free time, Mắn's mother often collects medicinal leaves to sell and instructs her customers on how to use them properly. But Mắn cannot remember all her mother has done or said.

Mấy, three years older than Mắn, has been married for three years. In the past, she seldom came back to visit, as if she feared marrying a drug addict had crushed her father's hopes. She would often return home right before Tết and gave her father a few liters of San Lùng wine and her mother a new scarf, a few kilograms of pork, and water-buffalo meat as New Year Gifts. Her father seemed not to appreciate them. Mắn and her entire family knew that he desperately wanted a son, but her mother was unable to have another child after Chanh was born.

Her mother paces in and out of their house anxiously. The door has been made. The pig has been slaughtered. Some chickens' legs have been tied for later slaughter. The scent of the medicinal leaves is filling the air. The family is waiting for Mấy to arrive with her newborn. Mắn's grandparents do not seem pleased with the situation. In Chu Lìn, few married women come back with their children to live with their parents and grandparents. If they do, they will build a new house nearby. No one has behaved like Mẩy—she is coming back with a newborn that will keep everyone up all night with his crying. How will the family save face in front of their Tết visitors who will see diapers fluttering in the wind to dry?

At noon, well after the sun has burned the fog off the mountains, Mẩy's brother-in-law arrives at the gate with Mẩy and her two children on his motorcycle. The family rushes out. Mẩy holds the baby in her arms, lowers her head, and mutters greetings to everyone. The baby's face is fully covered except for his eyes, but he is too busy sleeping to open them anyway.

Mắn's paternal grandfather is known for being difficult to please. Traditionally, the Dao people spend months preparing an elaborate ceremony to welcome a newborn boy. Witnessed by the gods, their ancestors, and a shaman, they must be extremely careful in naming him.

"Why is she coming back with her newborn on the twenty-sixth, right before Tết, and with only two hours' notice?" asks Mắn's grandfather. "What's going on with her husband's family? Why are they treating their grandson with such little kindness? Do they think the gods live too far away to notice and the shaman is useless? Have they lost their minds?"

Per custom, Mẩy and the baby enter the maternity chamber through the new entrance. It is temporarily covered with a canvas that she pushes aside to walk through.

The baby squalls ceaselessly but his skin is glowing. Mắn's mother pulls up his shirt to take a look at his bandaged navel and says, "May the gods witness! Look at his round belly and skin. He'll grow up very fast. We'll celebrate Tết early this year to welcome you."

Mắn knows that her mother is trying to direct everyone's attention to Tết so that they will be less irritated about having new family members.

The baby is well behaved during the daytime, but he bawls constantly through the night. When the roosters start crowing, he is still bawling. He only takes a break from screaming for thirty minutes and then starts up again, as if something is irritating him. Mẩy tries to force him to nurse, but he flat-out refuses. In the morning, when everybody gets out of bed, exhausted from a sleepless night, the baby closes his eyes and sleeps. As Tết approaches, there is so much to do, and everyone works all day long, which aggravates their lack of sleep. Chanh stares at the baby snoozing under a mosquito net and says sarcastically, "Sleep well so you can torment your mother at night."

With heavy arms, Mẩn soaks bundles of bamboo strings in water to soften them to tie *bánh chưng*, sticky-rice wrapped in banana leaves. Her grandparents sit next to the fire with bloodshot eyes. A cat sits between them, also exhausted. Every now and then, her grandmother nods unconsciously. It is a pitiful scene. Mẩy asks Mẩn to look after her baby for a while. Mẩy covers herself carefully and runs out to buy something. She comes back an hour later, and thankfully, the baby is still asleep.

That night, the baby sleeps well. He only mewls a little every now and then as though he has heard all the adults' complaints. He sleeps well for three consecutive nights, and Mẩn's mother is obviously elated and offers flattering words to everybody in the family.

Mẩn's father invites Chá over for the family's year-end dinner. Chá is in his early thirties and works as a physician in the village's clinic. At dinner, Mẩn's father tactfully invites Chá to move in with Mẩn's family after the wedding. Everyone at the dinner table is astonished.

"Dad, what are you talking about?" Mẩn says, irritatingly. "Chá would never move in with us. His family's affluent."

A couple moves in with the wife's family only if the husband is destitute. In this region, thanks to cardamom, no man is so poor that he cannot afford to offer engagement presents to the bride's family and no man needs to move in with his wife's family. Chá and Mẩn's wedding date has been scheduled for the fifth of January.

Mẩn looks at her father as if trying to remind him it is not the right time to talk about this.

Her mother also wants to direct her father's conversation else-where, suggesting, "It's the Tết holiday. Let's talk about delight-ful things."

To her mother, this means the slaughter of their smallest pig to celebrate the Lunar New Year. The bigger ones with less fat will be saved for Mắn's wedding. Another subject of conversation is how this year's cardamom price is higher than last year's, and her parents will soon build a new house. Only after bringing up these positive things does her mother mention Mấy's return and her baby: "The baby only cried the first night he came out of his mother's womb, and since then he's slept without disturbance."

After dinner, when everyone is gathering around the living-room table drinking tea, Chá appears restless and asks for permission to visit the baby. Mắn's father waves his hand in rejection, saying, "No, you can't. Dao people have a custom. No man can visit a new moth-er's chamber until a month after she has given birth. Even family can't break this custom. And you're our guest."

"Am I just your guest?" Chá smiles and asks. "After the wedding, I'll live here with you. Will you still consider me a guest then?"

Mắn's grandfather is so surprised that he puts down the bowl of rice wine he is about to sip. Mắn's father grows excited and holds Chá's hand, insisting, "Say it one more time. You will move in with us?"

"Of course!" Chá replies honestly. "I've told my family about your request, and my parents are perfectly fine with it. Please let me take a look at the baby."

"Let our son-in-law see the baby," Mắn's mother says. "He's a physician."

Mắn now understands why her father is so fond of Chá—because Chá has many brothers and Chá can become "his son."

It is the first time the electric light in the nursery chamber is turned on. For the last five days, an oil lamp has been the only source of light. After taking a look at the baby's belly and face, Chá picks him up and examines the bottles of medicine Mấy keeps in the basket that contains his clothes. Chá says something very softly that Mắn cannot hear clearly from outside the room. Mắn sees Mấy lower her head and wipe tears from her face.

Chá exits the nursery chamber and takes a seat in a chair. After drinking a bowl of water boiled with leaves, Chá seems to regain his composure and stares into the yard for a long while, although the darkness makes it impossible to see anything. "Dark as the night of New Year's Eve," as the saying goes.

Finally, Chá speaks.

"Do you know why the baby stopped crying and now sleeps so well? His mother made him drink sleeping syrup for kids, which is not good for newborns. He was crying because he needed to grow accustomed to the new environment. Once he does, he will be fine. If he persists for more than a few more days, we'll need to take him to a doctor. When you allow Mấy and her newborn to stay with you here, you need to accept the fact that there will be some changes to your daily life. His mother probably didn't want the baby to disturb everyone's sleep, so she made him drink the syrup every night . . ."

Nobody says a word. Mắn's mother rushes into the chamber and bluntly, but compassionately, says to Mấy, "Why are you so foolish, my dear?"

Chá has to return before the New Year countdown, so no one dares ask him any questions. Mắn's father sees his son-in-law off at the gate and holds Chá's hands tightly as if he doesn't want Chá to leave. When he comes back inside, the sound of Chá's motorbike has not yet begun to fill the darkness. Mắn slowly walks out from her room. Since Chá arrived, she and Chá have not had a chance for a private word. During his visit, Mắn, every now and then, has secretly looked at her fiancé and caught him glancing at her as well.

Mắn walks to the gate and approaches Chá's motorbike. She stands next to him, and although she keeps an appropriate distance, she can feel the warmth coming from his body, and her face turns red.

"It'll be this way just a little longer," Chá says comfortingly.

"Go home," Mǎn says as she pushes Chá's shoulder. "Look, the rain has made your jacket wet."

"I can't leave unless you do something," Chá suggests endearingly.

Mǎn comes a bit closer to Chá.

"Come closer," he insists affectionately.

She steps forward, leaving just enough space for her to burrow her face against Chá's back.

Mǎn cannot remember what Chá said at that moment. Her feelings are indescribable. It feels as though she doesn't walk with her legs back to her house—as though some kind of affectionate silence had carried her away for a long while and just then brought her back to the veranda. Inside, the five-day-old baby is sobbing to express his infantile sulkiness with his mother.

LATE MOON

NGUYỄN THỊ CHÂU GIANG

My grandmother had given birth to eight children, six of whom died. Grandma died when Aunt Duyên was nineteen, and I was sixteen. On the day Grandma died, the sky erupted in a downpour. Fallen leaves littered the ground in the garden beside disheveled trees.

"She died at an inauspicious time, and is a frightened spirit," Mr. Nhiên said after counting his fingers. "Get a piece of white, homespun fabric and hang it on the altar. That will drive away any bad luck."

That year, Dad left Mom due to complicated, inexplicable reasons. Mom's life was caught in the doldrums. One day, I got up and noticed a piece of white cloth on the altar.

Since then the aroma of burning incense has filled our home. The red and blue pieces of paper on the wall make the rooms look like a Chinese restaurant but the atmosphere is deathly quiet. The three women in the house—my mother, Aunt Duyên, and I—are like shadows living and moving in our own private worlds.

The rainy season ended. The sky became limpid and the air cold. The trunk of a plum tree had been eaten by worms and stood in a corner of the garden among a tangle of weeds. In the morning I went to get my bicycle to go school and experienced a great sense of foreboding, as if Grandma were sitting near me and telling me,

"That tree is dead." I lowered my head and said to myself, Life and Death—that's the law of the world. I shuddered at the idea that one day I could die without having accomplished anything, just like that plum tree.

The older Aunt Duyên got, the more beautiful she became. Her eyes were bright and her eyebrows arched elegantly. Her light-skinned face was framed by a unique haircut that swept her black locks toward the back of her head. Auntie was passionate about several things but indifferent toward everything else—so capricious. Her life resembled an abstract painting characterized by large, barely visible black strokes among which thin red strokes slithered in no particular order. These strokes were like the smoldering remains of a fire that could burst back into a blaze and burn everything into ashes.

To her, I was merely a naïve young girl. I was studious but ridiculously and pitifully ignorant. To me, Auntie was neither too close nor too distant. She led an unusual life, often exaggerated things a bit, and then laughed at herself, which I found rather annoying. But sometimes, I wanted to be like her—leaving everything behind for the sake of living completely carefree. But I remained a good and meek girl living in my own realm of love and hatred, and nothing could change me.

I climbed up to Auntie's small room in the attic a few times. Several unfinished paintings lay about, and even the finished ones were incomprehensible to me. A few dust-caked bookshelves held some Bibles, Buddhist books, Kim Dung's novels, thick classics, and a few books about palm reading. Once, Auntie was sitting with her legs on the desk, extending her arm to turn on the cassette player. The horrible noise that came out seemed to harmonize with the big cobwebs hanging in the room's corners.

"Do you like it?" she looked at me and asked.

"Not really. I prefer relaxing music."

"What about the paintings? Are they beautiful?" Her mind was seemingly wandering elsewhere. "My friends gave them to me."

I smiled, and neither nodded nor shook my head.

"Yes. They're beautiful, but I don't understand them."

"You don't need to understand them. If you think they're beautiful, that's enough." She smiled slightly and then looked up at the window. A bright star in the sky shown at the corner of the view. "It's a lonely star." Auntie sighed.

She then hummed a song, her eyes watery. After a while, her head dropped to one side, her eyes and mouth closed, and she fell asleep. At that moment, Auntie looked like Mom sleeping peacefully when she was younger.

Gradually, it dawned on me that Mom was lonely. She relied on spirituality and everything else besides me and Auntie to give her life meaning. But Mom was still lonely. Her deep feelings and longing for Dad made her age rapidly. He never came back, but Mom remained hopeful and kept waiting for him.

"Why do you torment yourself over that bastard?" Auntie said boldly to Mom. "Even if he comes back, he brings you nothing good."

"I'm not tormenting myself," Mom defended herself feebly. "But in life, we must be forgiving."

Auntie pouted and immediately turned her face toward the door. Mom and I were sitting on the couch. It was late in the afternoon. As usual, the spirit of Grandma returned wearing a white silk blouse, and her hair tied in two buns. She wandered around the garden reliving memories although she could no longer touch anything.

Auntie coughed and told Mom, "I'm going on a field trip with some guys tomorrow. Living in the city is stressful."

"Nonsense!" Mom shook her head. "You're an adult now and should get married. Young people like you are immature and reckless," Mom frowned and exhorted. "A woman must be gentle and know how to manage a household efficiently. Look at yourself."

Auntie was stubborn and shook her head in defiance.

"I'm leaving tomorrow, even if you don't approve. You're a gentle and responsible woman, but that bastard left you, anyway."

Mom's face turned pallid and she frowned. I looked at Auntie and said nothing. If I were my aunt, I would leave, too. At least, I would be able to change my monotonous life for the better, so that in my old age I would have something interesting to look back on.

Hội came over. He sat next to a vase of withered asters in the living room with a jaded expression on his face. I didn't like Hội but didn't want to upset him. I found him boring. He always surrounded himself with books and wore glasses with very thick lenses. Hội seemed to be floating on the surface of life. My aunt once said he was a pitiful chump.

"Please tell him I'm not feeling well, so I don't have to see him today," I mumbled to Mom.

"You can't do that. Be polite," Mom said while arranging the paper offerings for the dead on her bed. "Go out there and talk to him. I think he's a fine man. Nothing's wrong with him."

I obeyed Mom reluctantly and felt drained of all my energy. I put a cold expression on my face. Auntie stood at the door and pulled my hand, saying, "If you don't like him, tell him so. It's best for both of you."

I looked at Hội sitting on the couch, leaning forward, and wondered to myself how he could be so pitiful. I worried that one day I would be as pitiful as him.

"Hoi, you should leave. Our relationship isn't going to change. I'm actually seeing someone," I said.

I then saw him off at the gate. It was a moonlit night and the wind blew the leaves off the trees. I closed the door, went inside, and felt relieved.

Aunt Duyên had been gone for over a month without sending any word home. Mom became quieter amid all the incense smoke and the somber garden full of rustling leaves. I biked to school every day and frittered time away in the library or in coffee shops with friends.

One day, Auntie sent home a letter, informing us that she was dropping out of school. She wanted to test her luck by joining an affluent man from Hà Nội on a business trip. In today's society, having a lot of money meant living in paradise. All life's values were impermeable. She wrote, "I'll be away for a few days. I'm not sure about the future, but I remain optimistic. One is happy when one has something to wait for, right?"

The letter left my mother dazed.

"How come young people nowadays are so different from my generation? This is not a good idea," she complained.

"Auntie is just trying to make a life for herself," I defended Auntie. "As long as she's happy, that's all that matters."

I climbed up to the attic. Through the window, I gazed at a single star that looked as if it were nailed onto the sky. I thought, wherever Auntie is now, she can't be as lonely and dismal as that star.

One day, Auntie came home. She had gained some weight. Her beautiful eyes were partially hidden under an even more unusual haircut. She wore an elegant, expensive dress, but I detected anguish in her eyes. I could tell immediately that she was no longer the same person. She had become more experienced, more mature, and charier.

"How have you been?" she caressed my hand and asked.

"I'm still in school, studying International Business. I'll graduate very soon."

"That's great! A bright future lies ahead of you. But don't be too practical."

"You're funny," I said while sitting and fidgetting in my chair. "Everybody told me not to be too dreamy. Only you say the opposite. Is being practical bad?"

"No, but money doesn't bring you happiness." She rubbed her belly, then lay on the couch and asked, "Are you in love?"

"I don't know, but I'm feeling exhilarated," I replied.

That evening, we sat around our small table in the corner of the kitchen. The delicious aroma of cooking food filled the room. After putting a spoonful of rice into her mouth, Auntie placed her chopsticks on the table and announced, "I'm pregnant."

My mother and I were stunned. In her letters, Auntie had always talked about how much she was enjoying single life. My mother took a napkin and wiped the grease off her lips.

"When did you get married? Why didn't you inform me? Where's your husband?" my mother inquired.

"There was never a wedding," Auntie looked at Mom and said glumly. "The guy disappeared."

My mother's lips quivered. Her face turned white.

"How many months along are you?"

"Almost three months."

"You can still get rid of it," my mother frowned and suggested coldly. "Tomorrow, I'll take you to Từ Dũ Hospital. They'll take care of it quick."

Auntie stood up and smirked.

"Thank you, but I must take responsibility for what I've done. Don't force me to get rid of it. I'll leave if you don't want me to live here."

"You've tarnished this family's reputation," my mother exhaled loudly and cried. "It's shameful!"

I didn't know what to say or what to do in this situation. I merely stood there with a heavy heart. I asked myself, why do young people never learn from the mistakes made by older generations?

We didn't finish the meal; the dishes grew cold. My mother got up from the table and staggered to her room. Auntie rubbed her belly with a pained expression on her face. She was powerless and bitter.

"Please don't be upset at Mom," I came closer to her and mumbled. "She's very strict about everything. It'll all be okay. Your baby won't be a mistake."

"Is what I'm doing wrong?" Auntie looked at me regretfully and asked.

"I don't know. But I don't think freedom means that you can break all the rules."

I held Auntie in my arms and felt that I had become more mature. I had never felt so close to her, nor felt so sorry for her, either.

I walked into the garden. The moon had risen. The moonbeams illuminated the corner where the plum tree stood dying. I saw some young new buds and sighed with relief. There was no need to torment and hurt each other. Spring had finally come, and everything was starting to change.

THE ETERNAL FOREST

TRỊNH BÍCH NGÂN

T he enticing words from a TV commercial for an eco-friendly tour caught her attention: "Discover the sublime beauty of the lake at night, enjoy the moonlit sky, and watch the sunrise." Unable to resist the idea, she decided to book a weekend getaway. As recommended by the travel agent, she bought a bottle of mosquito repellent, a small flashlight, and a high-collared, zip-up jacket. She packed all of the necessities neatly into her suitcase and looked forward with great excitement to the excursion. She imagined how magical it would be to sit in a boat beneath a moonlit sky and drift across a serene lake surrounded by a forest.

She and her fellow tourists got off the bus and followed the tour guide on a well-worn path into the woods. The forest was half old-growth, half new-growth. The travelers acted like rambunctious children—they were curious about everything and asked the guide and the forest ranger all kinds of questions. Questions about the birds and butterflies. Questions about the plants and the flowers. Questions about the monkeys, weasels, and foxes that were probably hiding somewhere in the bushes. Questions about endangered wild animals. Questions about which plants were edible before they broke into small groups and trekked along the edge of the woods to pluck the recommended leaves. After a few hours, everybody returned to the guest lodge and enthusiastically handed the chef their baskets filled with edible greens.

By the time dinner was served, it was dark outside and multiple twinkling stars lit the sky. They made a toast to the chef while he shared his recipes. After dinner, they sat around a fire and sang together until nearly midnight. Then they each returned to their rooms for a few hours of sleep before they would wake up at 4:00 AM to get on a boat, floating on the lake to greet the sunrise.

She put on her nightgown, got into bed, pulled the blanket up to her chest, turned off the light, and tried to get some sleep. In the other bed, her roommate, Hạnh, was snoring. Although they sat next to each other on the bus and shared the room, they had only just exchanged phone numbers and barely looked at each other's faces. They only shared necessary words, like "Go ahead and use the restroom first," or "I have shampoo here if you need some."

She did notice clearly, however, Hạnh's long slender fingers while she sat transfixed with her iPad. They moved quickly across the screen as if grasping for something in the virtual realm. Her fingernails were painted purple with a layer of silver glitter. Sometimes Hạnh snored loudly as if the air had gotten trapped in her throat and it sounded like she was suffocating. She thought about getting up and adjusting her roommate's head into a proper position on the pillow but didn't do so in case that would startle Hạnh, who might then blame her for interrupting her sleep. Normally, we can't hear ourselves snore or detect our own body odors. Yet, when you desperately want to fall asleep, the slightest snore becomes a tormenting train engine.

When the tour guide knocked on her door to tell them to get ready, her head ached and she felt dizzy. As soon as she got out of bed and paced around the room for a while, she lost her balance and plunged back into bed. Hạnh, on the other hand, woke full of energy. She loaded her backpack, unplugged her iPad from the charger, and quickly scrolled its screen before looking up and asking,

"Why are you still sitting there? I'm heading out now."

After Hạnh and the entire group had left to join the tour, her dizziness subsided. In the dark room, she lolled for a while and fell asleep. When she woke up, the sunlight already had reached her window. She opened it wide and from the second floor she could see the carpet-like green lawn and yellow flowers below. A path. Two rows of areca palm trees. A tree branch quivering in the breeze. A yellow dog wagging its tail while burrowing its nose in a pile of pebbles on the ground. The scene was tranquil. The air was fresh. She saw no one and heard only birds chirping in tree branches.

She left her room and ambled along the sunlit path, quickening her steps as she approached the road that joined the national highway. A few bicycles, some motorbikes, and every now and then a few small trucks passed by. She turned left and arrived at a small but crowded open-air market that was selling a variety of products, vegetables, food, and household necessities. It was a typical countryside marketplace, and the sellers and buyers were hardworking, frugal people. Not far from the market stood a hat shop with purple bougainvillea vines framing its entrance. The glaring sun was stinging her eyes, so she walked into the shop and bought a basic, floppy camouflage hat. She donned the newly purchased hat and stopped at a food stall for a bowl of crab noodle soup. It was a bit salty, even after she had squeezed four pieces of lime into the broth.

After breakfast she walked around to find a coffee shop, thinking that she would enjoy a leisurely cup of coffee while waiting for her group to return from the early morning hike. Suddenly a blue sign that read *Eternal Forest* caught her attention. She had no clue why the adjective *eternal*, often associated with things that are not materialized, was named for this place, where everything was so worldly. She was enticed by the word and walked toward the sign.

She took out her iPhone, held it as far from her face as she could, and captured two selfies with the sign in the background. She looked at the photos but wasn't pleased, thinking she looked goofy in them.

When she was about to take another photo, someone offered, "Let me help you."

She turned and saw a man wearing a brand new military uniform and a fresh camo hat. He was strong, tall, and handsome, resembling the actor Nguyễn Chánh Tín in the movie *Cards on the Table*. She was taken aback by his attractive face and handed him her phone without hesitation. He graciously took several photos for her, politely gave the phone back, and asked if she was pleased with them. The photos were perfect—she looked much younger and prettier than she had in her selfies. She couldn't have asked for better images. She sat down, posted the photos on Facebook, and waited to see who among her friends clicked the "like" button first. The man was still standing there, so she put her phone into her bag and stood up. The sunlight made the word *Eternal* sparkle but also cast shadows on the stranger's face, which made it impossible to see clearly.

"Follow me if you want to take some nice photos," he moved closer and suggested, as he pointed at the straight path stretching under a row of trees toward the forest.

She was mesmerized and walked at his side without saying a word. He took several photos for her with sunbeams shimmering through the foliage in the background. Stubble covered his attractive face. His mustache and beard must grow in thick if he doesn't shave for a few days. She thought about how she liked to look at and touch her husband's facial hair as it grew in. She bought him razors so often that he sometimes reminded her affectionately, "Are you buying razors for an entire military unit? I still have plenty."

"I like to," she barked.

To her, the word *like* didn't need an explanation because it was a matter of emotions, and thus liking something didn't require a justification. However, since she created a Facebook account, she had vaguely realized that the verb *like* oftentimes involved fears. Fear of being neglected. Fear of loneliness. Fear of being lost in a crowd. She was no different from other Facebook users who were trapped in their own egos and loneliness, surrounded by hundreds of virtual friends. Like everyone else, she had experienced the vicissitudes of life. She reflected on herself and her life and dared not abandon the online masses to be alone. In addition to her few close friends, many people whom she had never met in person "liked" her photos. That was sufficient for her—the "likes" she received filled the days' emptiness. An emptiness that consumed her heart even when she and her husband were making love.

"Do you know the longjack plant?" the stranger asked. His question interrupted her wandering thoughts.

"I've never seen it but I've tried the alcohol infused with its roots."

"Do you like it?"

"Not really. I had a shot last night but it tasted rather unpleasant."

"What you had must've been counterfeit."

His comment was irrelevant because she had consumed the herbal wine to help her forget her unfulfilling marriage and loneliness, rather than enjoy the taste. She wanted to be free during her weekend getaway. But the man's face looked sincere and he was a good listener. He was probably right about the wine.

She recalled that once on her way to work, she had purchased a liter of honey from a vendor sitting on the pavement. The honey came directly from a pot with a beehive above. The seller, a member of an ethnic minority group, wore his clan's traditional outfit and looked like a genuine man. When she got home, she realized that she had been cheated—it wasn't real honey; it was water mixed with honey-colored sugar. She was often lied to and cheated, and her gullibility made her bitter. Sometimes she even knew that she was being led into a maze but she wasn't mentally strong enough to free herself from it—the maze where lies were embellished or camouflaged with beautiful and realistic images. She couldn't explain why sweetness and bitterness were often intertwined.

"I'll find and dig up some hundred-year-old longjack roots for you," the man continued.

She followed him without asking how he would dig up the roots with no tool in sight. She felt safe walking behind a man in uniform who didn't carry a weapon. His bright eyes weren't those of a hunter or criminal, and his face was warm when he looked at her. The path became narrower and the forest grew gloomy thanks to the shadows cast by old trees with thick foliages. She almost asked, Seriously, are you taking me to where the longjack is? But somehow the words got trapped in her throat. She quietly walked at his side. The sunlight gradually faded on his hat, clothes, and face.

It wasn't his handsome features, or his broad shoulders, or his uniform that enthralled her. It wasn't his promise to find the longjack roots that enticed her. It was a mystical and alluring power held in his empathic eyes and the way he had seemed to appear out of nowhere to take photos for her. Maybe he was a soulmate who would always be available to provide solace via Facebook when she needed it. She wanted to say something but was tongue-tied. She felt comforted in his presence and could sense that he was genuine, affable, and reliable. They walked quietly in the woods among whirls of colorful butterflies fluttering past, a chorus of birds singing morning songs from tree branches, wildflowers blooming with timid, quivering petals, and delicate leaves floating down from branches.

She stopped at an ancient tree whose branches held a broad crown of leaves. Rough bark covered its trunk that rose with a gentle bend; the tree resembled a giant bonsai. Its thick foliage occluded the sunlight, which made the man's face inconspicuous when he bent down.

"The more bitter the roots," he said, "the more you remember the taste."

She felt his breath rush past her ear and blood surged in her veins. Submerged in nature, she inhaled deeply and her mind went blank as his sturdy arms pulled her toward his muscular body.

"Are you cold?" he asked.

She was overwhelmed by his irresistible aroma. Her entire body tingled, her lips hurriedly found his, and, clumsily but passionately, he pulled her closer, claiming her mouth, hungry and intense.

During the brief rush of ecstasy, her phone rang, jolting her from the moment. It took her a few seconds to regain emotional balance as she leaned her body slightly away from the man, took a few clumsy steps away from the tree, and reached into her bag for her phone. The screen announced the caller's name—her husband. She pressed the answer button.

"Where did you put the razors?" he asked. "I can't find them."

His voice was a bucket of frigid water splashed onto her burning face. She wiped away the sweat that had gathered on her forehead and replied placidly, "If there are none left in the bathroom, check the top dresser drawer where I keep your underwear."

As usual, he hung up without asking how she was doing or if she was enjoying the trip. He often said he respected people's privacy and thus did not want to pry. Once, while he was shaving, she had become infuriated by this perpetual indifference and shouted, "What would you do if I slept around?"

"I would cut someone's throat," he replied coldly. He, of course, couldn't have cared less about the question.

"Whose throat?" she responded.

"Both of your throats."

The terseness of his answer enraged her.

She looked back and the stranger had disappeared. Maybe he had left or possibly ducked into the vegetation to find the longjack roots. Perhaps he had to return to his unit after what was just a break. Her phone rang again, but this time it was her roommate, Hạnh, calling.

"I'll be back soon. Where are you?" asked Hạnh.

"I'm on my way to the lodge. I left the room key at the front desk."

"You're lucky that you didn't join us today."

"Why do you say that?"

"Because my legs and arms are swollen with mosquito bites. But the tour was wonderful, otherwise."

While walking the worn path back to the asphalt road, she kept picturing the man in his uniform, his warm embrace, and passionate kiss. She tried to understand everything that had happened. His unexpected presence while she was taking photos. His eagerness to find longjack roots for her. His intimacy, and the inexplicable feelings they conjured, which were probably related to her desire for adventure and discovery.

The experience forced her to reexamine the emotions she was suppressing and the loneliness that led her to escape into the woods. She contemplated death and the continuity of life; the small, secret worlds all individuals hold inside themselves; and nature's complex, intertwined operations. According to the tour guide, this region had been the site of a bloody battle in which *we* and *they* fought vigorously. It bore witness to tragic separations, deaths, sorrows, and sufferings. But nothing could extinguish humanity's aspirations for life. The woods, the trees, the river, the soil, and the lake had been a refuge for thousands of soldiers. Many of whom had lost their lives, and their bodies then become fertile soil that nurtured the trees and plants around her.

She walked slower and reached into her bag for her phone. She opened the photo album to look at the shots the man had taken of her. But none existed. She turned the phone off, restarted it, and searched through the album again. But again she found nothing. She turned it off and restarted it one more time. But the most recent photos were the two selfies in which her expression looked silly and her face distorted due to poor lighting, and the string of her floppy hat hanging down like a noose.

The sun had risen high into the sky and the asphalt road was roasting under her feet. She adjusted her hat to avoid getting sun-burned. Sweat slicked her face and a glare danced across her phone's screen. She opened Facebook, hoping to find the photos that she had posted earlier but they were gone too. A shiver slinked up her spine. She scratched her wrist and pinched her forearm. She could indeed feel pain, but she was sweating and shivering.

Had she been hallucinating?

The desires she had been suppressing could have led her to imagine the man she had encountered.

Did she wake from a dream?

She was grateful for whatever it was that had given her an opportunity to meet him, to discover herself, and to mentally escape, for even a few hours. Touching and talking with the man, feeling desired in the dark, ghostly forest where death had an important place in the cycle of life was an invaluable gift. Her heart had leaped up when the stranger looked at her with kindness, and the photos that were now mysteriously lost had captured a moment when she felt younger and freer than ever. That ephemeral instance came and went like a gentle breeze. But she believed the stranger must be around somewhere. She quickly looked back at the worn path that distance was swallowing behind her.

She saw a motorbike driving toward her, and her heart beat faster.

Could it be the man she just met? Could it be the man who awakened desires she thought were long dead?

Her phone rang again. It was her husband. She could tell that he was drinking in a swarming, clamorous bar.

"If you see any raw wild forest honey there," he said loudly in the phone, "don't forget to buy me some."

"I'll try, definitely."

"In fact, not just for me," he added, "but for our family to use."

"I know," she said gently.

"By the way, I've heard that Tri An Lake's dried *chach* fish are pretty . . ."

"OK. I'll buy some," she interrupted.

"Oh, and don't forget to buy a few bottles of longjack wine. It's good for one's health and improves virility."

"I'll remember."

"Make sure it's made with authentic longjack roots. I don't want any fake stuff."

The lone motorbike passed her, kicking up plumes of dust. She could only see the driver's helmet and its white and blue stripes.

On her way back to the lodge, her husband called again. He was drunk, and over the phone he cursed the wicked, greedy, filthy world they lived in. She knew her husband was reveling in a bar with a mug of sudsy beer in his hand, but somehow she pictured him shaving in the bathroom, with white foam all over his face and mouth. The white foam looked like the clouds above her. She didn't know why she suddenly thought of the flashlight and the mosquito repellent she had bought for the trip but never used.

SELECTING A HUSBAND

KIỀU BÍCH HẬU

"**W**here are you, my darling kitty?"—a text message from Takashi punctuated with bright, throbbing hearts pops up on her phone.

Ân is inundated with business matters and anxiously awaiting the arrival of shipping containers from China that are stranded at customs, but wants to cast everything aside. She wants to be able to savor relaxed moments, free of any obligations. Pursing her lips, lust swirls between her legs. If she were not so busy, if it were not a workday, she would have dropped everything and raced to Takashi's.

"I'm starving," Ân texts back. "Can you feed me today?"

"You'll have a feast, my love." His message is a promise that makes her heart race. She holds her breath, attempting to contain her excitement.

Ân's assistant rises to his feet and strides across the room. Ân tries to avoid his inquisitive eyes, flipping her phone upside down on her desk and handing him a signed contract. Alas, she didn't have time to read it closely. But she trusts karma, and the contract isn't worth much anyway. The only problem left to deal with is figuring out how to retrieve the cargo stuck at the border. Everything must be resolved by noon. The spa chain in which she invested in Hà

Nội and Hồ Chí Minh City is always packed with customers as the weight-loss industry is booming. The slimming procedure they offer, which combines fat-burning therapies with weight-loss pills to enhance a body's firmness, makes her beauty salons increasingly lucrative, with profits pouring in every day. The stress is worth it. Ân marvels at how she is able to make such a fortune, when only five years ago she had to struggle to make ends meet. Where had all that money been when she needed it?

Ân is relieved when she is finally able to get into a cab. She took care of the customs paperwork. Thousands of packets of weight-loss supplements have been rescued and are on the way to her warehouses, which will bring in even more cash. Now, she doesn't have to worry about anything, not even money. She turns off her phone. Her head is empty except for Takashi and the meal that awaits.

Ân reaches for her key to Takashi's apartment, but as if the door recognizes her, it swiftly opens before she touches it. The magic eye on the door blinks in complicity. Ân sheds her jacket and transforms instantly from an iron-minded businesswoman to a tender woman craving love as she enters Takashi's living room.

Takashi opens his arms wide and then holds Ân tight. She snuggles her head against his shoulder, inhaling his Hugo Boss cologne. Leading Ân to the couch, Takashi hands her a glass of cold mineral water with lemon slices. It calms her. Takashi lifts her left hand to his lips and kisses it. In his rough hands marred by age spots, hers seem smaller and softer. She is twenty years younger than him and their age difference allows her to appreciate her own youthful, supple allure.

As she approaches the dining table, Ân is amazed by Takashi's flair for preparation and presentation. The broiled salmon topped with orange sauce resting on a white porcelain plate is the perfect harmony of colors and flavors. Takashi pulls out her chair, places a napkin in her lap, and pours wine into her glass as if he were a professional waiter. When she closes her eyes to savor the food, Takashi stares at her. She can feel his gaze admiring every inch of her body, which makes her cells tingle. More than anyone before, he knows her most sensitive places where pleasure resides. She drops to the floor, inviting Takashi to join her. He is powerless as she holds him down. Overwhelmed by passion, she swirls like a raging storm. It's too much for Takashi who tumbles off the cliff in ecstasy before she has been fully satisfied.

In the haze that follows, Ân drifts back to Núi Xẻ Village. She was just a young nineteen-year-old, gleefully following her new husband to his family home. She rejoiced in the fantasy that she eventually would become a mother, holding in her hands a little baby she would cuddle and breastfeed. Her breasts hardened with anticipation at the thought. But Ân didn't even know where the baby would come out from. Ân's mother never taught her about that. Neither did she learn it at school. She did know, however, that all married women sooner or later did have babies. She only desired to have her own child so that she could nurture it herself; it didn't matter whether her husband would be Quân or Hùng or any of the other men in the village. Ân had no special feeling for Hùng, except for the way he looked at her like a dog staring at a bone being dangled above its head. She would have to end up as someone's wife, anyway. Marrying early would make Ân more popular because, unlike many other girls her age in Núi Xẻ Village, she would no longer be available.

While Ân was carefully hanging their bed's mosquito net, Hùng shoved her back onto the bed. The foul smell of alcohol suffocated her. She tried to endure it. But when Hùng pressed Ân's head into the wall, she grew terrified and struggled. Hùng almost tore her apart. He acted like a crazed beast tearing into its terrified prey. He ripped off her pants, flipped her upside down, and split her legs wide so she was splayed out like a frog. She snapped back and forth as he thrust over and over from behind. It felt like her bones would snap.

That wedding night's brutal rape was repeated again and again. Ân was always horrified by the sight of the sun slipping below the horizon. She grew paler and gaunt. It was as if she had developed a serious illness. Every night, Hùng flipped Ân upside down and pinned her legs back; the crushing pain seemed unceasing. After a year, Ân still hadn't gotten pregnant, but she kept enduring her husband, never telling anyone about how he tormented her. She assumed all women had to undergo the same trauma to have babies. Only when she had a baby would the suffering end. She would take the baby with her and leave.

Ân is so thankful for Takashi's love. When he drops to the floor, she takes possession of him and regains her femininity. Ten years earlier, Hùng killed himself, and Ân left Núi Xẻ for good. Hùng died only after robbing her of her virginity and destroying her capacity to love. She had become scared of men. Deep down, she believed relationships with men would always lead to dreadful anguish. It was too horrifying to imagine.

For many years, Hùng's ghost haunted her. Night after lonely night, Ân would return to that first dark night in Núi Xẻ. Eventually, when a baby had still not appeared, despite her husband's nightly, merciless rapes, Ân fled to her mother's house. She didn't return until her husband threatened to kill himself if she didn't. Ân was packing her luggage to go back when her mother held her back. She locked Ân in her bedroom because she worried that if she let her daughter leave, she would never see her again.

That night, Hùng tied a rope around his neck and killed himself. He left Ân a scathing letter blaming her for forcing his suicide. Hùng's family and everyone else in the villages blamed her. Ân's mother used her entire savings to pay for her son-in-law's funeral and then secretively helped Ân escape far away from Núi Xẻ.

Ân was blessed. Her mother sent her to a teacher named Thanh in Hà Nội who became Ân's second mother. Thanh was her mother's former classmate, but Thanh left Núi Xẻ as soon as she graduated from high school. Ân's mother stayed in Núi Xẻ and got married while Thanh found work as an assistant to a director of a Japanese company. She taught Ân Japanese, and it was through her work that Ân met Takashi.

What Ân had been expecting eventually came to pass. Takashi proposed. Looking into his eyes, Ân didn't dare say no. But she asked him to give her some time. Her business was going strong, and she wanted to focus on developing it further while enjoying a few more years of freedom. She didn't want to tell Takashi that her mother didn't like him. Her mother thought he was too old for Ân and didn't look like a trustworthy person. Ân kept asking her mother to explain why she didn't approve of him, but she never did. Ân's mother also had disapproved of Ân's father marrying her off to Hùng, arguing that she feared he would be violent, although she had no evidence.

Ân's mother seemed to have a supernatural ability to judge people. Although she never could provide any evidence to back up her claims, Ân trusted her mother's intuition. Still, Ân was grateful for Takashi as he entered her world voluntarily and re-awakened her ability to love men. He played a very important role in her life. But she wouldn't marry him.

So, how would she select a husband? Ân sat down, overwhelmed by the idea. She had never before listed all of the criteria her husband must fulfill. Absurdly, before she married Hùng, she hadn't even taken the time to picture what married life would be like. It had happened so quickly, and to this day, she still couldn't visualize the type of husband she wanted.

"Go for a young, masculine man. One with sturdy legs, so you and your children can travel the world, exploring all sorts of splendors. A man with a broad back will be able to carry you and your children to the hospital in case of an emergency. A man who can be a friend to your children. Think about such a man, and one day you'll definitely meet him," Thanh advised.

"And he must be wealthy so that the whole family can travel by air and stay in nice hotels," Ân added. "You wouldn't want your student to have to walk across the world, would you?"

"No. You should never rely on a man financially, whether it's your husband or any other man," Thanh said. "A relationship based on money is fragile and will ruin your talents."

"People say a woman who has to earn a living by herself suffers a poor fate," Ân stubbornly countered her teacher. But Ân knew Thanh would never concede.

"That's the reasoning of a spineless, inept, scumbag. I don't care what they think. They own nothing, not even their own lives. Parasites. Making money is a pleasure that is its own reward. Treasure it."

Thanh was right. What's wrong with making money? Ân's business had thrived despite the occasional hassles. She was thrilled by the many opportunities it granted her. She had risen from a miserable woman in Núi Xẻ into a wealthy urban dweller. It seems that a very thin line exists between the rich and poor and one must be daring to cross it.

But she also understood that she needed a real husband—someone who would always be waiting at home for her after hectic days in the office. Her husband should be able to control the wild instincts that Takashi had awakened in her. Since meeting him, she had become so empowered that whenever she saw an attractive man, she felt an urge to have crazy sex with him. Before he could make a move, she always initiated a flirtatious conversation. She explored different types of men, to satisfy her curiosity and to explore her libido to the fullest. But she understood that when she did marry, she would need to contain her monstrous lust.

Ân often gravitated toward adventure. Sometimes she traveled for business, or to visit a faraway friend, or simply to discover somewhere she had never been. She said she traveled to re-energize her mind, but in truth she was looking for the man that Thanh had described. Or some other rare creature she couldn't fathom, but who must exist somewhere. Thanh has dwelled in the same corner of the capital city for most of her life, surrounded by pollution, rapacity, and vanity. Yet Ân, who traveled extensively, was still unable to picture who her husband would be. Who would be the best of all the bad choices? What about love? Why does Takashi only arouse her sexual desire, but not her deepest love?

In a world where everything is automatic, designed and programmed to function with complete efficiency, is love an antiquated, secondary luxury, too ludicrous to be desirable?

But Takashi persisted. During the Tết holiday, a time to spend with one's family, Ân would complement his life in his luxurious nineteenth-floor apartment. Unlike the Ân of the old days—a country girl with a soul scarred from the wounds of a shattered marriage—the Ân of today could enjoy an extravagant dream-like experience with a foreign businessman. She could spend the five-day holiday feasting and having passionate sex.

On the night before the Tết holidays begin, Ân leans against the window, contemplating Nguyễn Trãi Street stretching below. The lights shimmering on either side resemble two lines of stars streaming endlessly into the distance. Ân wishes she had wings so that she could fly off among those dazzling stars.

Back in the kitchen, Ân watches Takashi lower a tray brimming with Tết specialties. He arranges the fried spring rolls, fermented pork, *bánh chưng*, and pig bladder soup into the traditional Hà Nội peacock and phoenix shapes. This Japanese man is a genius for being able to make such authentic local dishes. However, this artistic ability is not enough to win her heart.

As soon as Takashi loosens himself from her body after having taken his pleasure, Ân whispers, "Takashi, will you go with me to the end of the world?"

"I want to stay by your side forever," Takashi says with a curious expression, as he stares into her eyes. "But we should stay here, in Hà Nội. This city is large enough for me. We'll be safe and happy for the rest of our lives."

"But the world is immense, full of amazing things, incredible foods, enchanting lifestyles. I want to explore all the best, the most beautiful places out there."

"Those things are appealing merely because they seem exotic," Takashi explains soberly. "By nature, of course, you should be unique. You don't want to blend in with others or become someone else. But you need to stay here with me, indulging and exploring yourself. Otherwise, you'll never be able to understand yourself fully."

Ân silently nuzzles her face into Takashi's chest, refusing to contend. Because he is from Japan, Hà Nội is far enough for him, but it's not far enough for her. Takashi's experience isn't hers. When she was in Núi Xẻ, Ân naively believed that all women would have to get married and birth children after suffering painful sex and a husband's violent abuses. Only when she left Núi Xẻ did she realize that women deserve to be loved and cherished. She came to understand that sex satisfies both one's physical instincts and one's soul. Women can have children without entangling themselves in a marriage. One's life can always be improved if one is daring enough to abandon one's comfort zones.

Ân still intends to find a husband for herself. Or so she tells herself. After staying with Takashi for the five days of Tết, Ân leaves. But she plans to introduce another woman to him—someone who can explore herself with him.

She then spends a steamy night with an Indian businessman seven years her junior who considers sexual intimacy to be a religious ritual. It's then Ân realizes that she has been wrong from the start. The ideal man in Thanh's fantasy, or the man young women imagine meeting and marrying, doesn't exist. That's why Thanh had never been able to describe an ideal man vividly.

During their carnal ritual, Ân was able to achieve an until-then unknown ethereal passion and satisfaction only because she made the Indian man understand and attend to what she wanted. Ân thus came to the epiphany that the perfect man is one she must make for herself.

THE HAUNTED GARDEN

TRẦM HƯƠNG

I called and called outside the gray wooden gate beneath a trellis overflowing with buttercup flowers. Nobody answered. A chain dangled on the unlocked gate. I left my suitcase on the ground. A text scrawled across the gate's walls read *The Haunted Garden*. The door cracked open, the face of a young woman poked out, dazed, as she approached the gate.

"Is Hằng home?" I asked.

At first the girl said nothing and only stared at me. Then she likely didn't see me as threatening and replied timidly, "Hằng is still at the brick factory. She hasn't come home yet." She then slammed the gate.

"Come on! Hằng and I have an appointment today," I cried out. "I'm Phương and I've come to help design this garden."

She shook her head and then jumped up and down like a kid.

"Ah! Ms. Phương. Hằng told me about you, but I forgot. Come on in!"

The girl opened the gate and greeted me with a strange hospitality.

The gate opened onto a poetic scene. A concrete bridge spanned a canal that flowed through the front of the garden between the north and south walls. I was mesmerized by the glamour of this haunted garden. Apricot trees lined the two main paths. Spring was already over but yellow flowers continued to blossom gorgeously in the tropical sunlight. Pure white grapefruit blossoms emitted sweet fragrance. Bees and butterflies hovered in the tranquil, serene slice of nature. The girl who answered the gate carried my suitcase in for me.

I was about to turn toward a two-story, red-tiled house, with its ostentatious architecture, but the girl stopped me.

"Not that house. Yours is on this side. Hằng told me to take you to the retreat."

I followed her.

Maybe she could read my mind. She scratched her head with embarrassment and said, "The main house. . . . Hằng has never received guests there before."

"So who lives there?"

"Hằng and Tuấn."

"Hằng isn't married yet, is she?" I asked, full of shock.

"Well, she has never been married," the girl explained but seemed embarrassed. "Tuấn is her brother-in-law."

Realizing her careless disclosure, the girl fell silent. She was demure and passive as we walked down the path. I followed her, looking at the plants in the garden while my thoughts went wild. Ripe grapefruit swayed on branches on either side of us, which no one had bothered to pick. The girl stopped at the southwest corner of the garden beside two clear creeks. Amid yellow bamboo and bodhi trees, a lotus pond, and a cluster of flowers, I noticed a humble dwelling.

Why am I here in this utterly deadly, desolate place? I asked myself, resentful of the owner of the garden. But when I climbed the steps and entered the retreat, I felt calm and peaceful. All my anger evaporated as I immersed myself in the serene atmosphere. It was neat and simply decorated inside: a mattress spread on a glossy black ebony floor, a desk, and a bookshelf. I suddenly didn't want to go anywhere else.

The girl helped me arrange the furniture.

"Aunt Hằng built this retreat for uncle Tuấn to come stay and practice meditation," she said. "Since he left, she's told me to clean it as if he were still around."

Her words made me curious about the relationship between Tuấn and Hằng.

"Is he Hằng's younger brother? Why does he practice Buddhism?"

"After Hằng's older sister suffered burns and died, Hằng didn't get married but stayed to raise her six nieces and nephews and support her brother, Tuấn, as he finished his studies," the girl hesitated and then said. "After Tuấn finished college, he became a monk in a temple and didn't return home. Hằng was depressed and she kept looking for Tuấn wherever he went to receive alms. But whenever they saw each other, Tuấn ignored her. She was devastated."

The girl's naiveté and honesty were so attractive. Without her, I never would be able to understand the secret behind the mossy gray gate.

"Hằng is pretty, so why did she stay single?"

"What a question! How could she get married and support her mother, brother, nieces, and nephews? She's stayed here with Tuấn."

The girl pouted, shrugged her shoulders, and began to sulk.

"Our neighbors envy Hằng for her prosperous business and talk behind her back a lot. They said a brother-in-law and a wife's sister only live under the same roof if they're having an affair. They urged me to leave. They said Hằng was wicked and the whole family was cursed. But that's not true. She loves me like a family member."

"What is your relationship with Hằng?"

"I'm an orphan. My name is Bí and I had scabies. She adopted me and raised me. I'm grateful for that, and I'll live with her until I die."

"She's so kindhearted and generous. So why do people say she is evil?"

The girl shook her head, frustrated.

"People hate her, so they spread that rumor. Please don't ask further. Hằng would scold me if I said anything more."

She quickly walked away, disappearing into the bushes.

"Spooky house," I murmured, looking around exhausted. I had to arrange everything in the retreat myself. After bathing and changing into my pajamas, I felt relieved. Leaning back on the mattress, I wanted to read something. Bí suddenly returned, bringing a platter of fruits.

"Are there any books for me to read and forget my boredom?" I asked.

"Yes, Tuấn has a lot of books about Buddhism," Bí frowned before responding. "Hằng stores them in a closet to keep them safe from insatiable moths. Let me see."

Bí ran toward the big house. Moments later she returned with a black, musty notebook in her hand.

"Hằng used to read this book frequently, keeping it hidden the way a cat hides its shit. It must be a good one!"

Sheesh, Bí couldn't even differentiate between books and notebooks! Reluctantly, I took it and casually flipped through it—*Diary of the Haunted Garden*. I sprang up. This was Hằng's diary! She wrote in lofty but assertive handwriting that drew me in.

> . . . Karma and retribution? I heard this phrase uttered briefly when I was a kid. My family was well off and employed many servants. My mother was beautiful, diligent, and kindhearted, but austere. One day, she caught one of my father's sisters stealing ten silk sheets. Mom didn't care about losing the silk but hated the act of stealing. She was furious and whipped the woman ten times in front of the servants. The relative was so ashamed that she committed suicide and left a curse that someone from each generation in my family would burn to death. I don't believe it, but that curse keeps haunting my sisters. They continued to pray about it, but I forgot the curse when I went to school. My older sister had been married for a long time. My brother-in-law is a handsome, rich, and wise businessman. Thanks to my sister and

her husband, my family continued to live a comfortable life even when experiencing economic calamities. My sister gave birth to seven children—one died, six survived. My sister carried the burden of the entire family. She contentedly accepted that mission.

Bí suddenly became upset.

"I smuggled this book from Hằng's room. Please take care of it after you finish reading it. Don't get me in trouble!"

"I'll be careful. She will never know," I said softly, fearing that Bí might take the diary back.

To assure Bí, I gave her a hair clip with a beautiful white bow. Bí was so thrilled that she left right away.

The curse became obvious. Oh God. Why it was my sister and not someone else. Her death was hard to believe. It seemed like there was some invisible hand that arranged all this. It happened when she was making a fire to cook dinner for my brother-in-law and the children. Did she mistake the fuel tank for the kerosene because she was distracted? The fire was inevitable. Her nylon clothes were so flammable. She died a tragic death. During the funeral, looking at her children, standing by their mother's coffin, wearing standard white mourning headbands with tears streaming down their faces, I felt like someone was rubbing salt into my intestines. My brother-in-law was still young. What future would my nieces and nephews have? What if he remarried a selfish, evil wife? Where would our properties end up? What would our future be like? Countless questions tormented my heart. I had just finished my undergraduate studies and wanted simply to enjoy my life. But misfortune fell on our family. I loved my nieces and nephews. No, from now on, I would replace my sister by raising them. I would protect our family's properties and not lose anything to anyone. And I would bravely face all venomous rumors. What else could I do when the responsibility I shouldered was so enormous?

So, I had already opened the gate of this haunted garden. The next pages made me admire Hằng enormously. Who could imagine that beneath the woman's fragile, glamorous, peaceful façade, an immense power lurked. I was drawn to her beauty the first moment we met. It was the same with this wild, mysterious garden. It turned out this splendid, verdant space had a tumultuous history.

Then a day came when I didn't want to be made into a shadow by some man. I have shouldered. . . . Over the past ten years, my nieces and nephews have grown up. The first three have become doctors, the next two are engineers, and the last one is going abroad to pursue further studies. Only Tuấn remains. My brother-in-law doesn't want to get married. He is obsessed with the curse. After finishing his undergraduate studies, Tuấn left our house for the temple. Seeing him commit himself to an arduous life breaks my heart. I'm also terrified of the curse. But what can we do? How can I leave my children for the temple? No, I have to make a living, I have no other choices. I'm indifferent to the rumors, indifferent to those who say I am some selfish hoarder. Indifferent. It's time to make a living on my own. My brother-in-law didn't know my plan. Leaving the three-story house downtown, I went looking for a good piece of land. The soil here is fertile but desolate. I bought a few acres. Broken roads. We would have to cross several canals to reach it. I was wearing a silk outfit. Who cares? I waded through the stagnant canals. Woods rife with snakes and weeds. Then I looked at my hands. I told myself, Hằng, you can't give up. And I bent down, uprooted a tuft of grass. I will turn this forest into a well-trimmed, spectacular garden. I will let Tuấn inherit it. He is more than forty years old. C'mon, Hằng, stop day-dreaming. Don't you already have six grown-up children? Tuấn, where are you now? If only you were here, I would be much more bold . . .

I stopped there, hiding the diary quickly in a desk drawer as a car honked outside the gate.

"Ah, Hằng is home!" Bí shrieked with joy while standing behind me.

Leaving me there, she darted toward the gate to greet her. The burgundy car pulled into the driveway. Behind the wheel was a tall middle-aged man with graying hair. His square face was stern. Beside him was Hằng. She signaled him to stop the car and got out to walk toward me while the man calmly turned the car around toward the big house. Her silk blouse and sweater made her look even more enigmatic than the last time I had seen her. Perhaps what I had read in *The Haunted Garden Diary* was still resonating with me, making me see her differently.

She rushed to me, offering a convivial hug.

"Did you just arrive? How's everything so far?"

"Yes, and I love the retreat."

"I thought you would," she smiled and said. "That's why I asked Bí to take you there. She's dull and knows nothing. Don't listen to her gibberish."

"See, Hằng said you know nothing!" I turned to Bí and said jokingly.

Bí shot a slanted stare at me and then left with a raised fist as a threat. I smiled in solidarity with her.

"Call Bí if you need anything," Hằng said. "She may not be smart, but she is kindhearted. Now, please go take a shower and have dinner. Make yourself at home. When you are ready, we can talk. I have a brick factory a few kilometers away from here, so I'm quite busy. I knew you would come today, but I had to pay my workers their monthly salary so I couldn't stay home to welcome you. I hope you aren't upset."

I wandered through the haunted garden and reached for a ripe orange, not expecting to be stung by bees. I flung the orange away and sat down on the grass and held my swollen hand, moaning. Bí quickly picked a Katuk plant near me, chewed it up, and dabbed the pulp on my swollen thumb.

Bí pouted.

"C'mon, it's a minor injury, stop moaning. When we first came here and planted this garden and built the house, Hằng and I had so many challenges. We slept outdoor and got soaked overnight by the dew. We lived like that for a year before the house was finished. Back then this garden was a wild forest filled with snakes and wild animals. We finally were able to move into the home, once we had tamed everything. There wasn't even a bridge to the house back then," Bí proudly added. "From the main street to the garden, we had to wade through the two cold canals!"

I looked around the garden. I could leisurely stroll across the bridge thanks to its owner's sweat, which had once moistened every concrete block. The bridge spanned a human life. The fragrance of the flowers, the sound of the bees hovering, and the garden's sweet honey hadn't come about naturally. I sensed the pain of the person who had made it possible. Even if she was not an exceptional girl, Bí had the right to be proud of her work. I couldn't imagine an elegant, gracious lady like Hằng ever rolling up her pants to wade through canals and weed and till the soil, and plant trees in a place filled with dangerous creatures while enduring the scorching heat and the frigid cold.

"Did Tuấn help you? Is he strong?" I asked Bí.

"Can buffalos fly?" Bí pouted her lips and said. "He went out to receive alms during the days. At night, he would meditate under some trees or simply wander about. Hằng cried her eyes out because of him."

Bí pointed at the trees. Hằng had planted those because she wanted Tuấn to be comfortable during meditation. But after we had planted them, he stayed only a couple of days before leaving. Hằng and I were deathly afraid of ghosts. Thus, Tuấn had to come stay in the big house with us."

I smiled and looked at my shoes, thinking how strange Tuấn was.

I knew enough about the haunted garden to start my work at the retreat. I didn't explain why I had made this trip to the "haunted garden." Perhaps spending the Tết holiday alone in Sài Gòn would be unbearable for me. Or maybe it was because of Hằng's kind eyes when I first met her at the architectural association meeting where she invited me to visit her hometown to help design some vacation homes that would complement her garden. She wanted to turn the garden into an ecotourism site.

I could already envision the surreal but familiar houses I would design so that tourists could get lost in the haunted garden and feel as if they were living in a modern fairy land. It would be a tough task but I would work tirelessly at it. Throughout all my efforts, Bí was a good companion. She quietly brought me trays of bananas, milk fruits, grapefruits, and apples from the garden. During breaks, she entertained me with endless stories about the people in this desolate garden: "Tuấn is very picky. He only eats what Hằng cooks. Because he never remarried, his possessions were split up evenly among his children. People said Hằng hindered Tuấn. I despise those widows so much that I just laughed and told them, 'Hằng lives as if she were married to Tuấn, and it's good for both of them.' I lash out whenever someone says something repulsive about them."

Bí smiled at me. Her meandering stories made me love Hằng even more. Everyone has secret places in their lives and I dared not tread into those dark shadows. Whenever Hằng dropped by the retreat, I made only small talk and didn't inquire about her private life. She was very upfront when talking about business matters but more cryptic when discussing personal affairs. Her enigmatic nature intrigued me. The big house belonged to another world, a world that no one, including myself, was invited to explore. If I knew what life was like in that house, the world would become boring. Having read *The Haunted Garden Diary* was sufficient.

The retreat where I stayed had a sacred, religious atmosphere. *Adhere strictly to oneself is the motto of a Buddhist practitioner*, and *We have to die with what we know*—these two beautiful aphorisms were inscribed in white chalk on the retreat's walls. They revealed that Tuấn was a knowledgeable, gifted person. Why did a handsome, wealthy, and highly educated man confine his life to a temple? Was it because of his promise to break his family's curse or was he always destined to devote his life to prayer? Well, forget him. I had to return to the work of designing the houses that would harmonize with the unsettling garden.

I offered Hằng several designs to choose from. She was amazed that I could finish the project so quickly.

"A charismatic, beautiful, and smart girl like you must have plenty of suitors!" she said while looking at me.

I laughed, casually.

"How naive you are! I'm the least fortunate girl ever to have lived. I've been alone for the last thirty years."

"You must be kidding!" She pinched my nose, thought for a moment, and said, "If my brother Tuấn were not a monk, he would be a great match."

"Why did he opt for that life?" I struggled to suppress a laugh and asked.

"It was his choice," Hằng looked into the distance and said. "I disapproved but ultimately realized that he must have his reasons. I've also wrestled with my difficult life, but I have no choice. I almost died in a fire, too!"

I understood that Hằng was opening the door to her soul. Perhaps she had suffered alone for too long and wanted finally to confide in someone else. Thus she invited me to partake of her innermost secrets.

"He went everywhere in that orange robe with an offering bowl in his hand," she explained, with misty eyes. "He endured place after place just to lift the curse. I've tried all kinds of things to break it, too. My way was to stay here and support this family. While doing that, I had to deal with rumors that I was a home-wrecker, a wanton, a gold digger. Alas, what else could I do to support my sister's children who had lost their mother at such young ages? I'm so isolated in this garden, but I won't give up. Thank you for coming to help me. One day this garden will be a popular tourist destination and no longer be seen as a haunted garden."

Hằng's chin widened. Her bold nature returned to her face and I could again recognize the practical businesswoman who meticulously calculated her workers' salaries and tasks. Her head was once-again filled with figures and plans. What for? Of course, not just for herself. Her youth had passed while she was doing those endless transactions to support her mother, her brother, and her six children. But there was some regret in her voice when she talked about her brother.

"For my kids, I've fulfilled my duties, now I'm worried about Tuấn. I'm saving this land for him, but he's left for some unknown place. Is he cold? Hungry? I don't know. My heart will ache when I see the apricot flowers blooming this spring."

"How old is he now?"

"Forty."

"Why don't you find some girl to keep him back here?" I said with a mischievous smile.

Hằng shook her head.

"I did everything, but beautiful girls are like logs to him. I've never seen a single flame of lust in his eyes!"

"Want to bet? I'll win his heart!" I said. Something reckless broke out in me.

Hằng just smiled.

"I would be so thankful if you could do that. I would gift you this entire garden!"

"I'm afraid that you'll regret that offer."

"You won't be able to do it," Hằng said with great confidence.

"If I really want something, I always get it!"

"Let's wait and see. Well, I must go to the factory now," Hằng said, hesitantly.

Once she left, I grabbed a book from the shelf to read. The cool breeze lulled me to sleep.

I woke up to the sound of footsteps on the stairs. Standing before me was a young, tall monk. He looked at me with indifferent eyes as he dropped his bag onto the wooden floor.

"I'm sorry. I didn't know someone was staying here," the monk said.

He joined his hands in prayer before his chest and looked off at the yellow bamboo trees. He seemed undisturbed by the scattered furniture and the clutter of home designs I had spread on the table. I quietly observed him to be a strange creature who came from another world—one that held some sober, sophisticated charm. He had a strong body with stout legs and an aloof facial expression. If he didn't have a shaved head and orange robes, he would be the most perfect man I had ever met in my life. It seemed that he was able to pick up on my mischievous thoughts and a canny smile flashed across his face.

"When did you come back?" I asked, unable to stand the silence.

Tuấn frowned.

"Did my sister Hằng tell you about me?"

I pointed at Tuấn's inscription on the walls that read, *We must die with what we know*, and then teased him, "You must know many things."

"No one dares say they know everything."

"Someone like you'll never die."

"That's not important. Everything changes over time, especially a fragile human."

"I'm not fragile," I argued. "Humans like me can craft gigantic architecture."

"Who can say nothing will collapse someday?" Tuấn said while glancing at the mess of designs on the table.

I was speechless, realizing that this man must have caused Hằng limitless torment over the years. He had become someone who placed faith in the act of praying and he would die for his belief. I became embarrassed by my mere presence in his space, but I had no choice because Hằng was not home yet. Ah, while waiting for her, I would pick at this man.

"Why did you choose to be a monk?" I asked, looking at his fading bag.

Tuấn seemed to grow pale. He inhaled deeply and exhaled slowly. After a while, he pointed toward the lotus pond and said,

"Mud, water, and lotus. I want myself to be as pure as those lotus flowers that reach for the light even when submerged in muddy water. What's wrong with trying to submerge one's troubles?"

I stared at him, with an open mouth, feeling something burning in my heart. I couldn't control myself so I walked downstairs.

"I'm going to take a walk in the garden," I said.

He remained silent. I had to stay away from that weird monk in his orange robe. Damn all his things scattered around the retreat! Lost in my thoughts, I stepped on a shriveled slug. The effluvium of mud troubled my nose. I headed toward the lotus pond to wash my feet. Ah, lotus flowers, what a gentle, pure scent! My eyes suddenly stung, my feet tried to grip the steps of the pond's dock. So, he decided to become a monk because he was afraid of a curse and thus found himself a vagabond. Wearing an orange robe, carrying a bowl in his hand, the monk kept walking, weightlessly, but leaving immense burdens on a woman's shoulders. Hằng had to take care of his six children, her mother, her brother, confront the curse, and deal with all sorts of painful rumors. The haunted garden and an unmarried wife were almost burnt in a fire. Hằng—a stern boss, workaholic, money-lover. She had to rise above all that responsibility and carry on. She didn't fear slugs and snakes; her slender, torn hands built up this splendid, poetic garden. Oh, I loved her deeply. Perhaps, because I was also a woman, I shared her perspective. Perhaps a woman like me, who had to strive every day to achieve a good life, wasn't able to understand the meaning of a lotus rising from mud and water.

I was thinking about this when Bí appeared before my eyes.

"Uncle Tuấn's back. You're wooing him, aren't you?" she laughed and teased me.

"No, I am not. Did you think I would do that? Forget about it!" I slapped her shoulders, explaining.

Bí pouted and then left me alone.

Learning that Tuấn was back, Hằng was overjoyed and immediately ran to the retreat. I happened to see their reunion. Tuấn joined his hands together before his chest as if waving away the sister-in-law who was about to hug him. Tears streamed down her face.

"Tuấn, is it you?" asked Hằng.

She rushed to him but stopped mid-way because of his distancing pose. She had to lean against a bodhi tree so that she wouldn't fall as she held her face and sobbed like a child. I couldn't detect any emotion on Tuấn's face.

"I'm going to attend a Buddhist academy for senior monks. I'm here just for a visit because I'm not sure when I can be back," Tuấn said while looking away.

Hằng pursed her lips and wiped away her tears.

"So please stay here with me for a few days before you leave. I'm glad that you look healthy. Don't torment yourself anymore. Let me clean this retreat for you. Phương will come stay with me in the big house."

Tuấn shook his head.

"Let her stay here. I'll come stay with you in the big house."

Hằng's eyes glistened with happiness.

Night fell. Suddenly, the southwest corner of the haunted garden felt desolate. I would be leaving tomorrow, too. This retreat would then become extremely melancholic. I imagined that tomorrow, once night fell, Bí would come and clean the retreat as if her Tuấn were still here. And I would never come back again. A sadness took possession of me. I shooed the girl away because she was always asking questions that would ruin my sweet but painful ruminations.

"Do you know if Tuấn will come here tonight?" Bí turned back and asked before leaving.

Her question frustrated me.

"You're crazy!"

Walking for a while, she suddenly remembered something.

"Hằng would like for you to join the family for breakfast and then say goodbye to him."

I looked at the light in the big house. It was Hằng's world, her private space that I couldn't and didn't want to intrude. I loved its mystery. My task in the haunted garden was complete. I would return to my own world, taking with me the secret of this garden. Anyway, I learned something from this journey that made me want to share.

Breakfast was prepared in one of the big house's rooms that overlooked a grapefruit grove. Hằng's brother-in-law nodded his head slightly and started eating. Bí carried a big bowl of rice and went to sit in a hidden corner. She was excited about the food but didn't want to share space with the home's owners, because she didn't like being reprimanded. Although Tuấn sat at the same table with his family during his farewell meal, his behavior kept him at a distance. He held his bowl in his left hand, a spoon in his right as he slowly stirred and ate the food. He focused on his rice as if the whole universe had converged there, in the bowl. Even though his sister-in-law wanted to put food in his bowl, she refrained. It was silent at the table and I regretted joining them.

Hằng kept putting food in my bowl. She herself could say nothing. Never had I attended such a dour party. I put my bowl down once the tea was ready. I didn't know that Hằng was so talented. It turned out she had done all the cooking. Bí was responsible only for some simple things like watering plants and weeding. After the third cup of tea, Tuấn stood up and joined his hands before his chest. Hằng dropped her piece of ginger mid-bite. It was time to say goodbye. She was about to touch the shoulder of her beloved brother, but stopped herself; instead she quietly walked out behind Tuấn. I followed as if in a trance. Our footsteps crunched on the gravel. When we reached the apricot tree that grew beside the wooden gate, Hằng and I stopped as Tuấn waved at us. Without lingering, or looking back, he walked away, step by step, slowly, and placidly.

The monk had left, carrying his alms bowl in his hands. He was walking his path. Yellow apricot flowers blossomed in the sunshine, shivering in the spring breeze, harmonizing with the monk's orange robe. He disappeared into the line of apricot trees, becoming a small dot atop the bridge. The wind blowing across the canal made Tuấn's robe billow. I glanced at Hằng—her eyes were filled with mist.

DESOLATE GRASSY HILL

TRẦN THANH HÀ

Grandma reserved a small area in her yard for planting vegetables, such as spinach, Chinese plantains, fish mint, and amaranth. She put up a thick reed fence around the garden so chickens couldn't sneak in and eat the plants. Most of her days were spent watering, pulling weeds, and sowing seeds. Everything she planted had medicinal value, she said. In the summer, she boiled and ate purslane and spinach because she believed they cooled down one's body. But our family normally consumed only a little of what she grew because it all tasted rather plain and slimy. If I had a minor fever, Grandma would chew some unpleasant-smelling Chinese plantain leaves and place them on my forehead.

On Aunt Sửu's wedding day, the young men in the village trampled down Grandma's reed fence so that they could sneak into our yard to watch a Hong Kong martial arts movie that my father was playing inside. The following morning, Grandma went out and saw shoe prints, trampled vegetables, and cigarette butts everywhere and cursed loudly until my mother told her to stop. In the afternoon, Grandma busied herself repairing the garden. Uncle Thao, my father's younger brother, brought her a bundle of reeds from the other side of the hill and made a new fence for her.

"Just stay inside, Mom," my father suggested. "You don't need to tire yourself out gardening."

Grandma sighed, "Don't forget to pee in the trough at the back of the garden," she reminded him in a gentle voice, "so I can use it to water the plants."

To reach Thao's house, one had to cross a hillside full of *léc* grass that was taller than one's head. The frightening *léc* leaves grew bigger, greener, and thicker near the creek and they were the only plants in the forest with sharp, blade-like edges that could easily slice your fingers. But Thao did not clear the *léc* grass. He simply stomped it down, cracking the stems and eventually wearing a path over them. In the dry season, villagers who collected *léc* leaves for their pigsties and wild animals used the path. When it rained, leeches and snails would sometimes take over the path and people avoided it for a while. Eventually, young leaves would rise from the roots of trodden-down *léc* and quiver in the wind.

In our village, Thao was the last person to return home from the war. Everyone thought he had died. By the time he arrived at our gate with a worn bag slung over his shoulder, his wife Hồng had already remarried and had two children. They lived together next to the market, separated from us by a river and a street. Grandma hugged Thao and sobbed while mumbling stories from the past. My mother and Aunt Sửu remained motionless, sobbing. He stood in front of the altar Hồng had erected in his memory and said nothing. The muscles of his left cheek quivered. He did not look like the man in the photograph on the altar. Thao's left cheek now had a discolored patch of skin and several small scars.

At the market, Grandma apprised Hồng of Thao's return. When she came to meet him she knelt down and bowed to him. The muscles on his left cheek trembled faster.

"Don't worry," he said. "Try to live a blissful life with your new husband."

Hồng left and never came back.

After coming home, Thao built his own house. The tall, thick *léc* grass that surrounded it made it impossible to see from a distance. He hoed the soil to plant sweet potatoes and cassava. The soil was fertile so it didn't take him long to produce a good harvest. Sugar apple and mango towered above the *léc* grass. It was said that Thao had asked the local authorities for permission to clear the other side of the hill to plant eucalyptus trees, but his request was denied. Mr. Bính, the village Chairman, said the area was riddled with unexploded bombs and nobody could be responsible if someone was injured.

Thao asked my father to put in a good word for him, but my father said, "It's not easy." "You're right—not easy." Thao nodded in agreement and left.

In the late afternoons, buffalo herders listened to the sound of a flute wafting in from the other side of the hill. The melancholy music drowned the entire *léc* hill. The buffalo herders stood to listen and forgot that the day was ending, that their stomachs were empty, and that their bodies were trembling in the cold twilight. When the music stopped, they led their buffaloes home and talked among themselves: "Thao looks scary but he plays the flute so well."

As claimed by Grandma, Hồng used to be the most beautiful girl in Thượng village. Long ago her family had arranged her marriage. At first she refused to comply because she was still in love with the sound of Thao's flute. It was as if his flute had magical power. Whenever Thao played at an event, all the village's young women became enchanted. Thus the village's young men once threatened to break all of his flutes and forbid him from playing in public.

As the Lunar New Year approached, the lemon trees in Thao's garden yielded their first fruits. Their enticing aroma filled the air. The sweet scent attracted bees that danced among the white flowers.

Thao sat pensively, gazing wistfully at the *léc* grass bent by the wind. The muscles of his left cheek shivered.

Once the lemon flowers in his garden bloomed, Sửu occasionally asked me to go to Thao's garden and bring back some flowers for her to wash her hair with. She was addicted to the scent of the white lemon flowers boiled with honey locust fruit because it lingered in her hair for several days. Lemon flowers bloomed seasonally, but Sửu enjoyed them all year round because she asked Thao to collect the fallen flowers, dry them in the sun, and save them for her.

"I was able to get married thanks to Thao's lemon flowers," Sửu once said jokingly. She proudly thought of her generation as romantic, stating, "And your generation is so materialistic, so forget about lemon flowers. Tell your father to buy you a few gold bracelets to attract men."

Sửu was unattractive; she had a dark complexion and bulky figure. She spoke in harsh, clipped sentences. After obtaining an associate's degree in agricultural studies, she worked as a technician. She was by no means a refined, elegant woman, but whenever a man in the village flirted with her, she would pout because she thought she was out of his league. She said she preferred educated men. She was over thirty but remained single. Eventually, she consented to marry an engineer at my father's company.

Grandma often asked me to pick some of the vegetables from her garden to bring to Thao, and whenever I did, she told me stories from before he was a soldier: how he had caught fish and asked her to cook mixed vegetable soup for him, or how skillful he was at hoeing the earth. She told me many stories about him, and my mother had to interrupt and tell me, "Run there quickly and come back to do your homework."

Thao didn't come to my house very often, but when he did, he brought a dozen eggs and some wild game meat—porcupine or weasel. We spoke only briefly and he left quickly.

"Thao, you should get married," Sửu once said. "You're not an old man. I'll introduce my former classmate to you . . ."

Before she finished her sentence, he glared at her and she accidentally broke the lipstick she was holding in her hand. She frowned.

"He's such a weirdo," she said out loud after he had left. "Nowadays, many women will marry a man whom nobody pays attention to. Although a small part of his face is burned, he is still a man. It's better to be married than to be single. He works hard and lives a frugal life. It won't take him long to become wealthy. Well, maybe he still loves Hồng, but she is already remarried, so what's the point of his waiting for her?"

"Stop talking nonsense, and hold your tongue," my father reprimanded Sửu.

"I'll say what I like," Sửu argued vehemently. "Do you think you *really* care about him? If you did, you wouldn't let him live in the woods all by himself. Why don't you try to get him a certification of disability? You could put in a good word with the village officials so that he can rent the *léc* hill, instead of leaving it for weeds."

"I told you already. There are lots of unexploded bombs there."

"Bullshit! You don't give a damn about Thao's life. You care about something else. You're such a hypocrite."

"Don't be idiotic. Shut up!" my father bellowed with rage.

"Who do you think you are?" Sửu wouldn't comply and continued mocking him. "Don't raise your voice with me. You can't shut me up. I know very clearly about the thousands of things you've done wrong. I even know about the enlistment letter with your name on it and how you evaded it by going abroad while scheming to get Thao drafted in your place. All your success today is due to your brother's willingness to enlist on your behalf. It might have been better for you if Thao had died.

"You . . . you . . . you . . . ," my father stammered and his face turned red.

Sửu turned and walked away.

"I'm so unfortunate, so unfortunate . . ." Grandma whined.

My mother said nothing and bit her lips while sitting alone in her bedroom. My father got on his motorbike and raced to the center of the district, although it was a Sunday.

A year after Sửu's wedding, she suddenly returned home. My mother
pulled my aunt into her bedroom. My mother's face was pale.

"What's happened?" she asked.

"I was stupid," Sửu cried and replied. "I should've remained single for the rest of my life. Getting married was a mistake."

My mother was terrified and looked around the room.

"Lower your voice and tell me what's going on?" my mother
whimpered.

"I was born under an unlucky star," Sửu wiped tears from her
face and explained. "People laughed at me for still being single in my
early thirties. I married an educated man, I get to wear nice clothes,
and everybody thinks I live an enviable life. But my husband is impotent. After finding out I was pregnant, he beat me."

"Oh, my God!" my mother exclaimed, with her face in her hands.

"I'm going to get a divorce. I don't care what you all say," Sửu
later announced in front of the entire family.

"You've disgraced this family. You've thrown mud on my name,"
Grandma screamed and yelled. Then she started crying.

"It's a dishonor to the family," my father said nothing for a while
and then started. "You can't hide it. In the future, villagers may come
here to see whom the baby looks like."

"I don't give a damn about what people say. I've got nothing to
hide," Sửu defended herself.

"Is this something you are proud of? Go downtown and listen to
the gossips about you and your husband. You might not be ashamed,
but I am."

Sửu looked at her big belly and sobbed. Our family treated the
day like a funeral.

In December the following year, the lemon flowers bloomed in Thao's garden but Sửu no longer asked me to get her any. When the cold autumn breeze danced through the green *léc* grass, chills rose up my spine. It often drizzled in the late afternoon or early evening when ushered in by a thick layer of fog. Grandma warmed her hands next to the fire all day long. When Grandma went to bed, my mother had to put burning coals under her bed to keep her warm. Every now and then she reminded us to pee into the trough at the back of the garden. Long, grayish-green amaranth flowers had begun to peak up between the pink-flowered weeds. The reed fence trembled gently in the wind. My mother threw the wooden handle of a rusted hoe into the fire, and Ki later sold its iron blade to a scrap dealer.

Sửu's baby was beautiful but he often wet the bed. No villager came to see him like my father had warned. Mr. Bính, the childless village Chairman, came to claim the baby as his, but Sửu smiled and said, "He's my son, and nobody else's." Then she put the baby into a cradle, covered him with a white mosquito net, and sang a lullaby: *Go to sleep, little heron. When you grow up, find a good girl to date.*

"Keep an eye on the baby for me," she then said to me. "I need to run out for a second. I've been staying inside since he was born. It's boring." She tied up her hair, covered her face, and left. She came back a few hours later yelling, "Crazy! Thao is crazy!"

My mother rushed into the living room from the kitchen. Sửu removed her face covering and said, "There're several unmarried women in this village, so why did he choose that disgusting Nền? Marrying her is like wearing a neck shackle. Everyone will ridicule him for the rest of his life."

Nền moved in with Thao. Her house had been near the school. Nobody ever saw her husband, but she had three children. School kids often dropped by her house to ask for drinking water, or unripe papayas and guavas to eat with chili pepper salt. Some kids even stole some eggs and one of her hens. Nền saw them do it but didn't discipline them. She simply told them not to steal. But the mischievous kids wouldn't stop.

Nền was a frequent topic of gossip among the men who sat around killing time. They joked and slapped each other's back: "Nền is so easy. Just make up stories about your miseries and she'll pity you and let you have her."

The women in the village found Nền disgusting. They called her a slut, a whore, a bitch. Nobody ever came to her house except for the school kids during the day.

Sửu gently shook Grandma and complained about Thao. Grandma was sitting quietly in the kitchen warming her hands by the fire, and she seemed not to listen. Her eyes were blurry as if filled with smog. She smiled and showed her gums. Every now and then she asked my mother, "When will the anniversary of Thao's death come?"

"He's still alive, and he's come back," my mother rubbed her eyes and reminded Grandma gently.

"Oh, I see," Grandma said. Her eyes brightened a bit and then became blurry again. My mother and Sửu looked at each other and remained silent.

The hill was empty except for a few buffalo herders. They crouched in their cloaks made from dry leaves while the cold wind turned their skin pale. The sound of Thao's flute meandered through the *léc* green leaves. Accompanied by the late afternoon's drizzle, it sounded melancholic. None of the buffalo herders said a word. They held each other's hands and looked at the little house on the other side of the hill where a streak of smoke curled up and wafted away.

LONGING IN VAIN

NGUYỄN HƯƠNG DUYÊN

Mom sat on a corner of the bed facing the window and Dad by the tea table. Outside, waves playfully rippled one after another. Dad's empty stare landed on his teacup. After a long while, Mom sighed quietly. Dad remained seated, motionless.

"Why did you come back? Have you forgiven me?" asked Mom, in a soft voice. She seemed on the verge of sobbing.

"It's time for me to come back," Dad exhaled loudly and answered in a deep voice. "I'm glad that you are *not* with anyone."

Tears crowded Mom's throat. The bones protruding from her skinny shoulders trembled. Dad stood up slowly and walked outside. The waves continued to murmur, accompanied by whispering winds.

Dad finally came back. He was my father but also a stranger. He looked rather relaxed and confident as if his twenty-year absence from the family had been merely a routine adventure that Mom, my brother, and I, had no right to complain about. His return meant there was a male voice in the household. Mom became happier and had more energy. I, on the contrary, felt deeply hurt and wallowed in self-pity and resentment. During my childhood, I had longed for his presence and protection. *Dad, where were you during those years?*

Mom never told us the reason behind his absence or where he was. My younger brother Tít and I grew up as witnesses to the sorrow Mom endured due to her love and longing for Dad. He left when my lips were only first beginning to babble the word *Daddy*. Back then, I ran after him, grabbed his shirt and beseeched him to hold me. That stormy afternoon lodged itself in my mind and haunted my sleep every night until I became an adult.

Our house was located on a sandbar where the river spills into the sea. If you walked through our village past a poplar forest you would reach the ocean. Its little houses seemed to crowd closer to one another when the sea was turbulent. The river flowed beneath the shade of coconut trees out to the ocean—as dictated by the laws of nature. The river isolated us from a bustling town that stood across its banks. For my entire childhood, I thought that if I could cross the river I would be able to find Dad. At night, when the moon shyly peeked above the horizon, Mom would stare across the river as a breeze rustled the leaves of the coconut trees.

Despondency welled in Mom's eyes as she watched the current slip past. Those melancholic eyes were burned into my adolescent mind. Dad remained elsewhere. Day after day, some unspeakable secret weighed Mom down.

"Don't hate him. It's all my fault," she wept and said when I spoke ill of Dad.

"Tell me why?" I cried loudly.

Mom remained silent and refused to answer my question, her eyes reflecting more anguish than ever.

At midnight, it was tranquil but the air was stifling. It made my handicapped brother Tít uneasy and he writhed on his bed because he couldn't breathe. He was asthmatic and sudden changes in the weather affected his condition. Thus my mother and I had to take him to the clinic near our house. When he saw a syringe, he recoiled and sulked.

"I don't want to be injected. It hurts." Tít opened his mouth wide and gasped for air.

The nurse soothed him with a gentle voice, as my mother often did.

"Be a good boy. Tomorrow I'll give you a whistle. Be good now! That's right. You're doing great. See, it doesn't hurt at all."

Tít immediately returned to his normal self, goofy laughter and all. But normal for Tít wasn't normal for most. His pupils constantly darted back and forth. Two long, large, welt-like growths stretched from his ears to his mouth and made his lips grotesquely thick and ugly. Tít fell asleep on our way home. Mom carried his forty-kilogram body on her back, moving at nearly a run. It started to rain. The teeming rain always ushered in an increase in Mom's uneasy sighs and festering sorrow.

I had to get ready for my teaching assignment in the mountains. As always, Mom packed for me as if it were her lone remaining pleasure in life. She bent her head to conceal tearful eyes as she meticulously filled my bag.

"Try to take good care of yourself, and don't worry about anything. I can take care of your brother," she assured me.

I ran to the river pier and cried in solitude. Early afternoon, the sun's yellow reflection bobbed atop the surface, which was beset by floating algae. Out of nowhere, Tít ran toward me and whistled loudly. A piece of red cloth was pinned to his sleeve. He waved a stick that had one end painted red and the other blue. I wiped away my tears and realized that I needed to help Mom with something. Tít was well behaved and stood still while I gave him a bath, pausing every now and then to pucker his lips to tease me. Mom stood on the veranda, her eyes sparkling with unusual gaiety.

Without a man in our family, all the burdens fell upon Mom. I taught in a mountainous region far from home and thus couldn't be of any help. My detached attitude toward Tít saddened her even more. But I realized I didn't hate Tít as much as I had thought, back when I used to blame my disabled brother for Dad abandoning us. If Tít were a normal kid, Mom would be less disconsolate.

My boyfriend Vũ had lost his patience with me and didn't want to wait until the day I could move back to the Mekong Delta to make things work. The last time we met, he said he was no longer excited about traveling nearly two hundred kilometers through the mountains just to hold me briefly in his arms. It wasn't enough to satiate his longing every week. I jerked my head away from his face proudly and refused to ask him for an explanation. When there is no love, all attempts to hold on become ridiculous. In my mind, I thanked him for not telling me the real reason for our breakup—his mother didn't want him to marry me because Dad left Mom. His mother was afraid that I would have Dad's bad genes. Her rationale helped me forget Vũ and come to terms with the end of our relationship without anger or bitterness. Vũ was like everybody else. He didn't like conflicts or complications. I decided that I didn't want to be a burden to anyone, so I embarked on a carefree life.

I visited Mom twice a month. She refused to entertain any suitor, although two men admired her beauty. At night, Tít slept in a swinging hammock in a corner of the house, forgoing a bed because he preferred the hammock's rocking motion. He didn't sleep much and opened his eyes while holding his whistle between his lips. He placed his stick across his belly while the piece of red cloth remained on his shirt. He didn't blow the whistle loudly at night. He only blew it gently, generating a mere flutter.

At first, I was irritated because I couldn't sleep.

"Leave him alone. He's always like that," Mom sighed and said.

At four in the morning, the river pier grew busy. Tít jumped out of his hammock, running excitedly toward the gate, blowing his whistle loudly.

"Recently he's been flirting with girls. Poor thing!" Mom turned over and said.

It dawned on me that Tít was already twenty years old. I had often counted on my fingers to remember his age and also to remember how many years it had been since Dad had left us. I used to wonder where Dad was, whether he knew he had a son who was his age when he had left, and which of his biological urges were starting to express themselves in his handicapped body. Tít kept teasing the girls, which frightened them so that they would screech and throw rocks at him. Days went by and Mom's sighs filled our house even more frequently.

Winter nights on the mountain were extremely cold. High, steep cliffs emitted frigid air that made me shiver. I nestled in my warm blanket and listened to the wind ripping through my thatched roof. The locked door shuddered, making a ghostly sound. The night was long. My despair froze when I thought about my parents, and I warmed myself with memories of Vũ, but, ironically, a feeling of loneliness and self-pity filled my heart.

I was pregnant. A bold man who was infatuated with me had knocked on my door one night while I was living in an abyss of desperation amid the windy hills. The animals out in the wild couldn't stand the cold either and their terrifying howls echoed across the forest.

"Oh, no! I never taught you to act so foolishly! Do you want to kill me?" my mother bellowed after learning about my pregnancy.

I felt dead inside.

"It's because of Dad. Do you know that? It's your fault, too," I argued. "Neither of you was ever there when I needed you the most. You never gave comfort in my life."

Mom collapsed on the floor like a fallen tree.

When I was fifteen, I once accompanied Mom to the poplar forest to collect dry leaves. It was windy in the forest. I kept walking negligently until I got lost on a beach. A man with a thick beard stopped me and asked, "Do you want to meet your Dad? Come with me."

"How do you know my Dad?" I inquired as I opened my eyes wide and looked at him skeptically.

"I'm his friend," he replied.

Then he grasped my wrist and pulled me. My legs seemed shackled by a ghost and I followed him.

Suddenly, out of nowhere, Mom rushed toward me and cried out, "My daughter . . ."

She was like a mother hen stretching out her wings to protect her chicks. The bearded man disappeared quickly. Mom dropped to the ground, felt my entire body up and down, and hugged me.

"Thank God! My daughter is OK." She exulted in my safety.

"Why are you crying, Mom?" I remained aloof and inquired. "The man told me he would take me to see Dad."

"That man is not a good person," she glared at me and warned. "Don't ever trust him. Your Dad is far away." Her voice was drowned in the vastness of the area; her eyes filled with sorrow.

The incident terrified Mom and afterward she watched over us even more attentively. My pregnancy traumatized her to her core. I secretly had an abortion and bore the pain alone. I avoided the father of my unborn child like the plague. I dismissed his hope of having me when I ground my teeth during the abortion. I had already lost my virginity and with it my opportunity to marry a worthy husband.

"Nobody can be a virgin twice in their life. Women are shallow-minded," Mom reprimanded me.

Filled with despair, I looked at the blue sky and her words were like salt grating across my heart.

Dad hadn't come back. Tít became feebler when winter came. His asthma tormented him constantly, and one day he was unable to blow his whistle. Tít lay on the bed, his eyes lifeless, his breath heavy. The two growths on his face turned red. He died in pain, not knowing how many of the girls that he had teased cried upon hearing the news. Mom grieved by his cold corpse. I hugged her and my chest ached. If paradise existed, I hoped that he would go there, because he had lived a life of agony predetermined by fate.

After Tít's death, our house became quite empty. In the early morning, the river pier was depressingly quiet. Shadows circled Mom's dark, sunken eyes. I rolled up Tít's hammock, hoping that it would alleviate Mom's sorrow, but she still cried every night. I started to have nightmares about Tít.

On the ceremony marking one hundred days after Tít's burial, Dad came home, carrying a big, heavy suitcase. Mom was astonished when he arrived at the door. He gently patted her shoulder, nodded his head, entered the house, and looked around. Mom ran out to find me. I could hardly understand what she mumbled upon seeing me.

When I followed her home, I was neither happy nor excited—I just stood there staring. My longing for Dad had long ago become hardened, petrified into hatred. My indifferent attitude was like a declaration of war on him. I rejected his caring gestures, and Mom looked at me anxiously. I said to myself, Mom, please don't be mad at me. Dad wasn't around during my childhood. When I was growing up, he wasn't there to teach me right from wrong. He comes back when I have nothing to lose, when feelings of loss have already permeated my heart.

I wanted to cross the river and return to my windy mountain. It was the first time I left without telling Mom when I would be back.

"I beg you. Please don't hate him. He's heartbroken, too," she held my hand and pleaded.

"Is he really heart-broken? He doesn't deserve our longing," I argued bitterly.

"Honey, everything is my fault," she said regretfully. "He isn't as bad as you think. In fact, he should be pitied."

I stared into her eyes and detected an unspeakable desolation. My heart sank into exhaustion.

"Tít is the evidence of my betrayal to your father. I must tell you about my sinful secret. When he was in my womb, it was already too late to hide him from your Dad. Tít's father was my first love. I lost control with him and we slept together. I lied to your Dad. After learning of my affair, your Dad was mortified. I tried to get rid of the baby in my womb but I failed, and Tít was born—a pathetic, handicapped boy. Dad left. Back then I wanted to commit suicide. Only death could free me from my guilt. But I had to live for you and Tít, and I've been tormenting myself with the glimmer of hope that he eventually would come back."

My ears popped as if an arriving storm plunged the air pressure. Mom's loss of self-control had caused my family turmoil. Dad's self-respect and masculine pride forced him to refuse Mom's attempts at repenting. My respect for Mom was gone, but I thought back to how I lost my virginity on a cold, windy night in the mountains—an experience that I wished to forget—and realized that my experience allowed me to understand Dad better and forgive Mom.

I walked to the river's pier. The light from the other side of the shore reflected on the currents in front of me. Dad was sitting in a small boat that Mom often used to cross the river. He held a paper bridge to offer to the dead. He lit a match. White ashes fluttered into the air and landed in his hair. When Tít was alive, he had always dreamed about a bridge that would connect the two sides of the river and the sand bar with the busy town. A half-moon had risen and the wind rustled through the coconut trees. I hoped that my mind could hold this memory forever.

THE BITTER HONEY

NIÊ THANH MAI

"*T*omorrow *you come beneath my longhouse, when the rooster
has yet to crow, you stomp your right foot, I know, you stomp
your left foot, I see.*
"*You and I go down the hill together; my eyes in yours.*"

Dung couldn't stand the way her sister-in-law Phen's singing
floated in the mountain air. She sang incessantly from dawn to dusk.
When in the fields, her trilling voice pierced her thoughts. It wove
itself into the branches of the coffee plants laden with fragrant, white
flowers. Phen's eyes sparkled and she smiled to herself when she was
alone. Only a person who is in love smiles like that.

The fire that raged in Dung's heart revealed itself when she performed quotidian tasks. For example, when she went to make rice,
she burned it three or four times in a row. It was so inedible that her
mother no longer asked her to do it.

But Dung couldn't stay still. She had to do something. She
swept the house, and then brought out the loom to weave a brocade. The sound of shuttles flowing back and forth all night left her
mother sleepless, but Dung feared that if she stayed idle, her head
would burst.

"Is something wrong?" asked her mother the night before.

"Nothing, mom."

"You know how to lie, but your behavior gives you away. You've done nothing well recently. You mess everything up. You're an adult now and you don't have a boyfriend, so what could possibly be making you so upset?"

Dung's mother looked deeply into her daughter's eyes. Dung's heart felt like an uneven thread in the loom. Alas, how could Dung confide her heart in someone, while withholding it makes her life unbearable?

Until the previous day, it had been quite some time since it last rained in Jin village. Under her blanket, Dung could hear the heavy rain furiously pelting the metal roof. It rumbled all night long. Dung tossed and turned sleeplessly until the rooster crowed. When she closed her eyes, the images reappeared vividly. Dung pictured again and again Phen's wet body seen through the bamboo screen. And the suppressed moaning, heavy breathing . . .

The sun hadn't risen yet, but Dung was sitting up, holding her knees against her chest on the mat. She sat like that until the day began.

"Didn't you sleep last night? You have dark circles around your eyes. What's going on?"

Phen was tightening her sarong as she spoke. Dung said nothing in return and simply stared into her eyes. Dung noticed a flicker of embarrassment in them, but her sister-in-law looked away and said, "I'll head to the farm early today. Despite the recent storm, it hasn't rained much this year and our coffee plants will wilt if they don't get some water."

Dung was left to sit next to the window alone. The morning breeze blew in carrying her sister-in-law's voice.

In Dung's village, nobody wanted to live with the husband's family. Yet Phen came to stay with Dung's family after marrying Dung's brother. Êđê girls proposed to their husbands and after they married, the husband would move in with her family. The arrangement would last for three years, seven years, maybe even their entire lives. A husband could die, become a ghost and stay there forever. But Dung's brother was different; he wanted his wife to come to live with his family. She agreed and moved into their home.

But Dung knew that she came to stay with her family because she was like an orphan. Her impoverished family couldn't even build a bamboo screen as Dung's family could. In the summer and winter, wind tore through cracks in their home's wall, leaving it frigid every night.

When Phen arrived at Dung's house, she gave gifts to her in-laws. She presented a blanket to Dung's mother, a sarong to Dung, a scarf to Dung's uncle. Dung's mother said she didn't have to give anything else, but to simply have a congenial life with her son. Dung saw how emotional Phen became at that moment. Tears filling her eyes as she gripped her new mother-in-law's hands.

Dung's mother was so ecstatic to have Phen around. She was more elated than Dung's brother even. Whenever Dung's mother went to the woods to collect bamboo shoots, she woke Phen up to make rice balls for their lunch and they went together. When rattan shoots peeked out of the soil, she took Phen to the woods and picked some to make broth for the family. Dung's mother and Phen gossiped together all day long. Dung's brother acted upset at being abandoned like that, but Dung thought he actually liked it.

Phen didn't want her husband to go into the forest to collect honey. She said that her heart jolted when she saw him scale an enormous tree and dangle out on its far branches toward beehives. Besides, bees were just like humans, so how could we take their homes without feeling guilty?

Dung's brother laughed loudly, saying, "If we don't get them, others will. Beehives are lucrative. We only need a few to equal working the farm for an entire year. Besides, we take just enough for you to buy threads and weave new clothes for next year."

Dung continued to follow her brother into the woods for beehives, but she disagreed with Phen. As she watched her brother climb a towering tree, her pulse raced. Upon reaching a branch with a beehive, he would burn grass or dry leaves. He had to be careful not to start a fire but still to make enough smoke to drive the bees from their nest. The smoke made his eyes sting but once the bees flew out, he could grab the hive and put it in his basket. Some were so filled with honeycombs that he had to make numerous trips up and down to get it all.

He would give all the money he made from selling the honey to his wife, telling her to buy more thread for weaving brocades and to get some pork to make soup with the bitter eggplant for the rest of the family.

"Don't eat dried fish all the time," her brother said.

Phen said nothing, but quietly took the money and put it in a wooden box in her room.

One day in March. Dung's brother fell from the fork of an old tree while attempting to get honey. Perhaps the bees were especially aggressive and stung him repeatedly, so he lost his grip and fell to his death. He was dead before the villagers found him, crumpled on the earth in torn clothes, his hands still grasping the dripping honeycomb. The villagers informed his family and Dung dashed to look for her mother and Phen. When they arrived, Phen held his body tight, sobbing. Her face grew paler and paler until she fainted.

After her husband died, Phen paced back and forth like a shadow and neglected her meals. In the first few days after his funeral, she sat at the steps by the gate, her face constantly wet with tears. Dung's mother also wept from morning until night. Dung lay in the living room, wailing her eyes out as well. The house was in mourning. On the fourth day after the funeral, Phen went to the farm and got some vegetables for dinner. She prepared four bowls, and her voice was clear when she said, "Mom, my husband has passed away, but we have to live well. Mourning him forever would trouble him, and he won't be able to reincarnate. Please eat, mom, and drink some wine to live the life that my husband expects."

Dung, Dung's mother, and Phen all sat around the dinner table. Each one held a glass. They couldn't swallow the bitter eggplant in their bowls. Finally, Dung's mother started weeping and said she needed one more day to mourn before she could begin living the life her son would've wanted for them.

Dung's mother loved Phen like a daughter and never once yelled at her. When Phen's husband was still alive, the other villagers asked Phen why she hadn't gotten pregnant yet, as they had already been married for three harvests. They talked among themselves, "Why did her belly look as flat as a crepe myrtle tree in the forest?"

They then visited Dung's mother and warned, "Poisoned trees can't bear fruits, and cursed women can't conceive children. You should find another wife for your son."

"If you keep talking like that, get out of here, and don't ever come back," Dung's mother, out of frustration, yelled back at them.

After her husband deceased, the villagers spread the rumor that Phen must've been possessed by a ghost that brought misfortune to the family. If not, how could Dung's brother die from falling from a tree?

The rumor made Phen miserable. Every early morning, she would wake up before the rooster crowed and go to the farm and stay until well after dark. She didn't talk or laugh like she used to. She was a mere shadow drifting through the world.

Once, at dinner, Dung's mother told Phen, "We can't stop people from spreading rumors, but we don't have to take what they say to heart. Why must we let them disturb our lives? If a tree wants to survive in a dense forest, it has to grow higher and snatch the sunlight. We'll have to strive to grow above the gossip and grasp our happiness."

Phen burst into tears. She hadn't wept in two weeks but now she couldn't suppress her agony any longer and cried endlessly. Dung thought Phen had become emotional because her mother didn't truly understand what was in her mind. But Dung's mother loved her dearly. Dung loved Phen, too, and wished she had a good man whose shoulders she could lean on when exhausted, and someone to have children with and build a family together.

But when Phen did find that man, Dung was tormented. If it had been someone other than Y'Thôn, Dung wouldn't have been so bitter. Dung had loved Y'Thôn and his thick muscles and kind smile since her breasts were first starting to develop. She would blush and run to hide behind her friends whenever he came around.

Did Y'Thôn know Dung had had a crush on him? Dung had no idea. Accidently, on the rainy day a few days prior, Dung's mother asked her to take a raincoat to Phen as she was staying in a temporary hut to watch the family's farm during the cultivation season. When looking through the bamboo screen, Dung shuddered when seeing Y'Thôn and Phen so lost in each other's bodies that they didn't mind the torrential downpour outside, nor did they know that Dung was standing out there in the thunderstorm.

Dung sprinted through the field. She didn't go home. She didn't know where she was going. Running through thorn grass and spiky weeds she reached the top of a hill and dropped down to the ground beneath an imposing *knia* tree. The rain stopped and her body shivered but Dung still didn't go home. How could she? How could she fight back tears when she saw Phen?

After that day, Dung said nothing to Phen, and only replied to her questions with curt statements. After Phen went to the farm, Dung's mother held her hands with her bony fingers.

"Is there something wrong between you two? Bowls and dishes in the same basket can clash; it's the same with sisters. If you can, why don't you just let those troubles flow away with the stream in the forest?"

"How can I forget them, mom? Don't you know Phen is seeing another man?"

"Your brother passed away a long time ago. And your sister-in-law is still young."

"I'm your daughter but you don't feel sorry for me. Why do you love a stranger more? Only a stranger would steal your daughter's man like that." Dung groaned, dashed down the stairs, and ran to the entrance of the village. She went far away from everyone so she could cry alone.

Alas, Y'Thôn never smiled and chatted with Dung because of her sister-in-law. If Dung happened to meet him at a festival, his eyes were always longing for Phen's, even though Dung was younger and more beautiful. How could he love a widow but not a single girl like Dung?

Her heart was shattered.

Dung's mother sat quietly at the door and let Dung sob inside without saying a word. Perhaps her mother thought that if she let Dung cry till her tears ran dry, her agony eventually would flow out.

Three days went on this way until Dung's mother woke Dung up.

"How much longer would you stay in there? Are you going to die a spinster in that dark room?"

"What can I do now, mom? I don't want to see Phen's face again. My heart is broken."

Dung wept. Her heart pounded but her body was frail. Dung and Phen never hid anything from each other. But this time she didn't tell Phen about the cause of her anguish.

Dung's mother rose to her feet and turned on the light.

"In this village men were like leaves in a forest. If one doesn't love you, look for another. You'll find someone who loves you more than he loves himself. But you have only one sister."

"Mom, it's not that easy. Love isn't so simple. My heart is disobedient; it can't be forced to do anything."

Dung was so aggravated that she couldn't sleep that night, rolling side to side until the rooster crowed. Dung didn't know that on the other side of the divider, her sister-in-law was also awake. And across the house, in a small room, Dung's mother was also sleepless. Their home was frigid, even with a burning fireplace.

Y'Thôn's family ferreted out his affair with Phen. Early one morning, just as the sun had emerged from behind a bamboo ridge, Y'Thôn's mother rushed into Dung's house, yelling like crazy at Dung's mother, "Did you know your daughter-in-law is having an affair with my son?"

The two women faced each other, but looked like they were in different worlds. One was seething, the other sober.

"So what? My daughter-in-law is still young and has no kids. I consider her my daughter. Your son is an adult. If you approve, I'll take him into my family."

"Impossible."

Dung had never heard such a loud voice in her house. Y'Thôn's mother stood straight up, her hands shook frantically, her head jerking.

"I would never allow her to live with my son. Sleeping with a woman like her will make him a ghost the next morning. Don't forget how your son died. Please tell her to stop seducing my son. Otherwise, don't blame me for what will happen."

Dung's mother collapsed, enraged. Dung came to hold her. On Y'Thôn's mother's way out she passed Phen at the door and stared her down without saying a word. Phen was petrified, her face the pale color of a fever patient. Tears streamed down her face. Suddenly, Dung felt sorry for Phen and all her earlier resentment vanished in an instant.

Dung's mother skipped lunch and then dinner. So did Phen. The house was somber. Meals were prepared but no one bothered to eat them. Dung's tongue tasted bitter and she put the food away without being able to eat a single bite. She fed the pigs and sprinkled rice in the yard for the chickens, but her dolor lingered. Time and again, she would hear Y'Thôn's mother's shrieking voice reverberating in her head.

After Dung's brother died under a tree, the villagers spread a rumor that Phen had bad karma and whoever became her husband would die, sooner rather than later. Men in the village had been climbing trees for honey for generations and there had been only a few accidents that caused broken limbs but they got healed in a couple of months. Only Dung's brother had died. The villagers spread other rumors, but Dung's mother ignored them. She loved her son as much as she felt sorry for Phen's loneliness. When Y'Thôn's mother yelled at her that morning, she, however, was shaken, confused, and unsure how to talk to her daughter-in-law. Did she need to tell Phen to stop seeing Y'Thôn, or did she need to tell her to ignore what people said, since the villagers would soon find something else to gossip about?

She mulled it over that night but came to no conclusion about what to say.

It all made Dung love Phen more, especially when Y'Thôn called Phen softly from below the house one night. With a bamboo stick, he poked open the window above where Phen was lying. Dung was sleeping with Phen so the stick hit Dung's arm. Dung nudged Phen but she refused to sit up. Her face simply turned away toward the divider. She pretended to be in a deep sleep, but an occasional gentle sigh revealed that she was awake the entire night.

At dawn, Dung shook her sister-in-law, whispering, "Phen, do you genuinely love Y'Thôn?"

"I don't know. Come on! Please forget what you have learned. I enjoy living with you and mom like this."

Phen's voice was neither gleeful nor sad. She sat up and tied her hair into a bun. Then she sat with her arms around her knees, staring blankly ahead.

"How about you and Y'Thôn leaving this village for somewhere far away?" Dung suggested softly. "Live together for a few years, have kids, then come back. Nobody will blame you for anything."

"I don't want to leave our house. Must I leave this village to live a contented life? I love mom. I can live without men, but my life would mean nothing without you and mom."

Then she turned to touch Dung's face gently. Dung loved her sister-in-law's warm gesture. Just days ago, Dung didn't want to see Phen's face ever again and had wished she would vanish forever.

Phen went downstairs and Dung opened her sister-in-law's small window. Y'Thôn was standing below the window. Perhaps he had been there all night. His hair was soaked with dew. His eyes were deep and filled with sorrow. Dung felt a surge of adrenaline, but it wasn't the same as when she saw him and Phen entangled. She just felt sorry for the couple.

What could Dung do to help the man hold her sister-in-law's hand again? She couldn't do anything. Every day, Y'Thôn stood below the window where Phen sat weaving a brocade. Her lover was waiting, but she never opened the window.

One week. Ten days. Then one month.

She never went to the farm; she just stayed indoors and wove brocades. She said if she stayed inside like this, the thread of love would be broken; such a thread was fragile. One morning Dung didn't notice Y'Thôn at first when she opened the window, but then saw him standing right before her. Y'Thôn was bony, his hair fell across his forehead, and his beard was wild. He looked like someone who had spent months in the deep forest. His eyes were even sadder than the last time she had seen them.

"Phen doesn't want to see me anymore, does she?" he asked Dung.

"Please go home. How can you live like this, Y'Thôn?"

It was agonizing to see. Y'Thôn had stood for so long outside Phen's room. Why didn't he go home and persuade his mother and his family that Phen was a good girl? It was simple. Dung was only an in-law, but her husband's family loved her just like one of their own. Phen was talented, taking care of the housework and the farm work without complaint. And although Dung's brother had passed away a long time ago, Dung's family still lived a comfortable life— they had a motorbike, a TV, and everything else they wanted. Who could compare with Phen? Only a few could match up to her. He should've told his family about this, and if they still rejected her, he should've kept trying to convince them. But Y'Thôn only stood there and watched. He waited so long that the leaves outside the house turned brown and fell.

Early one morning Phen opened the window above the loom. Y'Thôn was nowhere to be seen. She told her mother that she would go to the market to sell the brocade that she had just finished weaving. While she was dissembling the loom to remove the fabric, Dung sat down next to her and spoke in a light voice, "Sister, I've heard that some girl in the village came to ask Y'Thôn for his hand in marriage."

"Uhm."

"Why uhm? Are you sad?"

"Dung, do you think this brocade is pretty?"

"Why do you ask? I'm talking about love."

"This morning, I'll take it to the market. If people don't like it, I'll bring it home and reweave it. If I work diligently enough, I'll have a worthy brocade to sell."

Dung didn't know if her sister was disconsolate at the news that another girl had come to marry Y'Thôn because she showed no emotion. In a few days, Y'Thôn would become someone's husband. After that, if Phen and Y'Thôn ever passed each other in the village, they would gaze at each other like strangers.

What does it look like when a lover becomes a stranger?

The thread of love, once broken, can never be mended.

Why not seek another thread? If it can't be found in the woods, it can be found in the mountains where birds sing and streams babble. Would there be men there? Very likely. Men always go to the woods to collect honey.

AFTER THE STORM

TRẦN THỊ THẮNG

I was looking for a caregiver for my hospitalized mother when I was introduced to a young woman named Cẩm Thúy from Cà Mau. She was carrying a duffle bag when she entered my mother's room and greeted her with a smile. When my mother sneezed, Thúy patted her on the back and quickly pulled out a tissue to wipe my mother's nose. Seeing that Thúy clearly had experience with this kind of work, I asked her to take care of my mother.

"Mom, I've got to go home now," I said.

My mother gently released her hold on my hands so that I could leave. I was her only daughter, so when I got married, she moved in with me. She was used to having me by her side. I was her breath; she was my refuge.

Sài Gòn was packed with vehicles and people. I didn't pay much attention to how crowded it was until my mother was hospitalized, which forced me to travel back and forth from the suburbs. I always wondered why so many people poured onto the streets every night as if there were a festival going on. A traffic jam ahead forced some motorbikes to turn around in search of another route. Cars and trucks stood still and I was stuck between them. I loosened my grip on the handlebars and thought about my mother.

I got home late and my husband and young daughter greeted me at the door. She embraced me, sobbing, and said, "I miss Grandma. I miss Grandma!"

We had to conciliate her for a bit before she stopped crying so that we could sit down and have dinner together.

That night, Thúy suddenly appeared in my mind: her oval face, ivory skin, bright smile, and maroon fingernails. How could a person like her become a caregiver? Although my daughter was sleeping next to me, I wanted to leave the house and run to the hospital immediately to check on my mother. But I had to wait until morning when my husband could look after my daughter.

Sài Gòn was rarely foggy in the early morning, and when it was, the cool air was refreshing. I gently pushed open the door of my mother's room and walked in. Thúy was lying on a mat on the floor while my mother slept peacefully in her bed. I quickly and quietly closed the door behind me and stood in the open hallway enjoying the fresh breeze. When Thúy walked out to get hot water for the thermos, I rushed inside.

"Was everything OK last night, Mom? Is Thúy taking good care of you?"

"No need to worry. She knows what she's doing," my mother replied softly as she caressed my hand.

The night before was the first time I had not been with my mother to take care of her, and hearing she was doing just fine was a great relief. Thúy entered with a smile. "You must be worried about your mother. Last night, I helped her walk to the restroom twice. She slept well. Please don't let her know you're worried. A patient needs peace of mind."

I gave my mother a bowl of porridge. She held my hands and then gently pushed them away. I felt comfortable trusting Thúy to watch my mom so that I could go to work.

Because Thúy had been with my mother for only one night, she remained enigmatic to me. I called my husband on the phone to ask him to pick our daughter up after school, and then returned to the hospital. After helping my mother eat her dinner, Thúy accompanied her for a walk on the rooftop right above her room. My mother needed to lean her old, enervated body against Thúy so that she wouldn't fall. When she was sapped by walking, she sat down. Her gray hair spilled across Thúy's shoulder when she rested her head on it. A breeze blew in and tussled her locks so they resembled a layer of fog. I whispered to myself, Mom, Mom.

I walked toward her and sat down. She intertwined her old, dry fingers with mine and moved them gently as if expressing endearing words. Thúy massaged my mother's shoulders. Her maroon fingernails moved back and forth like waves while my mother closed her eyes with a contented look on her face.

After putting my mother to bed, I asked Thúy to sit with me on the rooftop.

"How long have you been working as a caregiver?"

"Eleven years."

"You must have been very young and beautiful when you started."

"When I left home, I cried until I had no tears left. I told myself that I would be gone for ten years, until I was thirty-two, and then I would come back. It's already been eleven years. I have three children, and I haven't been back once."

"So when will you return for good?"

"It'll take me one more year to pay off our loan. After that, I can go home and we'll start from the beginning again."

Thúy had left her hometown of Cà Mau after the storm in 1997. The typhoon sunk her husband's fishing boat, but he survived. Her mother-in-law gave the young couple ten taels of gold that she had been saving her entire life to help them pay off a portion of the debt they owed to friends who had loaned them the money to buy their boat. Her father-in-law had been more fortunate in his fishing career than his son, so her parents-in-law had done quite well financially. Originally from Thanh Hóa, her mother-in-law moved to Cà Mau, where she had met the indigent young man who later became her husband. When their unfortunate son lost everything in the storm, they used their entire savings to help him.

The elderly couple was disheartened by their son's misfortune. After it happened they took a walk along the beach, hand in hand, and reminisced about the husband's life fishing on the open ocean. The old man had never experienced a storm like the one that stripped his son of everything. The son's misfortune became his father's financial burden.

"It seems like the sea provided us fish so that we could earn enough money to raise our kids. And then the sea took everything from us," the old woman said, looking out across the waves.

"That's not completely true," the old man refuted. "There had never been a storm in Cà Mau until this unfortunate year. Water is the most dangerous of the elements, followed by fire, our ancestors warned. It's lucky that he survived and came back unharmed. You and I have lived a hard life, but we have five sons, and they're all alive. That's a blessing from our ancestors. Expecting too much shortens your life."

The sea is vast and deep, and humans are small. As one ages, the sea becomes vaster.

After the elderly couple returned home, a loan officer from the bank arrived and said to their son and daughter-in-law, "This is your loan—two hundred million đồng. Please sign here."

The young couple had to borrow the money from the bank to pay back their neighbors and friends who had helped them buy the boat.

Tư Bảo, Thúy's husband, looked at the loan document as if it were a fishing net. Without hesitation, he signed his name. The movement of his pen felt like a knife across his mother's heart. Even though she had been in labor seven times, she had never experienced such pain—the pain caused by witnessing the scattering of her beloved.

On the rooftop, Thúy told me that, after the storm, she went to Sài Gòn and Bảo worked for his eldest brother taking care of racehorses in Long An. The family separated. Thúy's mother had to take care of her six-year-old son and two-year-old daughter. The boy looked like his father, the little girl looked like her mother. During her eleven years working as a caregiver, she hadn't spent a single Tết with her family. She had to stay in Sài Gòn during the Vietnamese Lunar New Year, not because she got paid double, but because Tết was when her patients needed her the most. Her mother-in-law did not complain about her absence, which was a way of showing Thúy that she supported and sympathized with her choices. However, her sisters-in-law showed disgust toward Thúy's low-class job, which, according to them, was full of temptation. It wasn't easy for a live-in caregiver to maintain her chastity, they argued. But because she had no formal education, Thúy had no choice but to work as a caregiver. She had to send home at least twenty-four million đồng every year to pay for her children's school tuition and to make payments on the loan.

Good caregivers must love their patients the way they love their own parents, siblings, or relatives.

"People normally don't trust caregivers," Thúy said. "And caregivers are fully aware of the dangers of sexual harassment and molestation."

"People need to overcome their prejudices to work together," I said.

"I'm still young, so I must resist temptations because I love my husband and my kids. It isn't easy."

Then she told me a story:

Once upon a time, I was the hired caregiver of a 53-year-old Korean man in the hospital. He had never been married and he fell in love with me. He invited his younger sister from Korea to visit Việt Nam.

"Thúy, please marry my brother and move to Korea with us. He never loved anyone until he met you. You're living a miserable life here. Why don't you take this opportunity and change your life for the better?" the Korean sister said.

"I have two children. The sea tore up our lives, but we still love the sea and our hometown, Cà Mau," I replied.

"That's the Thúy I know. If she went to Korea, she wouldn't be herself. And I can't live with a woman who has lost her true self," the Korean man said when we said our farewells.

To continue our conversation, Thúy clicked her tongue and said, "I have to uphold my dignity for myself and my family, and it's not easy for me. I've been in Sài Gòn for over ten years. I miss my family tremendously, but I have to pay off the loan. My husband's brother will give him a racehorse, and if he sells it, he might get seventy or eighty million đồng, if he is lucky. We can use that money to start over."

A month later, my mother's health improved, and when she was released from the hospital, she insisted that I go to Long An with Thúy to visit her husband. To our surprise, their two children were also visiting. Although Thúy's son was about to turn eighteen, he embraced her with tears in his eyes as if he were a little child. Her daughter hugged her tight as if afraid that Thúy would leave them again.

I had a little daughter, and whenever she visited her grandmother in the hospital, Thúy paid her special attention and gave her all kinds of treats. Thúy had become a member of the family. One afternoon, she took my daughter to the stairs leading to the rooftop, and said to me dejectedly, "The day I left, my daughter was about her age. She has grown up a lot, but in my mind, she's always a little girl, just like when I left her."

When Thúy looked at her children, her eyes grew wet. Thúy's children were summoned to the front yard to prepare fish for lunch.

"I have to work far away from home to earn money to pay back our loan," she said. "I feel guilty when I can't be with my children, especially when they're sick."

In the distance, yellow điên điển flowers blazed against the horizon. The breeze blowing in from the plains reminded the young couple of harrowing memories and their disconsolate, separated lives. When the typhoon hit Cà Mau in 1997, the entire nation rallied, and people provided the victims with aid. But many families still had to separate to recover financially. Thúy and her husband had been working extremely hard but hadn't managed to pay off the loan yet.

"When my father-in-law was a fisherman, he and his wife were able to earn enough money to raise their children and still save a little extra. My generation invested more in their fishing businesses, but the sea took everything from us. My parents-in-law gave us their entire savings, and I feel very guilty. What if it takes us twenty years to get back to where we were before the storm? Is this Heaven's will, or the result of something we did? Sometimes, I get so distraught that I want us to abandon the sea and do something else, but my son loves being a fisherman, just as all the villagers do. Sometimes I ask God what we should do, but He says nothing."

I didn't know what to say to comfort her, and words just slipped out of my mouth. "It's our own fault. We destroy nature, and as a consequence nature punishes us."

I immediately realized what I just said was disagreeable. The woman in front of me was victimized by the storm. Why did I blurt out such callous words?

Thúy suddenly looked stronger and said, "I already paid a great price for our wrongdoings. I paid with my youth. I understand that we can't abuse the sea. For years, I have been asking myself about our treatment of the earth. The sea wants to give us so much, and we should do it no harm. The sea will only get angry and angrier in response to our misdeeds."

Thúy's husband and children carried a pot of fish inside for us to boil. This was the first time I had tasted such delicious, flavorful fish.

During my visit, Tư Bảo's older siblings went to Sài Gòn to negotiate the prices for his racehorses. That year, pecunious horseracing fans didn't mind splurging money on fast and beautiful horses. In the evening, Bảo's children were drained from having been out in the grassland with their father the whole day, so they fell fast asleep. Bảo put a hat on and walked to the horse stable. He placed a wet towel on each horse's back.

That night, a female horse's neigh echoed throughout the stable. The sound of a female cantering and the smell of other horses could make male racehorses ejaculate. If they did, they would lose their energy for the race, and all the caretaker's efforts would have been for nothing. Humans must control horses' natural instincts. Every night, the caretaker had to be vigilant of thieves and of the horses' biological impulses. He could rest for a few hours, but then around four or five o'clock in the morning, he would bathe them until eight o'clock. After the horses were cleaned, he would go to a coffee shop to take a break. All the coffee shops in the area had places to tie-up horses, and their clientele consisted entirely of local horse caretakers. After the break, the horses were taken back to the stable and fed bunches of fresh, young green grass. Then, the caretaker spent time cutting, planting, and fertilizing new grass.

Being a caretaker was an exhausting job. Bảo had been working for his older brother for ten years without getting paid. Upon leaving, Bảo would ask his brother to give him a racehorse. During his ten years of toiling at the job, Bảo repeatedly asked himself, why is the sea so cruel to us, to our generation? The only way many of my friends could pay off their loans has been to leave their homes and work elsewhere.

If Bảo were able to repay his loan, his family could reunite. If he could sell his racehorse for upwards of one hundred million đồng, would he return to fishing? Although Bảo wanted to go back to his former job, he often warned himself, I've already paid a huge price; that should be enough.

During Bảo and Thúy's reunion, I had an opportunity to get to know more about the people of Cà Mau. When it was time for Thúy and me to return to Sài Gòn, the couple shared a tearful goodbye. Their son gripped Thúy while crying and repeating, "Mom, Mom, please come back to us."

Thúy's daughter held her mother tight, not wanting her to leave. Bảo held Thúy's hand and said, "I'm sorry that you must return to Sài Gòn and work there a little longer. Please come back to us soon."

"I don't like to visit my family, although I miss them tremendously," Thúy told me on our way back to Sài Gòn, "because it's unbearable to see everyone cry when we say goodbye. I live a hard life in Sài Gòn just to earn money, but there is no other way."

Thúy's family suffered for more than a decade after the storm. Storms ravish the region every year, victimizing how many similar families? I have seen and heard that after each storm, many people must separate and take on all sorts of menial jobs to pay off debts and loans. Thúy and Bảo were young, but what about older couples who don't have the time or flexibility to recover? Storm after storm humans deal with devastation generation after generation, but nobody leaves their homeland. People keep asking God why He roils the wind and sea, but never receive an answer. We must answer that question ourselves, for the sake of our own lives, our country, and our planet.

Could Thúy's hands, with their maroon nail polish, speak? Regardless of what we can accomplish with our hands, natural disasters can take it all away. Our ancestors said, "It's better to be a jack of all trades than a master of one." This didn't apply to Thúy and Bảo. He was a full-time fisherman, and he almost died at sea. Thúy did all sorts of jobs—she was a caregiver, a manicurist, and a maid. She could eke out a living, but she couldn't be with her children and husband when they needed her.

The couple wished that there would never be another storm to inflict such suffering, but who is there to listen to such a prayer?

MOTHER AND SON

PHẠM THỊ PHONG ĐIỆP

And now she knew that her son resented her. Wasn't her heart tormented enough, so why did he resent her? But if he hated her, she had to accept that. She could blame no one, nor did she have to let regrets eat at her. If she could turn back time and start over again, she would still call him her son.

No other mother in the Dứa neighborhood knew how miserable her life had been. Pregnant six times, with two miscarriages. But a miscarriage was better than the disabled children with deformed limbs or even limbless babies covered with slimy membranes that quickly died agonizing deaths. She passed out when she saw the creatures come out of her belly. Nightmares left her listless. Every time she failed to have a child, her dreams were shattered.

It wasn't because her husband didn't know that chemical agents had infiltrated his body. During the war, his engineering unit had been assigned to pave the road to the warfront at all costs. All sorts of toxic chemicals, especially dioxin-filled Agent Orange fell along with the bombs. There was nothing he was not exposed to. But at the time, he kept hoping that he and his wife would have a prosperous future, and that God would bless him with a son to maintain his family lineage. But now he knew that he would have to surrender to his fate. His ancestors, or maybe even God, could do nothing. Trying harder would only torment him more.

After months struggling with such thoughts, he drew up divorce papers and begged his wife to sign them. She deserved a better husband—someone who would give her a child. He was useless. He would be a selfish, heartless husband if he let her keep him by her side.

She felt something collapse inside her. What was her husband doing? Did he want her to die? She would have only one husband in her lifetime, and if she died, her spirit would stay with his family. How could he abandon her that way? If they couldn't have a biological child, they could adopt one. Living together for more than ten years, her hair was already gray, so if he didn't want others to mock him he must reconsider. He looked at her, his throat bitter, his heart in agony. He could hardly breathe.

"Darling, I owe this life to you," he said shakily.

Whenever someone told them about an abandoned child or a kid in need of foster parents, the old couple eagerly raced to investigate. But they always returned home empty-handed. Biological children were impossible and so were adopted ones, it seemed. They slept with their backs turned to each other. They suppressed their sighs so as to not anger each other.

Then, their ancestors blessed them with the greatest joy in the form of an offspring. She dared not believe it.

One night, after they had already turned off the light and were about to go to bed, they heard a creaking noise. Someone knocked on the door and whispered. First, they thought it was the wind. But how could the wind speak with a human voice? Or was it a burglar? He would starve if he tried to live off belongings from their home. Or was it a ghost coming to frighten them away? She trembled and leaned against him. He had been a soldier his entire life and refused to believe in ghosts. They just needed to open the door and see if it was a ghost or a human. What good was it to stay in bed guessing? They both gripped their canes as they approached the door.

It turned out it wasn't a ghost. Nor was it a thief. It was a tiny angel.

The angel was sleeping in a cloth sack. The couple then noticed a woman shuffling out through the gate. He wanted to run after her, but she held him back. In an instant, she understood everything. She was afraid that if she called out to the woman, the angel in front of them would disappear. She quickly cuddled the baby in her lap, retreated inside, and asked her husband to close the door. She stood at the threshold, nervously listening for anyone who might knock. Her heart was pounding as if she had committed a crime.

I'm not a good mom. I beg you to take care of my child. A torn piece of paper filled with scribbles and misspellings accompanied the baby. A red fingerprint stained the lower right corner. Perhaps it was the mother's.

A piece of paper floated in silence . . .

An hour floated in silence . . .

A day floated in silence . . .

A month floated in silence . . .

It was only then that she could believe it.

The boy was named Thiên Ân.

As Thiên Ân grew from a baby into an adolescent, she never spanked him. When she saw her neighbors chasing their children and whipping them repeatedly, a chill climbed up her back. Not once did she even raise her voice with her son.

Although she called him her son, she didn't bring him into this world. She had no right to assault him. He was a gift from God. She loved him and was so grateful to have him. How could she hurt him? But, seventeen years later, he started to hate her, and she could do nothing about it.

When he was still a baby, Thiên Ân suddenly developed a high fever one windy day. The storm blew in when no one expected it. Men and women rushed to secure their chicken coups and pigsties, hastily cut down their banana plants and collected chayote and loofah. Then they latched their doors and waited.

Thiên Ân had a high fever for two days in a row. She had tried everything her neighbors suggested to alleviate it and stop his seizures, but the fever persisted. His arms and legs were frigid, but his neck, armpits, and head were as hot as charcoals burning in a stove. How could she take her son to the clinic during a raging storm? It was far away and all nurses certainly would've left to secure their houses. Who would be available there?

"My son, you could be sick any time other than now. How can you be sick now?"

She wiped her tears away so that they wouldn't fall on her son. She kept wiping and wiping but they wouldn't stop streaming down her face.

Her husband moved back and forth through the house like a wild animal that had been stuffed into a cage. Outside, rain and whirlwinds tore across the sky, breaking trees and tossing garbage. Inside, his wife and son were curled up on the bed. What could he do? Never had he felt so useless. He couldn't even touch his son because their zodiac signs were not compatible, so avoiding contact was best. He counted every hour, waiting for the storm to abate. But the more he waited, the more hopeless he became. Wind hissed through the door. Rain bellowed outside. At midnight, the wind grew fiercer. The downpour intensified.

A shrub-covered mountain usually protected their home, but this time, the storm had found the "hidden victims." It didn't spare them. The wind tore in from the hilltop and rushed across the yard. Strong and soft winds. Mother winds and daughter winds. Their windows and doors rattled endlessly. The thatched roof he had carefully constructed trembled wildly. The steel cords that held it together broke, and the roof began to leak. Buckets and pots were placed on the floor to collect the water. The heavier it rained, the more worried he became.

He added more kerosene to the lamp and carried it all through the house, investigating what was happening. One hour, two hours. He thought the wind was going to persist for just a while and then stop. But it continued to hold the house in its grip. The thatched roof leaked even more. If he didn't repair the chords, the entire house would be ripped in half. Those ravenous whirlwinds wouldn't pass up that chance. What could he do? Hope his good karma would save them? Simply pray the storm would die down? His son still had a high fever, and if he got cold he would never survive.

The old man burnt three incense sticks at his ancestors' altar, grabbed his raincoat, and pushed open the door to reveal lighting streaking across the dark sky accompanied by crashing thunder.

She watched him, terrified.

"Please, don't go anywhere."

She couldn't finish her sentence before the door slammed shut. Gusts of wind raged through the crack below the door, and rushed onto the bed where she lay with her son. She bent over to shield him.

"Amitabha Buddha, Amitabha Buddha," she recited the Buddha's name reverently.

"My son, please . . . don't leave us."

The boy looked at her. The light in his eyes was starting to fade.

"Please don't . . . my son . . ."

"I'm willing to trade ten or twenty years of my life for your safety. You're a gift from God. Why isn't He saving you? My poor thing—you're not even old enough to have learned how to call me Mommy yet."

He grasped the house's pillar to climb onto the roof, but the deluge had made it too slippery and he fell again and again. His cheap plastic raincoat was torn to shreds. Damn! Was the universe challenging him? If so, he still would climb up at all costs. He fell again and landed on a sharp shovel in the dirt. His leg split open. The cold air and rain numbed his body but he continued to sweat. He had lost awareness of his senses. Everything was frozen except his heart—it continued to pound as it pumped hot blood. He was still alive but he had to finish his task.

Now he was on the top of the roof. What could mess with him now? Wind? Gust after gust gathered to lift him away from that sodden perch. He was like a frog on a lotus leaf that could be flung off at any moment. He bit his lips, grasped the roof's metal cords, and moved slowly. Every second felt like a lifetime. His frozen joints slowly worked him forward. Rain lashed his face. The droplets were like thousands of needles piercing his skin. But rain and sky and sun had fallen on his face for decades; what could a bit of weather do now?

He inhaled deeply, pressed his body against the metal cord, and crawled to the top of the roof. Below it were his wife and son. If he couldn't protect them, what kind of man would he be?

He reached the uneven top of the roof that had a gaping hole. He stretched his body across it and gripped a bamboo bar so tightly he might as well be nailed to it. He wouldn't let go. It was fine now. He had patched the hole. He would stay there. He would lie there, daring the sky and earth to try to remove him. If the storm was strong enough, let it take him before it touched his wife and son. Rain? He would stay there just to see how brutal it could be. Even if the downpour turned to ice, he would never let it harm his wife and son.

He fainted. His heart froze.

The entire Dứa neighborhood woke dumbfounded by the effects of the previous night's storm. People could hear sobbing coming from inside the house behind the shrub-covered hill. Neighbors rushed over with a ladder. The strongest young man climbed onto the roof. When he removed the thatching, he discovered a black body within an inch of its life. They weren't even able to perform CPR or pour ginger extract into his mouth. As they were about to lay his body on the ground the last of his life passed from his body.

Finally, he would return to the earth and join his ancestors.

Thiên Ân was never sick again. He never had so much as a cold. He was as strong as a buffalo. And he was rambunctious, and as recalcitrant as a demon. He terrorized the entire Dứa neighborhood with his pranks. Sometimes he scared girls with a dead rat's tail. At other times he sneaked into a chicken coop to steal eggs. He also threw snakes into pigsties and tricked dogs into eating chilies so they howled loudly all day long.

Thiên Ân also fought with children and made babies cry. He even dared to fight kids older than him. They would throw stones at one another, but even when his head was swollen and bloody, he still wouldn't look for his mother. Her neighbors constantly complained to her. All too often she had to drag her old body to their homes to apologize. She paid whoever demanded compensation. She knelt at the feet of whoever demanded it. She begged forgiveness from whoever asked her to.

She listened patiently to their insults: "Don't you know how to teach your kid? If he disobeys, hit him with a yoke. If he still doesn't behave, kick him out of the house. Why do you waste your rice on such a brat? Don't you know he could kill you one day?"

Those who loved her expressed their concerns: "If you don't teach him how to behave properly, he'll be spoiled."

He was already spoiled. She taught him right from wrong, but he never took her word seriously, ignoring whatever she said. He came home only when his stomach was empty, or when he was weary and needed to sleep. At fifteen he started raping girls in an open field. At sixteen he threw a hoe at another boy's leg and broke it. He also started stealing dogs to sell in the market for money to play games. No one could tolerate him. If she couldn't teach him, the neighbors would. Some neighborhood kids ambushed him and beat him up. When the village could no longer stand him, they shunned him. After that, they decided they needed to banish him.

Thiên Ân darted into the house and kicked over the meal she had placed out for him. His eyes rolled up to her.

"Why didn't you tell me earlier, *Ma'am*? Why did you ask the neighbors to spit on my face?" he asked insolently.

She thought she had misheard him. She had no idea what was going on. Who had picked on him? Why did he come home and start throwing a tantrum like this? And did he just call her *Ma'am*—the one who raised him up with countless hardships? Wasn't she the one who walked around the neighborhood and begged people, "Mercy, please. Forgive my son"? And now he called her *Ma'am*—so distant!

"My son . . ."

She had to crane her neck to look into his face. The face that she had once held and cooed over. The face that she had spilled so many tears over. Why was it so frigid now? Red veins netted across his eyes and his gaze sent a chill down her back. Her heart was broken.

"Don't call me *your son*. You didn't birth me, so you are *not* my mom. If you want, I'll get out of your sight. I hate you!"

"Don't . . . my son. . . . Please don't . . ."

She felt her breath rush out of her chest. Her limbs were shaking. She couldn't finish her sentence before he stormed out. She didn't intend to conceal his origin forever, only to ensure he would always be at her side. All animals have a history, and so do humans. She simply intended to wait until he grew up, and then she would tell him the truth. But before she was able, her neighbors, out of anger, threw those facts into his face. How could he bear such agony?

But the fury that overwhelmed him when he left for the district market soon dissipated; he no longer hated her. He considered himself fortunate. Because, at that moment, he started to believe firmly that his birth parents must be powerful people. They couldn't be anything like this rural, bleary-eyed woman living in crushing poverty. For some inexplicable reason, he believed that his parents must've sent him to her the way a prince was sent to live with commoners for the sake of safety. Whatever dangers his parents had been facing would surely have passed by now, and they would thus be eager to find him. And then they would surround him with luxuries to atone for all he had suffered during the past arduous years.

He returned to playing his normal games but didn't forget that strange vision that he had. He knew he would have to return to her house as she had all the information and contacts he needed to find his real parents. He popped through the door suddenly and startled her as she was reciting the Buddha's name. Was he back to take revenge on her? She was afraid. She sensed that he was no longer her son.

"If I find my parents, I'll compensate you." His voice cut through the air like a steel blade, slashing her heart.

What could she ever want from him? How could he compensate her?

Through three moves and five storms, she had been able to keep all of her son's keepsakes—the note with a fingerprint and the cloth he was brought in: *I'm not a good mother. I beg you to take care of my child, and raise him to be a good person.*

Thiên Ân snatched up that piece of paper, his eyes moving across it ravenously. Sixteen years had passed, so the ink was faded into a weak gray. But the handwriting brought tears to his eyes. The piece of paper would allow him to meet his parents. They would welcome him back with tears of joy. His life was going to change. He would spit on the Dứa neighborhood. He would strut and stride out victoriously.

Picturing the glorious scene made him tingle with excitement. He grabbed an old sack with his clothing and his real mother's note. He already had a plan.

A sentimental news television commercial announced: "Although sixteen years have passed, I've always missed you and dearly want to re-unite with you. Wherever you are, please call me at this number."

He was ready with the few mementos he had been given and his current portrait so that his parents would be able to recognize him. They only needed to rush to him and shower him with kisses, hugs, and money to erase his poor fate.

Everything was perfectly set up. Now he just needed to wait.

She knew this day would come. She had already prepared for it. Plants must always keep their original roots.

She was blessed to have had him for so many years. He had allowed her to endure the sixteen lonely, empty years spent mourning her husband. She was lucky to have had someone to take care of and to love.

She prayed to Lord Buddha, pleading with Him to unite her son with his family so that his shattered heart could heal. She couldn't be a good-enough mother for him. She had to return him to where he belonged.

She wept every night.

Whenever her phone rang, the sound was a lightning bolt straight into her heart. She always sighed in relief when it was only a friend on the other end looking to confabulate. She held her breath if the voice on the other end ever asked about him.

She was filled with conflicting emotions. She wished there were more hours in each day so she could stay with him as long as possible. She dipped deep into her lifesavings to buy him new clothes so that he would look smart and confident when meeting his family. She made chicken broth and bought roasted pork for him. She sat next to him while he ate so she could feel his warmth. She was afraid that when she woke up, his scent would be gone. Then she would be like a living corpse awaiting only the day of reincarnation.

Looking at her, he thought she would want to eat with him, so he put some meat in her bowl. She couldn't believe her eyes. It was the first time in her life that Thiên Ân did that. She still had a place in his heart.

She thought to herself, her son's life will have an uplifting ending. God and Buddha will still bless him. His parents got in touch three months after the message aired. They lived in another city, about five hundred kilometers from them. Thiên Ân was so excited. Although they didn't come by car to pick him up, their address gave him hope. It was an opulent city, with skyscrapers and magnates who were ready to squander their money without regret. His parents must be magnates too. They must have been waiting to surprise him when he turned seventeen. He would travel by himself unannounced and spend some time marveling at the luxuries that he would soon wallow in.

Since he got the news from his parents, he lost his appetite and couldn't sleep. He packed and asked for directions. He booked a taxi. He had a million things to do before he could meet his new family, so no time to care about that decrepit, bleary-eyed woman who silently wept in the back of the garden.

He left with a backpack over his shoulder without looking at her. Was it because he was so thrilled that he forgot to find her and say goodbye? She saw him open the gate and walk to the village road, his head high, his stride confident and excited.

She knew that she had already lost him. She went quietly back to the garden; she failed to compose herself to call him back for a proper goodbye.

Seventeen years.

Separation and loss, once again, gashed her fragile heart.

The Dứa neighborhood sighed with relief. Girls were less guarded. Chickens and dogs wandered around more freely. Fewer assaults and fights occurred.

She was the only one to be afraid of walking out of her house. Nobody called her Thiên Ân's mother anymore. They called her by her husband's name, Mrs. Sằng.

Mrs. Sằng was worried that Thiên Ân would not come back. Would he regret for not saying goodbye to her, and would he come back to bid her farewell? For seventeen years they had lived under the same roof and shared sweetness and sorrow. Would he simply come back to get something that he forgot? Was he nostalgic about this place, this house, this garden? He had found his parents by now. But he also would treasure memories of this home.

She couldn't walk out of the house, fearing people would ask about her son.

She wouldn't be able to bear it if someone said something to make her think of him.

She reminded herself that she would have to forget him, but failed. Her heart ached. Her eyes were sore. Excruciating pain permeated her body. She realized that she was already old. When she brought him into her family, she was only forty. But if they had lived together much longer, she would have become just a burden on him.

Oh, how silly she was!

He did, in fact, come back.

From a distance, he watched her go in and out of the house alone. He couldn't tell whether he despised or respected her.

He left again.

Some neighbors saw him roaming around downtown. His mustache was messy, his eyes protruded like a buffalo's, and one could see the hunger in his face.

A neighbor stopped him, asking, "Why are you here? Mrs. Sằng hasn't been well lately. You should go home to check on her."

He rolled his eyes. He grew cranky, irritable, and aggressive. It was as if by making such a suggestion, the man were asking for trouble. Fortunately, Thiên Ân recognized the man. He had saved him as a boy when a pot of boiling water had toppled onto him. If the man hadn't carried him to the hospital, Thiên Ân surely would be in his grave now. He wavered. He was about to walk away, but the neighbor insisted. He hovered around him, pestering him as if it were an interrogation.

"Get away! I'm mad, so fucking mad now!" Thiên Ân burst out cursing. He howled like a mad dog.

Later Mrs. Sắng heard the story from the neighbor without understanding what had happened. Wasn't Thiên Ân able to meet his parents? Or had a thug attacked him while he was on his way to look for his parents? Had the thug stolen his belongings and beaten him so fiercely that he became a crippled nomad? Were his "parents" frauds, and had they swindled him out of his traveling money? Thinking of all the possibilities was like rubbing her guts with salt. Thiên Ân was seen as a minacious young man in the Dứa neighborhood, but he was just a naive, foolish boy. She knew her son well.

Thiên Ân knew that she had given him her entire savings so that he could travel and reunite with his parents. She had nothing left to give him, so he had to toil in the district market to earn a living.

She knew why he had despised her but entreated a neighbor to take her downtown to find him. She would take him back. She would even borrow money to give him again, hoping that he could reunite with his family.

From behind the brewery, he saw her approach. That rural woman again—what did she want from him? He didn't know if he hated her or loved her. He wasn't even sure what to think about himself. Who was he, really?

He had already come to the address his parents sent him.

When he entered the house, three towering boys with hot pokers in their hands and menacing expressions stared at him. A shirtless man sat in the middle of the house beside five pigs whose bellies had been slashed open. He looked up and saw Thiên Ân. The man just grunted and called to his wife in the back of the house, "Your precious son is home!"

The boy could hear the sound of running water and then a woman appeared, her legs and arms wet. She looked at him awkwardly.

"Are you . . . ?" Thiên Ân asked with a visceral bewilderment. Was he confused? Or were they? He was excited to display all the mementos in his bag. The man slammed the cleaver onto the chopping board and snatched the faded piece of paper from his hand.

"Bitch, who could even read your horrible handwriting?"

The woman glanced at the piece of paper with embarrassment, and said, "Come on in, son."

The three brutish boys eyed him up and down as he moved past. Their faces shared no resemblances with one another.

He sensed that he had been fooled. They were tricking him to collect a ransom from his birth parents. He collected his belongings and managed to hide his emotions. If he made even a minor mistake, that cleaver might just slice his throat. It would be no different than cutting a pig's and then his life would be over.

He tried to look confident, but his voice was trembling.

The man laughed uproariously. "See, you aren't his mother."

The woman was awestruck.

"It was . . . when I was cheated . . . and I couldn't afford to keep you by my side . . ." she stammered.

Then she looked back and forth. Thiên Ân held his breath.

She approached the pot of pig's blood. Dipped her finger into it and pressed it on the newspaper as he watched.

"Here, compare the fingerprints."

The two fingerprints—one old and one new—were precisely identical.

She was indeed his mother. And with this, a sense of loss overwhelmed him.

The woman—his mother—urged him to put his stuff away and wash his face. By the time he was done, she had already disappeared into the back of the house. The overwhelming stench of pigs' feces made him gag. He couldn't do anything but find a corner and sit down.

He watched the man slashing meat in the middle of the house while his sons, who still gripped their pokers, were staring at him.

He didn't belong there. His arms quivered as they gave him a disgusting look.

It was lucky that the sons and their father had to take the meat to the market to sell. His mother asked him to stay at home while she ran some errands. He was all by himself now, surrounded by the stench of pig blood and shit.

Dinner wasn't ready until nine o'clock. He was ravenous by then. Nobody cared. They devoured the food without saying a word.

In the middle of dinner, his mother suddenly remembered his presence, pointing at the three boys and introducing, "This is Toàn, your oldest brother. This is Hùng. And here is Minh, your youngest brothers. You should get to know each other. And this is Hiệp, your stepfather."

"Your mother's so dignified. Four sons with three different men. What a productive woman!" Hiệp chuckled, mocking.

Thiên Ân swallowed rice and scowled at his stepfather for what he had just said about his mother. He was exhausted. He just wanted to sleep and escape this reality.

But he couldn't close his eyes while lying in bed. He and the other boys had to lie on a wooden board that reeked with pigs' blood and human sweat.

"What are you hiding? Money?" Minh slapped his leg and blurted out.

He thought of the money hidden at the bottom of his backpack. It was lucky that the boys didn't bother to wait for an answer and started snoring.

He stayed for a week and whenever he closed his eyes, he dreamed about himself as a pig. In the dreams, his stepfather chased after him, a cleaver in hand. The three brothers joined in. His mother pressed her bleeding finger on his forehead to make a print. He didn't want to be a pig, so he left for the district market. He strolled around. He picked pockets for a living.

He hated his life. He didn't want to live anymore. He spent all his money on alcohol. It could make him forget everything. Nobody could make him remember anything. He was crestfallen.

At Mrs. Sằng's request, the neighbors searched for Thiên Ân for three days. That bastard! The village was so tired of him. Even when he was gone he caused them troubles. But she loved him. She was his mother. She would find him no matter what.

BOOZING WITH A KHMER ROUGE

VÕ DIỆU THANH

"**G**randma, the Khmer Rouge!" Nga screamed before wading into the water to head to the home nearby where she lived with her mother and grandmother.

Uncle Ba's wife dropped her chopsticks and flung her rice bowl at the man as he moved through the water away from her house. Then she grabbed a broom and a chair, but Vân and Uncle Ba held his wife tightly. Uncle Ba winked at Sáu Khên, hinting that he needed to leave quickly.

It was pitch black outside and the floodwaters had reached the house's threshold. Sáu Khên jumped into the water with no idea where he was going.

Vân was confused as well, but she unmoored the sampan and followed her daughter.

Uncle Ba's wife was incensed and flung chairs in every direction.

Since returning to Nam Vang to visit her old house, Uncle Ba's wife became enraged whenever anyone mentioned the Khmer Rouge or Pol Pot. One day, twenty years prior, when she was a thirteen-year-old student, her teachers drove all the students out of the school to the border between Việt Nam and Cambodia. Arriving at the Tịnh Biên border, Uncle Ba's wife saw houses on the roadside burned to ashes. Grotesque configurations of bodies lined the streets. She wanted to return home to Nam Vang, but the Vietnamese who already had returned home after fighting in Cambodia questioned why she would want to do that, as Pol Pot's men had run rampant in the village, killing everyone. Uncle Ba's wife resisted. She assumed the Khmer Rouge would have left after ransacking it. Uncle Ba's wife just wanted to go home; she missed her parents dearly. But the ceaseless famine, Pol Pot's perpetual carnage, and Vietnamese soldiers who were missing, dead, and disabled were beyond imagination. Uncle Ba's wife simply had to grind her teeth and wait.

When tensions eased, and she had saved some bushels of rice, Uncle Ba's wife finally was able to return to her home in Việt Nam. The city was empty. Houses remained intact but unoccupied. They said nobody had returned after the massacre.

Nobody could stop Uncle Ba's wife from resenting the Khmer Rouge.

Was Sáu Khên a Khmer Rouge? Vân wondered while rowing the sampan back to her house. She saw him struggling in the flooded road. He tripped over something and disappeared in Uncle Ba's watery spinach swamp.

Vân also saw Nga flailing in an attempt to float in the waters near their house. She was sunk up to her neck and screaming, "Grandma, Khmer Rouge!"

Nga's grandmother, Năm, poked her head out of the window of her stilt house and asked frantically, "Khmer Rouge what? They no longer exist. Don't be crazy!"

"Over there! He's wading in the road."

In the dim light coming out from the house, Năm looked at the man stumbling through the water toward the market.

"Hey, where are you heading this late? Come in, over here."

"He's a Khmer Rouge, mom," Vân interjected.

"Really?"

"Yeah . . ." he muttered.

"You can't escape. Come on in. I won't kill you. I promise."

Sáu Khên reached the house when Vân's sampan touched its stairs. She was unsure what to do so she just sat quietly in the sampan, holding it while her mother tied it to a house's pillar.

Sáu Khên walked onto the deck. Water dripped onto the floor as he stood hesitating. Năm quickly went inside and came back with clothes in her hands.

"Go change your clothes," she said. "These are my son-in-law's. Don't get sick."

Sáu Khên was looking around for a place to sit while water continued to fall from his hair onto his shoulders. A bamboo bed covered with a mosquito net sat in one corner of the humble home, but he opted for a wooden board leaning against a pole. Năm was sitting on the opposite side of the room. She went into the back room and asked her granddaughter, Nga, to change her clothes. Nga was reluctant. She craned forward to peer around the room divider and get a look at the Khmer Rouge. Ever since she was young, she had heard countless stories about the Khmer Rouge. They burned houses, slaughtered people, and stabbed and tore children apart as if they were chicken wings. Nga imagined they had blood-red skin and sharp, pointed fangs. But this man had dark skin, and teeth as straight as Uncle Ba's.

"You aren't scared of Khmer Rouge, are you?" he asked.

"They have limbs just like me. The only difference is their brutality," she replied. "But being brutal is not a sign of strength, so why should I fear them? Do you drink?"

"Do you? But you're a woman."

"What can I drink, if not wine? When my husband died, his siblings came to visit me often out of sympathy for the tragedy that left me a widow with four fatherless children. They wanted me to heal with alcohol. But I was somewhat familiar with death already. Surviving is already a blessing and drinking is a celebration. Vân, grill some dry squids for us."

Năm went inside to fetch a bottle of rice wine and reached for a cup next to the teapot to cover the bottle top.

"I still have some jugs of alcohol. Do you . . . ?" Năm didn't finish her sentence because she heard someone wading next to the stairs.

"Năm, let me tell you this," came a voice.

Uncle Ba's wife was standing there soaked up to her chest.

"I'm sober and honest. I know you used to be very fierce. Pol Pot was nothing to you. And our neighbors in Phước Hưng Village could've escaped the slaughter like Ba Chúc's thanks to you. But do you know what you are doing? What if this man smashes your head while you and your family are asleep? Who would come save you? You shouldn't judge him by his appearance. When he bashed our people's heads in Nam Vang, did he look so nice to you? They change their faces but don't forget that they once murdered people as easily as they grilled rice paper. Will you stay up all night to watch him? Shoo him away! They are brainless, they are blood thirsty."

"Don't worry, I'll take care of him."

"No, you won't. We aren't living in wartime anymore. Killing a person, whether he is a Khmer Rouge or not, will get you locked up in jail. Get rid of him."

"What if he goes away and kills someone else? Do you want the entire village to stay up and watch him?"

"Turn him over to the commune Chairman."

"Who wants to deal with him?"

"God, is it . . . ?"

"Please go home and sleep well. If I can't take care of him, I'm not a true ethnic Cambodian."

"You're too stubborn." Then she called the kids, "Hey, come sleep at my place. Your mom is too headstrong; let her die alone. Vân and Nga, follow me."

Nga grabbed Vân's lapel. Vân was sitting quietly by the stove, staring at the dry squid being grilled. The entire house smelled like the burned squid.

Năm scraped off the burnt crust of the squid flesh with a chopstick.

"Don't you want to drink and chew on this dry squid? You speak Vietnamese, don't you?" Năm asked Sáu Khên.

"I speak some Khmer and some Chinese, but I'm best at Vietnamese. It's because I like it best."

"The woman you just met is also Chinese Khmer. When in Nam Vang, her family was very rich. But Pol Pot took power when she was still a student. The school wanted to protect their students so they sent them all to Việt Nam. She became homeless. Damn the war! Let's drink. How much you can handle?"

"I don't know. You?"

"I don't know either. Let's drink until we get sauced. Then crash."

"Did you fight the Khmer Rouge in this village?"

"Yes. No one was left alive."

"How many died?"

"Plenty. They swarmed us, killing three people at a time. Monsters."

"Three people is not many. In Ba Chúc, four thousand people were killed. In Cambodia, millions."

"Shut up. A single person killed is plenty. I would never spare the Khmer Rouge."

Năm slammed her glass on the table and it shattered. Her face became fiery red because of the wine and from frustration. Nobody would call her a woman. She must be Trương Phi or Quan Vân Trường.*

Sáu Khên knew she didn't mean it, so he remained seated and quietly picked up the glass shards before pouring another glass of wine and raising it without offering a toast. So did Năm. Everything was quiet. Vân could hear the sound of wine flowing in their throats.

The sound of wine brought her back to a bygone time.

---

* Famous second-century Chinese generals.

No, it was the sound of breathing. The water had receded and the land awaited the northern wind that would follow it. Yet tonight, Vân sensed strong overflowing currents. The water surged in the souls of those who had soldiered through the monstrous war.

Vân saw another battle happening before her eyes. The victims. The killers and the killed were victims. She recalled vividly the days the Khmer Rouge flooded the village. Life was hard but peaceful before a deafening explosion echoed in from a house adjacent to Tám Sớm creek. Blood overflowed in the main road. Năm rushed home from Châu Đốc and dashed to the creek. Vân ran after her. Năm told Vân to go inside and watch her siblings. Did Năm reach the trees at the border? Did she enter a bunker? Pol Pot's forces had gathered in the field near Dung Thăng River. Năm didn't know when they had retreated; she could only see a cannon left beside the trench.

Vân could picture the scene but never understood how her mother commanded those soldiers to lower their canon and target the Khmer Rouge who had swarmed along the Dung Thăng riverbank. They collapsed along the border as it went up in flames.

People died. Enemies died.

"Those Khmer Rouge were only seventeen or eighteen."

Năm told and retold that story to Vân, her siblings, and to soldiers who came to booze with her.

"They couldn't even grow a mustache yet."

Those Khmer Rouge teenagers died. They had been dying before they even entered this village and before they crossed the border. They were dying once Pol Pot came to power. They died once their parents and relatives were sent to concentration camps and held as hostages. They had lost their souls. Those men who marauded, gored, and murdered were only robots. They marched into this village like robots.

They swarmed in and mercilessly slaughtered people, but not for any sort of revenge. As killing machines, they didn't fear death nor have morals. They butchered any living creature, and they were butchered in return. The northern army was unfamiliar with the southwest's topology, and because they were ignorant of the ways of the devilish robots, they died, wave after wave. Recalling the deaths of the soldiers, Năm drank like a thirsty person consuming a jug of rainwater. The more she drank, the thirstier she became. It made her cry.

"Those strangers coming here could hardly go home again. Vân's father died in Châu Giang and my heart remained broken. I can't even think about all the parents in the north who lost their children. Pol Pot—a fucking bastard. How could he have risen to the head of the government? I'll chew him up."

"How could you be so fearless? They were so bloodthirsty. Who wasn't scared of them?"

"I didn't care. I had nothing to lose. The Khmer Rouge were so monstrous and brainless. Why should I fear them? They were so immature."

Năm started speaking about the boys again. She described the corpses of people who couldn't even tell the difference between right and wrong. They had no dreams, aspirations, or lovers. How could they love? Only their blood relatives remained, but they had been sent to concentration camps to tend cattle. Only by serving as killing machines could the boys assure their families' safety. If they had even an iota of human affection or faith, their families would be executed. They had no choice—either to die in combat or to leave the army and watch their families be killed. Becoming a zombie, an automated killing machine, was the only option.

That's how Năm was able to confront them. They were as young as Vân. When dead, the corpses of the soldiers were as small and vulnerable as Vân and her siblings.

"That Pol Pot. I'll chew him up."

Sáu Khên looked at Năm's fierce expression and his face became darker. Vân observed him closely. His skin was glowing. His eyes hollow. What was he thinking? Was he once one of Pol Pot's trained

assassins? Vân had read books about the carnage reaped by Pol Pot.
One story claimed that during a tranquil night, dogs started barking
in the distance as the Khmer Rouge entered a village. They raised
their guns. Death came so easily to what had been peaceful lives.
The floods today seemed to have made everything tranquil now, but
what remained submerged?

"Can I go into the back of the house?" asked Sáu Khên.

"Go ahead."

Vân hid behind the room divider and peeked into the kitchen.
Sáu Khên was sitting, staring into the distance as if he were waiting
for someone. It was dark outside. The floodwaters seemed to stop
seething. And Vân could hear his long breathes.

Vân listened to the sound of water in the distance. Was it a boat
or some other vessel parting the water, entering the village from the
Hậu River? What would Vân do? Vân would be like her mother
and confront whatever evil was coming. If Vân had to die, she
would kill all the devils first. She wouldn't leave any of those killing
machines alive.

He was still sitting there. He didn't pee nor drink any water. So
why had he gone back there? Who was he waiting for?

Năm staggered toward the back of the house, flashlight in
her hand.

"Why are you here? It is dark, so watch your steps. Don't fall. Oh,
God! Why are you crying? Come in here."

"I . . ."

"Are you repenting?"

He sat down and poured some more wine without putting it to
his mouth. Instead he raised the glass to his face. His hands squeezed
it as if it held something horrible.

"Would you like to hear my stories?"

"Please tell me. I want to hear your Khmer Rouge stories. I won't
kill you, so don't panic. But if Pol Pot were still in power, I would
never spare you. You were coerced back then. But today you are free.

If you hadn't been insane, you never would've killed anyone like that. But if you dare to kill my people now, your life is doomed."

"You sound like you know a lot about the Khmer Rouge."

"I stayed at the border after Pol Pot lost power. But honestly, I've only heard about the Khmer Rouge and never seen them. When leading the logistics team to Nhơn Hội where they were fighting the Khmer Rouge, I heard only rumors and saw the soldiers's dead bodies only after the war. Now I want to hear *your* stories."

"My stories aren't very long. In the 1970s, I was like the other Khmer Rouge who fought side by side with Vietnamese soldiers against the Americans. Back then Lon Nol ruled the country. The year I was stationed in Koh Kong, Pol Pot was a nobody. Suddenly, the government, or rather Pol Pot, ordered Koh Kong to attack Vietnamese soldiers. We had been sharing meals and sleeping in the same beds with Vietnamese soldiers. Then they ordered us to kill them. How could we do that? The forces in Koh Kong refused to participate.

"Not a month later, the Koh Kong forces merged with the central forces who had been fighting Lon Non's men. But then, in an act of great betrayal, the central forces turned their guns on us. We fled the bloodshed and ran toward Việt Nam. During the flight, all nine of my family members were killed."

Sáu Khên stopped talking. He lifted his glass to his mouth and emptied it down his throat, as though he were drinking poison. The wine didn't flow into his mouth, but into his eyeballs, and into his dark, glowing skin.

Năm stared at Sáu Khên, unconsciously waving her hands as if shooing something away. Her hands knocked against the wine bottle, sending it down to the floor. Nobody picked it up, so the wine flowed out.

"Nine people? Oh my God! How could you live with that?"

Sáu Khên took the bottle, muttering, "Displacement, war, and people were just like worms. Now, in retrospect, I don't get it—how could I survive? But the pain was part of the healing. If we hadn't been hurt, we all would've died after the war ended. You know this."

"So you don't hold any pieces of the Khmer Rouge in your heart? What did you tell Ba's wife that got her so agitated?"

"I didn't know I had upset her. Mr. Ba and I are friends. So during dinner, I told her who I was. She didn't let me finish my story but became furious. I had to swim away in mid-conversation."

"Nine people. Oh, God! Pour me some more."

Năm drank as if she were dehydrated.

"But if I hadn't fled when I did, I would've killed ninety or nine hundred people."

"Damn it!" Năm just mumbled the phrase over and over and then drank several more glasses in a row. The thirst crawled into her fingers and her hair.

Then she collapsed.

Tears were filling Vân's eyes. But what if he was making up this story? Was he plotting something? Năm was sleeping and Vân's husband wasn't at home.

Vân gripped a knife.

The man leaned forward to look at Năm. He walked toward her, his face next to hers, he touched her cheek with his.

"You could never kill me. My family brewed wine for twenty years. And don't you know that I'm a ladies' man? I could woo any woman. But when I look at you, the man inside me dies. You're neither a woman nor a man. You're iron. You're a rock. You're a stone—a kind of stone that holds no glittering crystal; tough, tough for a thousand years, ten thousand years. If it weren't for women like you, many more Khmer Rouge soldiers like me would've smashed in more heads. Thank you."

He hit his head on the table several times and then fell asleep right there. His hands still on Năm's shoulders on the dinner table.

Vân dropped the knife. She cleaned the empty wine bottles and put away the dried squid. She set up the mosquito net so it covered both Sáu Khên and her mother. He was so drunk. Any man who boozed with Năm fell asleep right at the dinner table. They often slept next to each other like that, like men.

INNERMOST

PHẠM THỊ NGỌC LIÊN

Sometimes, happiness is just paint that covers what is rotten inside.

One afternoon, while we were about to have dinner, Aunt Bảy pulled my mother outside and whispered into her ear. I heard my mother cry out like a chicken lost from its chick, "No! No! You're lying!"

Bảy said something else, and my mother burst into tears. I placed the stack of dinner bowls on a tray. Then my older brother Hai and I dashed to the doorway. Bảy waved her hand and said, "You two stay right there and don't come out here!"

My mother couldn't speak; sobs welled up in her throat. Finally, she turned toward us and said, "Go back inside," and pulled Aunt Bảy to the hedge where they could continue their conversation. When my mother returned, she looked like a completely different person. Her face was pale, her eyes were lifeless and her expression disheveled. Without looking at us, she said, "You two go with Aunt Bảy to find out where your Dad is. Then come back and tell me."

Bảy led us to the street, called a tuk-tuk, and told the driver to take us to the pier. After we had crossed the river, we walked past rows of coconut trees and turned onto a small road beset by Malabar spinach.

"See that house with the bougainvillea? Your Dad is in there. Wait right here," Bảy pulled us aside and enjoined us. "When you see him walk out with someone, keep shouting loudly and make sure he doesn't run away. Don't ruin this—we want to catch him red-handed. If he escapes, you'll be spanked. Do you hear me?"

My brother and I stood on the corner and waited for our father to emerge. The sun went down quickly and darkness surrounded us. Frogs croaked all around. A chilling wind blew in off the river.

"What is Dad doing in there, and why hasn't he come out yet?" I asked.

My brother and I huddled against each other to keep warm and eventually fell asleep on the ground. Suddenly, somebody twisted my ear and I woke up. My brother also had his ear twisted to jolt him awake.

"Good for nothing!" Bảy stood with her hands on her hips and scolded us. "I told you to keep watching and you fell asleep. He's gone. Let's go home."

My father was an elegant and refined man. A real gentleman. Back in the day, my grandparents didn't want their only son to follow in their footsteps by becoming a farmer, so they sent him to school in town. He was very handsome and didn't look like the typical farmer's son. He was good at singing and playing stringed instruments, which made him popular, especially among the girls. That was why he played more than he studied. His habits cost my grandparents a fortune, and there was no bright future ahead for him. A true wastrel.

Thus his parents decided to arrange my father's marriage. This was part of a typical countryside person's life-trajectory: get married, build a home, and start a career. My mother was by no means a meek and gentle woman, though. Although she was a country girl, she was known for her sharp tongue and acidic wit.

My grandparents considered her the perfect woman to tame and control my father.

"He needs a wife like her to keep him in line," my grandfather remarked. Then, he told his son to stand in front of the family altar and said, "You have two options: either get married or stay single and be disowned. Take your pick."

The wedding took place soon after.

During their ten years of marriage, under my mother's oversight, my father became the person my grandparents had always wanted: caring, responsible, and hardworking. Everything had been fine until one day when my father fell in love with a woman named Khuyên. She was a widow and a single mother in the neighboring town. My mother considered it disgraceful because Khuyên was neither young nor beautiful. She was my mother's age and worked as a lowly seamstress. Everyone concurred that Khuyên was in no way near as attractive or graceful as my mother.

My mother called Khuyên "a minx." Whenever my parents fought, the word *minx* slammed into my ears and heart, over and over. "Please lower your voice," my father pleaded, "or the kids will hear us," but my mother kept yelling and screaming, breaking things and bawling.

Hiding behind a dresser door, my brother and I covered our eyes with our hands and trembled with fear, like geckos that had lost their tails. Often, my mother rushed toward us and pulled us out from our hiding spot.

"Kill me! Kill your children!" she yelled at my father in front of my brother and me. "Then do whatever you want."

My mother was furious because my father had taken his lover out somewhere. That night, after we returned home with Bảy, my mother flung the dinner tray onto the floor. Vện, our neighbor Mr. Chín's dog, gobbled up the food. Mother sat on one end of the large wooden couch, her eyes roiling with anger under the soft neon blue light while my father sat on the other end of the couch with drooped shoulders. He admitted his adultery, stating, "I *thương* you and our children, but I *yêu* her."[*]

Once I grew up, I realized that my mother would never forgive him for saying that. There is a fine line between the words *thương* and *yêu*, but the distinction is clear-cut. My father married my mother, whom his parents had chosen for him, to fulfill his filial duty. However, at no point in the past ten years did he *yêu* her.

"You're very good and kind," he said wistfully, "and I can't blame you for anything. But Khuyên and I are more compatible."

Upon hearing his words, my mother felt as if she were being strangled. Outraged, she was determined to take revenge. That is simply the power of love. My father, on the other hand, couldn't care less about the ongoing fighting between him and my mother and continued to see Khuyên. My mother tried to catch him red-handed in the middle of one of his adulterous trysts but always failed because he constantly changed the location where he and Khuyên met. Bảy tried unsuccessfully to help my mother find him but finally gave up, saying, "Let him be. He'll come back to you eventually after he gets bored with that woman. You are legally married to him with two children. You can't lose him. Don't worry!"

After Bảy refused to accompany my mother on her "adultery-catching adventures," my mother made us accompany her. She had become a completely different person. She was skinny. The veins on her face popped out when she ground her teeth, and her eyes were reptilian in how they darted about. She was like a ferocious storm that threatened to destroy everything in its path.

One summer day, my brother and I were playing in a lychee tree when she summoned us down.

"I don't want to go with you!" My brother looked into her eyes and screamed.

---

[*] The verbs *thương* and *yêu* in Vietnamese are commonly both translated into English as *love*. However, in this context, *thương* is associated with unromantic love, while *yêu* is associated with romantic, passionate love.

"Neither do I!" I said, hiding behind his back.

"So, you don't want to go with me, do you?" She glared at us and smirked. "I'll chop you into pieces and kill you myself!" She held a large butcher knife in her hand. Its dull metal blade was terrifying.

My brother extended his arms behind him and held me tight. "Mom, please, please don't kill us!" he shrieked. "We'll go with you!"

We followed her to Khuyên's house. When we arrived, my father was inside sitting on a large wooden couch, eating lunch. A slight woman with a gentle face was seated next to him. Seeing Khuyên's dome-shaped belly, my mother yelled and stormed inside.

What happened next was like a horror movie. I don't want to remember it. I'm not completely sure but I think this is how it went down. My mother raised the knife. Khuyên fell to the floor. My father slapped my mother in the face. Blood flew everywhere. My terrified brother jumped up and down, trying to bite my father's arm, screaming like a siren that drowned me into unconsciousness.

My half-brother was never born. Nobody knew where Khuyên went after being discharged from the hospital. My father came home and became as quiet as a mute. My brother lost his mind. The doctor said that he was too psychologically sensitive to receive shock therapy. My grandfather had a heart attack when he heard about my brother's insanity and refused to look at my father after the incident.

My father said nothing to defend himself from my family's accusations. He tried to find the best doctor possible to help my brother, hoping that he would recover one day. He showed respect and deference to my mother, doing whatever she wanted him to do, except for sleeping in the same bed with her.

My brother's mental debility didn't get any better. Each summer, it became even worse.

Ten years have passed, and my brother's shouts still echo inside our house, as if he were still a boy. My father weeps when my brother kicks things around, or bites and pinches himself. In such moments, my mother goes to the back garden and sobs. I don't know if she feels remorse for what she did, but I wasn't moved by her tears. On the contrary, I felt sorry for my father. I had a girlfriend and understood how vexatious it would be to live with someone you didn't love.

I also understood my father's tormented feelings toward Khuyên's reaction to my mother's jealousy. Although my mother caused Khuyên's miscarriage and the latter had nearly died in the hospital, when she regained consciousness, Khuyên admitted that everything was her fault and requested the judge to exonerate my mother. Back then, I wasn't mature enough to understand all that was happening, but in retrospect, I have to say that my mother acted too balefully. When Khuyên left to live elsewhere, I forgave her for having dared to love my father, a married man.

For the last ten years, my parents have lived together with their crazy son. From the outside everything may look normal, but deep inside it is tempestuous. My father has aged rapidly; his refined, handsome physical features are long gone. His face now projects sorrow and wistful glances.

When we all went fishing together in the afternoons, my brother behaved like a normal person. He meticulously attached the bait to the hook and cheered jovially when we hooked a fish. Sometimes, he rested his head on the rice paddy dike's soft green grass and fell asleep like a baby. In those moments, I saw my father look at him carefully, turn his face and secretly wipe away tears. From behind, I saw his shoulders tremble as he sobbed. This saddened me tremendously, and I wanted to cry out, "Dad, Dad!"

My mother was even more miserable. Her resentment and pride made her do whatever it took to possess my father's heart and body, although it was a withered heart and a detached body. My father did whatever she wanted, just like a robot. They walked side by side at wedding receptions and parties. He was polite; my mother smiled gleefully. Who dared say that they were not two lovebirds? But nobody looked deeply into my parents' eyes to discern their true feelings.

One morning, my mother asked me to go to the adjacent village to buy some wine and a few areca leaves. When I returned, she had already cooked a pot of sticky rice and boiled a rooster. She quietly placed the offerings on my grandparents' altar and told me to go to the rice paddy to invite my father home.

When he returned, my brother was sitting on the floor holding a grasshopper made from palm leaves and smiling naively. My father stood next to him and quietly looked down at the floor.

"Please have a seat on the wooden couch," my mother said to my father in a low, gentle voice.

I stood behind the door and watched everything play out. I was perplexed and my heart ached. My mother burned incense, respectfully bowed four times in front of the altar, and turned toward my father. Then, she slowly knelt down and said, "Please forgive me. I am a sinner. I bow to you three times to ask you to let me live in the temple."

Tears rolled down his face, and he nodded in agreement. My mother had decided to do penance in the temple and spend her days chanting and praying. I realized that this was the best solution for them because they would no longer have to pretend to live happily together.

Sometimes, I missed her and secretly visited the temple. I stood behind a pillar or a wall to look at my mother from afar.

"Don't disturb her," my father had instructed me. "Don't take your brother with you to the temple, because if she sees him, she'll be distracted."

I obeyed him, although I felt a little uncomfortable. How could he be so unaffected by her becoming a nun? Ultimately, he was responsible for my mother's sins.

On my wedding day, as I joined the procession of vehicles driving away on the asphalt road, headed to my new home with my wife, I looked back and saw my father standing alone next to my insane brother in the twilight. Tears trailed down my face. This was the first time I realized that I would be making him suffer.

He had forgiven my mother and permitted her to become a nun so that she could leave everything behind and focus on her prayers. But every day, my father had to face my mentally handicapped brother. He had chosen the most severe punishment: to face his unforgivable wrongdoings until the day he died.

ON THE RẠNG RIVERBANK

TRỊNH THỊ PHƯƠNG TRÀ

A snippet of information brought me—a journalist working on an article for a newspaper's Tết edition—to her home in the late afternoon on New Year's Eve. The dilapidated house was nestled behind a bleak, barren garden with a few banana plants, some orange trees, and lemongrass shrubs growing beside weather-ravaged walls.

Her back was stooped and her hair was braided in a headband. Mịch stared at me in bewilderment. I told her I had traveled a thousand miles to hear her story. She smiled and then said, "Well, my life isn't worth that. It's quite late now. Let me go make us dinner."

I followed her to help wash vegetables and prepare the rice. Beside the flickering fire, she told me that perhaps I was blessed by the heavens to have been able to travel so far, and that our encounter was serendipitous because she had been nursing the memory of her husband for fifty years. She then sighed. "You know, I'm not the only one to endure such loneliness. I've thought it over. Tonight is the right time to share."

My face certainly revealed my confusion. She raised her two index fingers and brought them next to each other in front of her eyes. The stove's flames seemed to be dying, making her wrinkled, trembling fingers cast dark, blurry shadows across her face. The streaks danced apart and came back together. One fell down, the other pulled it up.

"It'll come like that. It's my turn for now," she said.

She repeated herself and then with the expression of someone being shocked out of sleep, poked the fire, making the rice pot boil more vigorously, the water overflowing the top and sizzling into the flames.

Glancing at her inscrutable, distant expression, I refrained from asking anything. There would be a better moment. After dinner, I followed her to the riverbank. I followed her hunched back to a wind-tussled field of white reeds. Quietly, I helped her break reeds and toss them up from the riverbank onto a nearby high, flat mound. We worked until we had woven together what resembled silk strips about three fingers wide. She had clearly been thinking about this moment and we sat down on the mat that was now spread out across the ground.

I began my question. "What does it mean? I mean . . ." My gaze stopped at the wooden box she held tightly in her arms, leaving the question unfinished.

"Well," she lowered her voice as if whispering to herself. She sounded like she had been practicing this soliloquy before some invisible audience for years:

> I stepped down clumsily into the boat, the vegetable basket on my shoulder, still wet with dew, was heavy. The plank bottom of the boat was also wet so I slipped slightly, clamping onto someone inside to steady myself and not fall into the river.
>
> "Let me help you."
>
> My shoulders became unburdened as I looked up and saw the man who had lifted my basket of vegetables. I could feel my face flush when our eyes met.
>
> "We once lived in the same village. Don't you remember me?"
>
> His heavily tanned face beamed with glee. The long lashes that

would make any woman envious caught the light as he opened his eyes wide. He smiled.

"You must've forgotten me. My father Mộc lives at the end of the village."

Who in the village didn't know Mộc? He was a carpenter who had been widowed when his only son was still a newborn. Alone, he raised his son until he reached puberty. Moc had a younger brother, who was also a carpenter living at the bottom of the Cẩm Mountain. One time when he went to the woods for logs, the younger brother was crushed by a falling tree and badly injured, so Moc sent his son to stay with him to help out. I had heard the story from the villagers many years earlier.

"I . . ." I started to say but froze.

"Do you sell vegetables at Hà Market very often?"

"Yes."

I looked down at my muddy toes and felt embarrassed.

The boat floated on as a curtain of mist enveloped the river. The man still had my basket of vegetables on his head. I could feel my heart flutter, drowning out the sound of the boat paddle hitting the water.

It was how we first met, at the wharf. Who could have known that one day we would become husband and wife? No one ever could've predicted that we would soon thereafter be separated.

She went silent. With trembling hands, she fumbled with the waistband of her pants, pulled out a drawstring bag, and removed a black and white portrait wrapped in a plastic bag. It showed an oval-faced girl with big round eyes and a man with a square jaw and rippling hair, smiling back at the camera.

"You and he were such a beautiful couple," I said enthusiastically.

"We didn't take any pictures together. I had his photo and mine developed and attached them together because he never returned." She smiled gleefully.

A wisp of clouds floated by. She gazed at the picture held tightly in her fingers. Her voice grew more youthful as she drifted further back in her memories.

Mịch's face was visibly flush as she traveled back further in time to recall her husband's tight embrace and her virgin body on their wedding night.

On our wedding night, I was on my period. For two nights, my husband and I could only cuddle and caress each other. Our bodies responded but we couldn't make love. But we knew this was our chance to have kids. . . . The thought made my breasts swell and ache.

After our unconsummated wedding night, eventually, my husband was scheduled to come back home for one night. The night before, I couldn't sleep, mulling over what I was going to tell my husband. On the ceiling, geckos ceaselessly chirped.

I imagined I would say, We'll probably have to fix our roof, dear. It has leaked terribly during the recent downpours. And also the pond deck. Uneven rocks there have to be moved around. I almost slipped and fell when I went to wash the vegetables.

I would tell my husband that a couple of months prior, my mother got a backache and had to go to the neighboring village for acupuncture. My father stepped on a bamboo thorn that was hidden in the mud and got a gash on his foot. Fortunately, there were some medicinal herbs in the garden. I plucked and washed them and pressed them on the wound. Now it was starting to heal. But I wouldn't tell my husband that we were running out of rice and I had to borrow some from my eldest uncle.

I didn't go to work that day but stayed at home. I swept the yard and the floor mat, I shook the pillow over and over again, I watched the front gate anxiously. Dusk finally arrived. My heart was pounding when someone's shadow in a soldier's outfit fell across the entrance to the alley. I rushed toward the man but stopped mid-step.

It was a soldier. But he was not my husband. He didn't wait to enter the house and took out a small parcel from his rucksack, handing it to me and explaining that my husband had planned to be marching with his unit nearby and thus could stay at home with me for just one night. Orders changed at the last minute and my husband was dispatched to another unit that had to depart for battle in the South.

After delivering the package, the soldier quickly left to join his unit across the river.

I saw him off at the dock during a chilling downpour, amid the vast white reed field. Suddenly, I feared that white color. The soldier got into the boat while I stood on the dock, staring as his figure disappeared. It was as if I was watching my husband leave. Who knows where the South is?

When she finished telling me the story, I asked what was inside the box.

"Here it is." Mịch looked at the box she was holding in her lap. Inside rested a hand-carved wooden soldier and a scribbled letter. "He wrote, in his spare time, and carved two wooden figurines. I keep the male soldier figurine; he kept the girl doll in his rucksack."

"Didn't you give him any keepsakes?" A handkerchief or something?" I inquired curiously.

"No, there was nothing to give." Mịch shook her head, smiling. "Our family was penniless. We only had a few areca nuts and a bottle of white wine for our wedding. He went to the battlefield, and I stayed at home farming, catching snails, and would one day raise our kids."

"You must've missed him terribly?"

"Alas, the picture of him taken when he joined the army, I had to leave it at my parents' house. I couldn't bear to hang his picture in our home. But I've always carried this box with me."

"How long had he been gone before you received his letter? Did he write you often?"

"It was wartime; it wasn't like now. He had been gone for almost four years. I had been waiting forever for his letter."

After the Tết holiday in 1970, I went to the commune for a meeting with the farming collective. As soon as he saw me, the commune Chairman exclaimed, "You have a letter from the South. Your husband's."

My heart pounded like rice being processed. The letter was tinged with gunpowder. It must've been carried through countless eruptions of fire and smoke to reach the North, to Thanh Village, now to my trembling hands. Tears streamed down my face when I read my husband's familiar handwriting:

"How have you been, darling? How are our parents? How's our brother's family? I heard that the US bombed the North, I was sitting on pins and needles, wondering if they would strike our commune. May our family, our village, our hometown be safe, and never suffer the misery of the enemy's bombs and bullets.

I miss you, our parents, and our village. In my dream, I saw you coming to the South, standing by my hammock, smiling. When I woke up there was nothing but the rustling, fluttering forest shroud in gloomy darkness.

I'm stationed in a sister province. Oh, I forgot to tell you, before going to the battlefield, I took a training course in nursing. Now I am in charge of a clinic in the liberation zone. You know, these days, my comrades and I eat only roasted corn or wild fruits gathered from the forest, saving our rations to give to patients and injured soldiers. We are starving for plain rice, yet we never have lost our will. Medication is scarce, so we have to search for herbs to use as medicinal alternatives. We clean wounds with herbal leaves, use cotton to filter coconut water as an alternative for transfusions. Medical supplies and rations are delivered from the North and from bases in the plateau. Some of the deliveries containing rice, salt, and medical supplies are covered with blood, so we have to be very frugal, saving every item. The other day, a comrade got injured in an ambush during a deployment. He was rescued by his comrades and transferred to the clinic. He had nine holes in his intestines and needed surgery. We had to put a wooden stick in his mouth so that he wouldn't bite his tongue, and we tied his arms and legs down so that he couldn't writhe in pain while we were operating on him. His eyes rolled back in his head. When the pain became unbearable, he passed out. The doctor injected a little anesthesia and continued operating before stitching him up.

He was fine then. A few days later we ran out of anesthesia and had to strap the left leg of a very young communicator down to remove shrapnel from it.

In my clinic (as in any other), we have to treat patients and do some farming to feed everyone in the area. You know, as soon as the crop is ready to harvest, the enemy sprays chemicals and all the plants are defoliated."

I held the letter's scribbled text to my chest. Returning home, I burned some incense at the family altar, praying to my parents to bless my husband and shelter him from bullets. Then I told myself that when my husband returns, I'll cook him fancy meals and make him new outfits.

That night, I turned up the oil lamp and wrote to him.

I told him only cheerful stories that wouldn't sadden him. I didn't tell him that two years after he went to fight in the South, our village was bombed. After several gloomy days, the sky was sunny. I collected all the snails I had caught the previous day and sliced a basketful of vegetables to sell in Ha market. Before it closed for the day, we heard the warning siren blare. Everyone rushed to the bunkers before the iron crows arrived.

When the sky became serene again, I took the boat down the Rạng River with other passengers going from the market back to their villages. I was devastated by the sight of the shattered homes belonging to my parents and my brother. "Mom! Dad!" I screamed, collapsing at the ruins. A strong arm held me back. It was a young soldier from the missile-assembling unit stationed at the end of our village. He visited my parents' house frequently. My body was trembling; I sat down and looked skyward.

The sky was blood red. I cried uncontrollably.

"Sister, I saw something."

The soldier handed me my husband's picture—the one taken when he first joined the army. Strangely, it remained intact.

Time was flying by.

The rain came early that year. The Rạng overran its swollen bank. Rain poured endlessly on days we devoted to planting, but I was focused on a burning sensation in my belly. One day, I arrived home and saw my husband's picture had fallen down. Washing off my mud-stained hands and feet, I grabbed some nails and secured it to the wall. Entering my room, I saw that the box my husband gave me, only God knows how, had dropped onto the floor. I was shocked to not be able to find the wooden soldier doll anywhere. I kept searching and ended up finding it in a mouse hole under my bed. A chill ran down my spine, giving me goosebumps and making my head spin. A vague terror took possession of me at that very moment.

The days of rain stopped that night. When I carried dishes to the water tank, night was falling across the treetops. From the reed field, the wind brought back the sound of a hawk. Its call was fragmented, low, and sad. If my husband had heard it, he would've said the hawk missed his lover. At that moment, when the sunset was fading from the Earth, my heart ached for him.

My feet led me to the Rạng riverbank.

A crescent moon glowed in the empty sky. The reed field was rippling in the moonlight. Each reed stretched its stem toward me.

"Mịch . . . Mịch . . . Mịch . . ."

Someone was calling. Was it my husband? Was he coming back? But the reeds were too thick and white for him to find his way through to me. I fumbled my way toward him.

"Mịch . . . Mịch . . . Mịch . . ."

My feet were frozen. Perhaps because of the rain, like on the day my husband departed. My shins grew numb. Something chilling surrounded me. In the misty, blurry curtain in front of me: my husband.

"Mịch! Don't!"

My husband's voice. It was his voice. I was going to him, to take him home. But he stopped me.

"Don't!"

The misty curtain splintered. I was jolted out of the scene by the appearance of my feet in the river water. The hawk was now quiet. The wind came in frigid waves.

I wobbled to the shore and ran to my house. That night I developed a fever.

Years slipped by with the rice I planted. It grew verdantly and the crop always came at the end of the year.

One afternoon, two men came to my house. One I knew was the commune cadre. The other was a stranger. They walked cautiously up the steps and quietly sat down on the splintered wood bench. I poured tea for them from a broken kettle while my mind was filled with countless questions. Finally, one of the two stood up and spoke.

I couldn't hear anything but the ground shaking under my feet. My fingers seemed as fragile as porcelain as I touched the cold paper. I collapsed.

Before submerging into darkness, I pondered in agony: I would never be able to make delicious meals or sew fancy clothes for my husband.

I couldn't cry anymore. A wife, after losing her husband, can never rise again. Neighbors brought me porridge but I refused to eat it. My husband had told me to wait for his return. He would fight in the South for a couple of years and then he would come back. Now his bones were buried there. I needed to visit him, console him.

Over the next three, four, five days, I grew frailer. My tears dried. I could only think, Oh God, my family is gone. If I also passed away, who would burn incense at our altars? This thought empowered me. I tried to swallow some spoonfuls of rice, waking up gradually.

But I became ill and anguished for many years. Whenever I touched his death certificate, tears filled my eyes. It said that my husband was killed on the first day of the planting season. Did he come back and call me in the reed field that night? Did he prevent me from crossing the Rạng River?

Every night, I held the wooden soldier figurine and stared at the ceiling, listening to the sound of hawks, which dredged up in me the feelings of that night when I went alone at the riverbank. I went to see healer after healer. I tried bitter and sweet medications, yet I could never sleep. I could focus only on the cries of hawks. A healer said my sickness was psychological. So I was the only one who could cure myself.

Whenever I walked to the front gate I felt broken if someone passed by with a child. My skin showed goosebumps. It was a mental sickness, wasn't it?

I sat quietly, feeling tears fall silently down my face. Mịch looked up, the sunset reflecting in her eyes, and stared at the picture.
A gust of wind blew past us.

People said my husband was killed while on duty. That's all I knew. Until later . . .

After the country was reunified, a man who came to Thanh village asked for me. He introduced himself as a soldier who had served in my husband's unit.

Burning incense and lingering for a while, the man said, "Month after month, the enemy sprayed Agent Orange across the region. Our vegetables all died. We ran out of rations and medical supplies. Our unit had eight people. Two nurses were assigned to buy medication for the patients and the men had to search for rice and salt. We traveled for five days, meandering through the enemy's checkpoints. On the sixth day, we encountered a group of South Korean soldiers from the White Horse regiment. Most of us hid in a cave beneath perilous rocks. Some others and I arrived late so we couldn't join them inside. When the enemy found the cave where our fellow soldiers were hiding, they used a loudspeaker to call for their surrender. And they counted down. From our hiding place, we held our breath. The enemy finished counting, but the creek at its entrance remained silent. So they flung a grenade into the cave and set mines to destroy the rocks above it. After the enemy left, we couldn't bring your husband and others out of the cave."

The man burst into tears.

Mịch looked at her husband's picture, her voice faded. "You promised to come home to me. Why did you break your word?"

I held her wrinkled hands, crying. "Grandma, when the pain subsided, why didn't you remarry, to have a companion as you aged?"

Mịch wiped her eyes with her shirtsleeves. "Others told me to do that. Some people even introduced me to a widower, but I resolutely rejected the idea. My husband was gentle and handsome. Where could I find a man like him?"

"Are you still missing him?"

"Yes, and I will until the day I die. I was so sorry that I was never able to cook him a fancy meal or make a beautiful outfit for him. I don't want to cry but whenever I think of him, it's impossible not to."

The sky again filled with the low, agonizing sounds of crying hawks. Oh, why are they screeching now? The crescent moon hovered above our heads while the river shimmered in the dim light. A mist started slowly to overtake us.

Mịch opened the box, gently taking out the wooden soldier, and stroking its face with her withered fingers. I imagined her eyes fifty years ago—the eyes that met the love of her life.

Straightening her stooped back, Mịch walked slowly, following the strip reeds toward the river. Winds blew like a prayer, waiving the plants like slender arms. Suddenly, the mist rose over the river as the wooden soldier plunged into its heart.

That night I lay beside Mịch. I couldn't close my eyes. It wasn't because I was sleeping in a strange house or because the old bed groaned whenever I tossed and turned. It was because the wooden soldier and the misty river kept flickering in my mind. The wall next to us creaked.

"They're termites nibbling my coffin."

It turned out that Mịch had prepared everything and was waiting for her last trip. She believed that when she entered the afterlife, she would meet her husband again, would cook for him and make new clothes for him.

An icy wind tore in through the window.

The next morning, I left her shabby house nestled in the garden to return to the newsroom. Mịch saw me off at the gate. I took a few steps and looked back. She was still standing there. My heart splintered when we made eye contact. She had the eyes of a wife who had never experienced a true wedding night and longed for it her entire life.

I held up my camera and captured the moment.

After the article was published, my colleagues told me that they were impressed with the picture of a stooped old lady, hair braided in a headband, standing in a fading field. Those eyes were indescribable. It couldn't be staged, could it?

How could one stage the eyes of a woman who spent her whole life loving a man who had lost his life to fire and bullets?

I edited some details from the article. Rickety boats no longer slid across the Rạng River after a solid bridge was built to link the two riverbanks. When I crossed the river, rain fell like a curtain. Strangely, I heard the sound of hawks again.

It was said that hawks cry in the afternoon, but I heard them before the sunrise when crossing the river. Those hawks still missed their partners, didn't they?

SPRING BUDS

NGUYỄN PHAN QUẾ MAI

Several readers were still waiting for Lan's autograph. Her hand had already grown tired, but she felt extremely happy. Lan smiled as she wrote the word *Peace* on the first page of her novel. When she handed the autographed copy to a young man with Asian facial features, she wondered if he was a Việt Kiều, a Vietnamese expat, and what he thought about her novel, especially about the American War in Việt Nam—a war that haunted her homeland though it had ended decades ago; a war that still resembled smoldering coals beneath the surface of restored peace.

"I really enjoyed your talk," a woman's voice interrupted Lan's meandering thoughts. Lan looked up and saw a kind-looking white lady smile at her gently as she placed two copies of Lan's novel on the desk and said, "My father fought in Việt Nam. I want to read everything you've written to understand why he became a completely different person upon his return."

"I hope your father has found peace of mind." Lan stood up and gave the woman a genuine hug.

After Lan autographed her novel for the last person in line, she put her pen into her handbag and tilted her head to look at the dark foliage above. She loved outdoor book events. Melbourne International Literary Festival. For the past three days, she had talked with hundreds of readers, and their love for her work moved her

NGUYỄN PHAN QUẾ MAI

deeply and made her more excited about her trip back to Việt Nam for Tết, Lunar New Year, after the book event was over. During her phone call with her husband earlier that afternoon, he said that he and their two children had bought a yellow apricot tree laden with flower buds at the Gò Vấp Flower Market for their home's Tết decoration. Very soon, she would join them in their cozy house nestled in a winding alley in Sài Gòn. Her children would rush out to welcome her back and then merrily show her the buds that were opening.

Janet walked toward her, greeted her with a bright smile, and said, "Congratulations! It was a successful event, even beyond my expectations. Are you hungry? The van is waiting for us."

"My heartfelt thanks to you and the organizers! I'm very honored to have participated in the event."

When Janet walked toward a group of international authors, Lan looked at the empty rows of seats and took a deep breath. She needed a moment of quietude to luxuriate in the fresh air and the serenity of the evening, because back in Sài Gòn, a city known for its unceasing materialistic competition, it was always crowded and stiflingly hot.

"Hi, Lan! Do you remember me?" A deep, warm voice startled her. A man in his early forties was standing in front of her. His blond hair fell across his high, broad forehead. His twinkling eyes resembled the lights of a boat. Memories from twenty years ago rushed through her mind.

"Anthony?" The name seemed to spurt from her chest and dredged up suppressed memories. For the last twenty years, she had called his name in her nightly dreams.

"My goodness! I found you at last." Anthony opened his arms and embraced her affectionately. His warm breaths traveled into her scented hair. You can recognize me because I fortunately haven't become a decrepit old man," he joked.

Lan closed her eyes and wondered where the uncontrollable emotions caused by this serendipitous rendezvous could have come from—her heart or his.

"Honey, don't cry." Anthony's soft fingers gently wiped off her tears. "You look so beautiful today. I don't want to ruin your mascara. How can a man land in Heaven if he ruins a woman's mascara?"

"You're funny!" She laughed.

How long had it been since her husband Chiến last made her laugh and cry at the same time?

"Lan, are you ready?" Janet's voice called from afar. "Everyone is waiting for you."

"Coming." She turned around and said to Anthony, a man whom she had missed and often thought about, "Anthony, it's been ages. How did you find me?"

"This afternoon, while I was reading a newspaper on my way home from a business trip, I saw your photo and the information about the book event. So I ran here, hoping to see you, of course." Then he put a piece of paper in her hand and said, "Goodbye for now! You've got to go. Call me later tonight when you can. I don't mind if you call me at midnight."

At the dinner reception, Lan was like a sleepwalker despite the lively conversations around her. She had been excited about this reception where she could get to know and talk with some literary luminaries whom she admired greatly, but somehow her excitement died and her mind was occupied with the beauty of Anthony's twinkling eyes.

After the appetizer, prawn and mayonnaise salad, she asked the waiter for the location of the restroom, stood up, and left the table. She kept the piece of paper Anthony gave her and her cell phone in her pocket. She wanted to call him and hear his voice, just to reassure herself that he was neither a gust of wind nor a dream.

St. Kilda Beach stretched vast in front of her. She took off her high heels and buried her bare feet into the soft sand, leaving behind the well-lit restaurant that looked like a huge lantern, and the conversations about literature and creative writing. In the dark night, she stood facing the ocean and listened to the murmuring sounds of the flapping waves. For thousands of years, the ocean emitted ceaseless musical notes and love songs, but humans seemed to live in a hurry and thus failed to appreciate these mellifluous sounds of love.

When she reached for the phone in her pocket, she thought about her husband, Chiến. It was 6 p.m. in Sài Gòn, and he was probably preparing dinner for their kids. Then they would clean banana leaves, soak sticky rice and mung beans in water, and marinate pork in preparation for the making of *bánh chưng* and *bánh tét*, holiday specialties, in the morning.

She would be back tomorrow afternoon and join her family in cooking a huge cauldron of *bánh chưng* in the small front yard. As usual, her kids would ask their parents to tell them stories about their childhoods; then they would fall asleep in her arms. Chiến would look at her affectionately while singing and playing the guitar.

Then, she thought about Anthony, who didn't live too far from her hotel. If she gave him a call, what would happen to her marriage? She had been married for seventeen years and sometimes her heart trembled when she came across a man whose infatuation with her stirred up indescribable emotions. But she reminded herself that she must return to her family and put her finger on Chiến's lips to reassure herself that she was his forever. She knew what she had to do, so she wouldn't go astray when men made her heart beat rambunctiously. She must take a step back and let them pass by her life like a comet, which shined for a while and immediately vanished into the dark sky.

Chiến remained a tranquil moon, a source of love and comfort for her and her children. He was a quiet and simple man but irreplaceable. He would never let himself become trapped in some lucrative business contract that stripped him of his ethics. Unlike his friends, Chiến rarely frittered time away. He would rather come home and spend time with his children, play soccer with them or teach them computer skills. Although he was an IT person, he was the only man to understand why his wife had to express her emotional pains in writing. He had taken her to the Trường Sơn Mountains and helped her stand up when she collapsed in front of the graves of unidentified soldiers. When the characters in her fiction haunted her sleep, it was he who managed the household and kept her from falling into a psychological crisis.

She asked herself how, if she loved Chiến that much, her heart could tremble as she stood on the St. Kilda beach in Melbourne, where she had spent only a few years of her youth.

Once, in her junior year in college, she agreed to cook for Huy's birthday. Huy, her classmate, asked Anthony to drive her to the grocery store. She recalled that the distance from the dormitory to the grocery store was short.

To her, Anthony was like an abstruse novel. He was born and raised in Australia, but he was fluent in Japanese, and before he attended college, he had been a globetrotter. He was confident and humorous—traits that she found quite attractive.

Her face turned red when she compared Anthony to her first boyfriend, whom she had broken up with over a year before. She regretted nothing. The end of their romance left no emotional scar because he thought she was too smart to pursue a worthless subject like creative writing. He said writing was not a career and thus she would gain nothing from it but trouble.

Instead of dialing Anthony's number, she held up the piece of paper. She had read and reread his note before sitting down for dinner. Standing on the beach and under the twinkling stars in the sky, she couldn't free herself from his words: *Lan, I have been looking for you for several years. I'm sorry for not realizing sooner how much you mean to me. Please give me a call at this number. I miss you.*

Anthony's words were like the kiss he had given her twenty years ago, when they went shopping for groceries for Huy's birthday at various Vietnamese shops in the Footscray market center. She had never laughed and talked so cheerfully in public until she went shopping with him. When Anthony helped her prepare food for the party, she watched his long, slender fingers struggle with wrapping the Vietnamese spring rolls. She had never thought she would fall in love with a Westerner.

While driving her back to her dormitory so that she could take a shower and get dressed for the party, Huy told her about Tracy, Anthony's Australian girlfriend. They were both in their senior year, finishing their degrees in Business Administration, and had been dating for more than two years. That night, she couldn't enjoy the food she had cooked. Everything tasted bitter, although Anthony sat next to her and told her stories that made her burst into laughter. The smile on Anthony's face vanished only when she asked him about his girlfriend. After a few moments of hesitation, he said Tracy was working the night shift. She was a sales assistant at a duty-free store and he hoped he would have a chance to introduce them to each other.

That night, back in her dorm room, she threw herself onto the bed without changing her clothes. Someone knocked on the door. It was Anthony. He stood in the empty hallway. She rushed to him. Her lips found his. Their first kiss was also their last.

She held up the hem of her dress as she walked closer to the ocean. The waves crawled up her feet and splashed against her knees.

"Lan, are you alright?" Janet's concerned voice echoed behind her.

She turned around and smiled gently. "I'm OK. I just really miss the waves. I used to come here to swim when I was a student."

"My goodness." Janet shook her head; the locks of her hair dangled in the wind. "Writers like you find everything inspirational. Let's eat. We don't want to let the food get cold. Then we'll take a walk together along the beach."

Lan followed Janet, letting her feet sink deep into the sand. She wished that Australians, instead of preparing seafood with mayonnaise or cream, would give her the chance to enjoy its original taste without additional spices or ingredients. In Sài Gòn, when she buried herself in her manuscript, and they had guests coming over for dinner, Chiến often bought fresh seafood and then steamed or grilled it. The aroma of cooked seafood was like an arrow piercing her heart. If she met Anthony tonight, she wouldn't be able to resist him, and Chiến's heart would be shattered if he found out about her infidelity.

The evening dragged on. It was the first time Lan found stories offered by other writers around the table tedious. During dinner, she sat quietly and kept thinking about Anthony's words. She glanced at the face of each writer around her and asked herself, who among them has committed adultery in order to find inspiration for their fiction?

Back at her hotel, Lan read Anthony's words again and placed his note next to her laptop on the desk. Was she ready to enter his life, a cryptic novel, and become a chapter in his book?

While drying her hair after a shower, the phone in her room rang. It was midnight. Who would be calling her this late? It must be her husband calling about an emergency. Maybe something had happened to her kids.

She ran to the phone and answered, "Hello!"

"I'm the receptionist. So sorry to call you this late but an Anthony Clark is waiting for you in the lobby. He said it was an emergency."

She held her breath and realized that his last name was Clark. Anthony Clark—a beautiful name. She glanced at the clean white sheet on her bed and pictured a romantic scene. Sài Gòn was too far away, and besides Anthony and herself, nobody would know what happened. She felt both excited and nervous, as though an electric charge had run through her body.

"How could you find where I am staying?" she asked and sat down on the couch. Anthony sat across from her and looked at her attentively as if he were afraid of losing her. His face hadn't changed much in the past decades, though he looked more mature and confident.

"Where there's a will, there's a way, you once told me that." Anthony smiled. "I have never waited for a phone call so desperately. Didn't you want to call me?"

"Waiting is joy. You used to say so."

Anthony laughed. "Incredible! You haven't changed a bit."

She looked at his attractive lips. After their passionate kiss twenty years ago, she had held his hand and led him into her dorm room, which had only a bookshelf and a single bed, but he whispered to her to stop. She trembled when he said he was in love with Tracy and didn't want to hurt her feelings.

He called Lan the following day and they talked for several hours in the evening. He said he had told Tracy about her, and Tracy had said it was up to him to continue or end their relationship. He had special feelings for Lan but needed to know more about the girl that came from another culture—someone born and raised on the other side of the ocean, someone who had endured unimaginable sorrows.

After two sleepless nights, she realized she couldn't date Anthony. Her student visa would expire in a few weeks. She had found a job in Sài Gòn, where her lonely mother was waiting for her. She decided not to meet Anthony again and returned to Việt Nam, carrying with her emotional scars caused by this separation.

From the other side of the table, Anthony looked at her without blinking. She returned his gaze with a smile.

"I've changed a lot. I'm married with two children. How about you?

Tracy and I got a divorce five years ago. It's a pity that we didn't have any children. But I'm doing fine. I lost contact with Huy a long time ago, so I couldn't ask him about you. I regret not having known your full name. I searched for your name on Google but millions of people have the same name, Lan."

"I also tried to look for you, with same results."

He stood up and came closer to her. Her small hand was buried inside his.

"Lan, I apologize for coming here without an advanced notice. But I was a fool to have let you go back to Việt Nam. How long are you here?"

"My last night here, actually. I have to be at the airport at 8:00 in the morning."

"Oh, so soon?" He grasped her shoulders with his strong hands and said, "Lan, we've never had time for each other. I've learned that I should never let someone or something precious go. I would never want to dishonor you and your husband, but will you please stay for a few more days? We'll go to Lorne, where I have my condo by the sea. We won't do anything that makes you feel guilty or uncomfortable. I only need you by my side. We'll cook together and take walks on the beach."

She looked at the clock on the wall behind the reception desk. Chiến already must have read bedtime stories to their kids. It was the hot and dry season in Sài Gòn. The alley leading to her house was covered in dust from new home constructions. Tall buildings quickly replaced trees in the city. An excursion with Anthony in Lorne, only a two-hour drive from Melbourne, would give her an opportunity to breathe some fresh air coming in from the tropical woods, and to swim in the ocean. The sound of the waves would ease her mind.

"Thank you for still thinking of me!" She looked deeply into Anthony's eyes. "Please wait until tomorrow morning. I need some time to think about it."

It wouldn't be difficult for her to stay a few more days because her visa was still valid for three more weeks and Janet could help her rebook her return flight. And Chiến, who was always so supportive, wouldn't question it if she told him she needed to stay a few more days to interview Australian veterans for her incipient novel.

Anthony's fingers gently weaved into hers like small waves.

"You must be exhausted. Have a good sleep, and wake up refreshed. I'll be back here at 7:30 in the morning. If you decide to go to the airport, I would be delighted to take you there. But I hope you'll accept my invitation for our getaway in Lorne." He kissed her cheek and continued, "I'm such a fool. I want to tell you I love you very much, Lan."

Lan sat in the taxi as it sped down the highway. The sky was blue and peppered with clusters of white clouds. In the winter, these white clouds floated lower and poured down heavy rains. During her college years, the downpours had drenched her and made her feel tremendously homesick.

Lan took out her cell phone and her fingers trembled as she texted, *Chiến, I love you.* Then she turned it off. In front of her, the driver was silent. It was 7 a.m.

In thirty minutes, Anthony would be at her hotel. He would be shocked to learn she had left. She would soon be at the airport for check-in. She had to return to Sài Gòn, to her family, because she knew that was where she belonged. Sài Gòn was crowded and polluted, but it was there that her hopes and inspirations bloomed.

She hoped that Chiến wouldn't be surprised when receiving her message. It had been a long time since she had last shared such amorous words. It was high time that she cultivated her marriage so that new buds of love could open into flowers.

She also hoped that Anthony would appreciate her novel, which she had left at the front desk. On the first page of her book, she wrote, *Anthony, please let the halcyon past rest. I wish you happiness.* She believed that after reading her novel, he would understand why she needed to go back to her homeland so that she could continue to write stories about her people.

She lowered the taxi's window and let the wind traverse her hair. Spring was coming. Though she was far away from home, her heart was filled with euphoria as she thought about her kids' chattering words, the melodies coming from her husband's guitar, and the aroma of boiling *bánh chưng* and *bánh tét*.

THE SMOKE CLOUD

NGUYỄN THỊ KIM HÒA

"**M**om, are you leaving?"

Little Đen rushed to the green grass on the side of the house where his mother, Năm Thúy, was squatting, burning leaves. The hill was quiet. Thin smoke rose from the fire in a single thread, streaking across the sky. The boy scurried in front of her and crouched down so that his shadow blurred into the smoke.

"Mom, did you hear me? Are you leaving?"

Năm Thúy looked up at her son. His dark skin colored his name, Đen, or Black, which could never be wiped off. He herded cows and cut corn for the expansive collective farm that stretched to a mountain village. Bare head, naked all day long, his pubescent body was wilted like a dehydrated tree and his messy hair was bleached from the sun. Wiping again and again the sweat trickling down his face and neck, Đen gazed into his mother's face.

He was waiting. Phillips was probably still in the camp in the mountain also waiting.

"Leaving or not?" Năm Thúy asked the smoke that was drifting apart into dull plumes above. Those plumes of smoke aroused memories that wouldn't dissipate into the sky but instead joined her beside the fire. Smoked-filled fragment after fragment of memories fell next to Năm Thúy on the yellow-green grass.

The memories stunk of smoke. But all the smoke looks the same when she tries to picture it. So when Năm Thúy tries to rummage through the memories in her head, she never makes it all the way home again.

Smoke was everywhere. It rose high like giant pillars connecting the earth with the sky. The pillars did not stand up straight, sometimes they twisted, sometimes they slanted, sometimes they jumped up and down with every bump of the rickshaw. Năm Thúy, just a young girl back then, leaned up from a vehicle's seat to look at the smoke.

"Mom, look at sister Năm Thúy! She's falling," her brother sitting next to her grunted.

Her mother said nothing, just raised one arm to grab Năm Thúy's shirt, and pulled her down. The rickshaw passed a neighborhood that must have been bombed or hit by artillery. The thatched roofs were shriveled due to the hot smoke.

In that same village, just a few days before, another fire had burst up, smoking like that. Walking, hopping on a bus, and walking again and then being jostled in this rickety rickshaw on the road, Năm Thúy couldn't remember how many plumes of smoke they had passed once they left their village. It was as if the smoke had been placed along their path to show them the way.

They traveled to an intersection near the airport where three Chăm towers thrust into the sky and blended in with the trunks of the surrounding trees. Năm Thúy's mother told her to stay put while she took her brother to the market across the street to buy water. The sun was hovering above the tops of the towers as the market closed up for the day. But Năm Thúy stayed at the fork in the road, dehydrated and alone.

An old woman named Mrs. Ba who was carrying trash bags found Năm Thúy and led her back and forth through the market several times, but not a single soul remained. Thúy bawled uncontrollably. Mrs. Ba was bewildered. She had no idea what to do with the child who clung desperately to her, so they both dragged themselves toward the neighborhood next to the market. Mrs. Ba had looked after her ever since.

It was then that Thúy learned what an airport was. The barbed wire that circled it reminded her of the fences in her once-burning village. Inside, a heaping pile of rubbish grew higher every day. In the burning heap, canned food, half-used rice bags, beer cans, steel mugs, and sometimes, if lucky, they would even find a watch or brand-new pair of glasses. But they had to be careful to avoid the sharp edges of the barbed wire fence. Bình, the boy who lived in a rickety hut at the end of the neighborhood, usually bent the barbed wires. His hands were stained by the familiar red of old bandages, rotten rabbit carcasses, and food scraps.

Living on the trash field near the airport, one's nose was good only for filtering out smells rather than for breathing. Children like Bình and Thúy, even after going all the way to the intersection, could still smell the trash, whether it was new or days old and reeking like hell. Although Thúy had a keen sense of smell, she could never smell the way back to her home village.

When she had to fill in for Mrs. Ba and sell something salvaged from the pile of trash, Năm Thúy often lingered in front of the market. She stood there with limbs thin as sticks and a scrawny belly until the day her cheeks became full, her waist lithe, her eyes dreamy. In those days, Bình still waited for Thúy at the top of the hill for her to finish her day's work, eventually going God knows where. Năm Thúy's mother and her little brother still hadn't returned.

From that hill, one could see the intersection where Thúy stood waiting for her mother. From up there, perhaps I will look down and see mom, Năm Thúy thought.

One day Năm Thúy walked to the top of the hill with several other girls who worked up there. Some of them cleaned rooms, another washed dishes, some waited tables. Their eyes were alluring, their waists tight, their cheeks full. Năm Thúy walked into the Starlight. Its lights lit up the entire hilltop.

It wasn't to put on a Western dress and wear high heels. It wasn't to slide on the wooden floor to music. And it wasn't to shake off the old name, Năm Thúy, to take a new one, Diễm Thúy, which sounded like the name of a celebrated dancer in Sài Gòn. It wasn't to receive dollar notes pressed into her cleavage. It was only because the Starlight was the only bar on the hilltop that kept all its windows open.

Loud music blared and the sound of high heels striking the floor echoed in the bar. But that didn't bother her. The only thing that bothered her was looking out the windows and seeing the intersection.

Only once did Diễm Thúy look out and not see the intersection, but instead, the mountain in the distance. That was when Major Thọ pressed her against the wall for what felt like ages, his hands groping underneath her dress up to her breasts and down to thighs and hips again. The dollar notes fell out of her bra and stuck in her hair when he pulled her to the floor.

"Your foster mother raised you to be a Việt Cộng, and she supplied them in the mountains for such a long time. Don't think I'm blind. If I want, I could send the MPs up there to bring them to the station anytime."

Diễm Thúy twisted and struggled on the floor, stale whispers filling her ear. Biting her lips to swallow a miserable cry, she saw the mountain through the window above her head. The mountain was not gloomy—there was no haze in the darkness. The mountain glowed with hundreds of thousands of eyes. Each eye was a light that shined on her naked, helpless body as it trembled on the floor.

"Thúy . . . please wait for me!" That pause after the first time she had held Bình's hand by the hibiscus fence was a piercing, throbbing toll. The boy who used to untangle barbed wires softly for her, the one who, rumor had it, recently had been seen holding an AK-47 and going up the mountain—why was he suddenly looking at her through a window obscured by smoke?

Major Thọ mistook the fearful tears streaming down Diễm Thúy's cheeks. He lifted his whiskered face and laughed uproariously, the stench of wine and self-gratification oozing out of him.

"Come on. I'm just saying. If you're as sweet to me as you were today. You could become the boss of this bar, honey."

"The boss of this bar" had to bite her lips and tongue while cleaning blood stains off the wooden floor where she was raped and bleeding and dancing on her own blood.

Ever since the night Diễm Thúy lay there on the floor beneath Major Thọ, she had to serve powerful figures in ornate outfits, coming from mysterious, far-off places.

"Here! I want you to meet the prettiest flower in our airport," Major Thọ had once said as flattering laughter fluttered out from behind his drooping whiskers.

Diễm Thúy was mortified when her first customer, an old bald man, laughed as he stared at her cleavage. But the next time, and the time after that, and the time after that, eventually she became familiar with the laughter and was no longer embarrassed, but simply disgusted. She was so nauseated that she wanted to vomit right in the middle of the dining table, or on one of Starlight's crisp white bedsheets.

Whenever the bald man came and dropped onto a bed, Diễm Thúy closed her eyes. Not all of the rooms in the Starlight had windows. But maybe the bright mountain eyes could gaze through the walls.

When the girls who moved to the top of the hill saw Diễm Thúy in a glamorous dress every morning, holding a handbag, sitting in

Major Thọ's jeep on the way to a coffee house, they couldn't conceal their envy and admiration.

"That slut has good karma. She's taken a step toward becoming a lady," a girl said.

But that good karma didn't bless Diễm Thúy for long. Major Thọ's wife flew straight from Sài Gòn to give her a slap on the face that left Diễm Thúy reeling as she descended from his jeep.

"Slut! How dare you sit in his vehicle?" she asked.

A crowd flocked to the Starlight only to regret having missed the moment when Major's Thọ's wife grasped Diễm Thúy's hair and dragged her indoors, slamming the door behind them.

Since the Major's wife often appeared unexpectedly, and Major Thọ sporadically came without notice, Diễm Thúy could only sleep on temporary beds, sometimes in the attic or the dimly lit wine cellar. The men also varied from those in crisp uniforms with fine cologne to those who were more rough, their sweaty skin stinking of the government-supplied Bastos cigarettes.

It was strange, but Diễm Thúy experienced only the slightest feeling of revulsion in her throat when encountering their cigarette smoke. Only once did the familiar fragrance of a young officer's hair shake her soul to its core. When she smelled it, she leaped up and grabbed the blouse she had just dropped to reveal her breasts. She stared at the client in astonishment.

"What's your name? Did you once live on a village farm? Did you lose a sister at an intersection?" Diễm Thúy couldn't help blurting out a torrent of questions.

A burning smell rose to her nostrils. She shivered when she realized what kind of smoke it was.

"Get out!"

The young client was embarrassed and confused by Diễm Thúy's yelling at him. He grabbed his pants and ran out of the wine cellar.

Dropping onto the not-yet-wrinkled bed, she shakily opened a full bottle of Johnnie Walker and poured the whisky directly into her mouth. Its acidic flavor slipped down and down, carrying with it the scent of smoke. The smoke that wafted from a thatched roof, consumed by the fire. The smoke that rose from the village their rickshaw passed through. The smoke that clung to the hair of her younger brother, who had been sitting next to her.

"No!" she screamed.

Diễm Thúy flung the Jonnie Walker bottle into the haunting, scented shadow of smoke. To hell with the skin-stripping squint of the Major's wife when she would see half the cellar smashed into ruins. After that, Diễm Thúy refused to let certain men enter her room. Sniffing their fragrance, she always searched for the scent of smoke. Some men even had to endure her endless rant about some mini pancakes sold by a kapok tree across from a thatched house.

Those mini pancakes by the kapok tree across from a thatched-roofed house rippled in Diễm Thúy's mind once when she happened to go home and see Đen squatting by Mrs. Ba, who was flipping a burning pancake. Đen's cheeks glowed and his eyes opened wide. Gazing into a molded clay pot another little face flared up into her memory. That child's face also possessed full cheeks like Đen and showed the same anxiety.

"Sister Diễm Thuý only messes things up," Đen grumbled.

Her heart racing, Diễm Thúy saw a little girl standing in a corner being punished, her arms folded. Above her, strips of white clouds floated past.

Staring into Mrs. Ba's pot of rice flour, Diễm Thúy saw puffs of white foam. Clumps and clumps of white looped in the pot: the same little piles of flour that little girl, in her memory, tossed into the pot by accident and ended up being punished as they became starker.

A slap on the hand from Mrs. Ba snapped her back to the moment.

Đen climbed up the bed to sit next to her, stroking her arm, babbling, "Did Mrs. Ba hurt you, mom?"

NGUYỄN THỊ KIM HÒA

Holding her little son gently, she sniffed the scent of his soft hair so the wistful fragrance could more vividly conjure that thatched-roof house to which she never could return.

On weekends when Đen came up the hill to see her, Diễm Thúy would show him the intersection marked with the three towers.

"When I grow up, I'll find grandma for you!"

As sweet as a tiny piece of candy, Đen had learned how to console and hug his mother while embracing the way her eyes looked longingly to the three Chăm towers.

That sweet piece of tiny candy had also learned to sit still at the ice-cream cart, waiting for his mother.

Diễm Thúy sometimes had to remain on those beds forever; and when done, she would find that the ice-cream cart had rolled elsewhere, leaving empty jars scattered behind. But Đen was still sitting where his mother told him to wait for her, chin propped up in his hands like an old man.

Diễm Thúy felt the burn of memory when she saw her son waiting for her at the corner across from the Starlight every weekend the same way that she had waited for her mother. How could she stop the Major's wife from grasping her suntanned son and scrutinizing him from brows to toes.

"Let me see. What bastard do you look like? Or are you a dead ringer of my Major!"

The Major's wife's saccharine voice would rise to a pitch when Diễm Thúy passed by, screeching like grinding teeth, making her dizzy—the same way it felt to have her hair grabbed, in great clumps, or when her cheeks were swollen by piercing sores.

Women in the bar adored little Đen's wise tongue. They loved how he crouched down, his chin cupped in his hands, waiting for his mother across the street. On weekends, they took turns walking him around the neighborhood near the Starlight when Diễm Thúy was stuck with clients.

On one weekday evening, when she went to pick her son up from the side of a theatre down the hill, she was awestruck to see a strange, blond man in a black jumpsuit. She was even more shocked to see her son riding on the man's shoulders with a great big grin.

"Are you the mother of this little angel?"

That was the first question she heard from Phillips. It came in broken Vietnamese, which was quite a surprise. She turned mute, nodding her head perpetually like a machine.

"Yes . . . yes," Diễm Thúy replied.

She nodded her head to whatever Phillips said but understood nothing, no matter how the young pilot and Đen tried to translate. One kept rattling in English, while the other offered babbled stories that sounded like riddles.

Mrs. Ba was the one who disentangled the confusion. Stirring her betel leaves, she yelled, "Ah! That Phillips. You've stayed up on the hill for a month without hearing about the incident. Fuck that American! What the hell was he doing? His parachute dangling up in the apricot tree at the end of our neighborhood. He dared not cut his parachute strings for fear that he would fall onto land mines and explode into pieces. From the apricot tree, he kept calling, 'Help! Help!' I intended to stay indoors and ignore him like everyone else in this neighborhood. Screw him! Their land mines crippled our people, so if he blew apart, I wouldn't care less. But because of this little dog." She then glanced at Đen who ran and hid behind his mom's back. "He scurried back and forth, calling 'American! American! The American is calling for help!' And the other kids in the neighborhood started yelling. I had no choice but to knock on the door of the village chief. The American was untangled. I thought you knew about it."

The story had several versions, each told differently. Mrs. Ba told it with betel leaves in her mouth, sounding as if her action was something unexpected. Đen interpreted it in a humorous way, and Phillips described it to Diễm Thúy as the way in which he met a little angel. A little angel with sun-bleached hair. A little angel that had lucid eyes and responded to the desperate cries of a neglected body suspending in the apricot trees with his rattling babble. Fortunately, Phillips would never know what that rattling babble meant: "That American is a piggy bird!"

Once Phillips came, Đen didn't have to sit around alone all the time, because Diễm Thúy could come home every day, for a couple of hours at least. Đen was overjoyed. He ran around his mom, then held Phillips's hands to ask him to play catch and chase him around his jeep. She looked at the colossal man chortling jocundly with her smiling son.

The American man never looked at her like the other men in the Starlight, nor did he forget to press some banknotes into the Major's wife's purse to trade for some free hours with Diễm Thúy. He called her Alice, his ex-girlfriend's name across the ocean.

In the shortcut that Diễm Thúy often took home, the American rolled up his sleeves, and bent a huge hole into the barbed wire fence. Those strange, hairy arms brushed against her for a moment, reminding her of the scrawny arms that used to disentangle barbed wire for her, wipe away her tears, and endure bloody wounds to help her. Was the man with those arms still living up on the mountain? Or did he leave the region where a woman, even after she moved to the hilltop, had never forgotten how they held hands?

Phillips didn't hold Diễm Thúy's hands. But beside whirring helicopter blades, she responded to his blue, articulate eyes with an embrace, unaware of Major Thọ's dark face in the distance. She had been paying attention only to Phillips's strong hand stroking her son's head.

"Don't cry. Little angel. Phillips will be back. I promise. Soon."

Diễm Thúy took Đen from Phillips as tears streamed down his face. He had been holding Phillips's legs and crying ever since arriving at the airport and seeing the lines of backpacks and blond heads disappear one after the other into the bellies of the iron birds.

"Will Phillips come back, mom? He will come back, won't he?"

His lips were quivering, and his grip on her hand was shaking when the last helicopter took off with a rumble.

She watched as it rose into the sky, failing to answer her son. During the tempestuous whirlwinds of her life, she had failed to follow through on the promise made the first time she held someone's hands, so how would a promise to a child be any different?

Major Thọ, the day after Diễm Thúy saw Phillips off, came to the wine cellar and repeated an old promise.

"Sooner or later, I would make you the boss of the Starlight bar!"

Lying under his sagging belly, she opened her eyes in full astonishment.

"But how can you do that? You would abandon your wife?"

Moving off her body, the Major didn't grumble or become riled as he usually did. Staring at the ceiling of the wine cellar, he sighed.

Not only Major Thọ but also other men who had lain atop her couldn't hide a secret or withhold sharing some regret when they were with her. Some of them even cried. Some muttered someone's name or the name of some distant region. Their sorrow mixed with terror that woke them at midnight, sweat trickling down their bodies, leaving them freezing.

The prostitute's breasts became a receptacle for the sighs and tears of men who rushed into battle like moths into a candle's flame.

The major's wife didn't care about that battle. She was more interested in how many people entered the Starlight. The more tenuous the war became, the more military men flocked to the airport, swarming into the Starlight. Her hands were always busy hoarding profits.

She hid the cash in iron boxes under her bed. When a grenade suddenly flew in out of nowhere, leaving a big hole in the door of the Starlight, the major's wife ran to a helicopter, unable to take any possessions with her. Women in the same bar rolled the boxes down the stairs. When the iron lid fell off the boxes, banknotes flew out like rain. Major Thọ drove home from his station, his gun muzzle covered with a green banknote.

No more grenades flew into the Starlight, but the entire hill was in turmoil. The noise of whirring helicopters mixed with rumbling jeeps, footsteps, and roars from voices cascading down the streets. In the dark, as seen from the gate of the Starlight, lights poured out of the mountain like glistening, glaring rivers. The burning currents flowed into the airport, which erupted in flames and smoke.

Major Thọ drove down the hill, but then turned back to pull Diễm Thúy out of a roaring crowd and into his jeep.

"Go get the little boy, hurry up! I'll save you a seat on the C119." One of his hands held the steering wheel while the other worked the buckles on his uniform.

As the jeep raced down the hill, the silver spikes on his uniform sparkled on the side of the road. A call came in on the radio: "Tinh Long calls Phoenix. We need help. Come help."

The sound couldn't compete with the jeep, however. The voice simply blended in with the cacophony of engine, wheels, and road as it rumbled, rattled, and thundered down the hill.

Diễm Thúy raced home beneath the thundering sounds. She stuffed some of her son's clothes into a bag and tore down the mosquito net before pulling her son to the hibiscus fence.

"Diễm Thúy, won't you wait for Bình?" Mrs. Ba's voice held her back. Yes, there used to be a young man who stood at that door waiting for her. A young man who held her hands right there by the hibiscus. That young man's eyes retained a longing for her.

She had traveled a long journey. She had abandoned those longing-filled eyes as her life careened along, but the memory of holding his hand remained.

That hand was holding her from moving forward. That hand now tethered her to the gate as she looked toward the airport and its glaring lights.

Yes. She had traveled a long journey. She would not travel any-more. She would stay there, waiting.

She thought about that man who longed for her while burning leaves continued to fill the air with fragrant smoke. Đen had gone inside by the time Phillips arrived.

"Diễm Thúy, aren't you leaving?" Looking at the smoke cloud that had enveloped the mountain and the airport in the distance, Phillips asked her the same question she heard from her son a few minutes ago.

She could feel Bình's eyes searching in the smoke. Those eyes that had never looked into hers, even on the day when they first held hands beside the hibiscus hedge or the times when he went up the hill to get her as she had waited for her mother. Those eyes had never looked straight at her, but Diễm Thúy could intuitively feel the wistful, pensive affection they held.

That was the reason why she was still sitting there, dawdling in the smoke, even after Phillips had shown up out of the blue and stood in front of her amidst the ruins of war.

"I came to get you both!" The American with fading blond hair was somehow able to say in Vietnamese.

He had kept the promise he had made to the child.

Phillips tried time and again to persuade Diễm Thúy to follow him. And then Đen joined him in his enthusiasm, urging her to leave the hilltop.

She had experienced countless promises in her lifetime. The eyes of that man on the other side of the smoke cloud didn't need to lin-ger. She wanted only to fulfill the promise she had made him, not to try and connect the woman that she was now to the innocent girl that made it so long ago. In her mind, however, Bình remained the same Bình from so many years before. One shouldn't have to suffer such a feeling of indebtedness.

"Diễm Thúy, if you need to have your paperwork signed in the commune headquarters, let me do that," Phillips said.

From the other side of the smoke cloud, where Bình used to get his arms torn by barbed wires, a man rose to his feet, muttering, choking.

She didn't mean to look at him. But her eyes followed him as he walked down to the T-junction, his back stooping, his head leaning forward.

Afternoon sank in. The imposing mountains cast their shadow on his burdened shoulders. He left, carrying the afternoon's shadows, the shadows of the mountain.

Before her eyes, the smoke cloud dissipated.

In its wake, men, one after another, returned.

Yet her mother and brother never did.

AT THE BORDER

VÕ THỊ XUÂN HÀ

Raging floodwaters washed nearly everything away. The entire region became an immense lake with trees, houses, and light poles submerged in turbid water. The stink of rotten fish, dead livestock, and garbage hung over the scene.

The seasonal floods engulfed riverside villages every year, and thus young women, mostly unmarried, traveled to big cities in search of jobs. No perfume could mask the smell of stale fish and dirt that clung to their clothes.

But they couldn't afford perfume anyway. At least none except for those who became "bar girls" in big cities and returned when the work robbed them of their beauty and they were no longer desirable. Normally, these urbanized women painted their fingernails, dyed their hair, and kept a few fancy bottles of perfume in their closets. They returned to their village to live with their parents after realizing that earning money in the big city wasn't so easy and not worth the price of losing their youth. Dark spots started to appear on their skin, and their bodies lost their soft curves. If they were fortunate they would be able to get married, normally to someone who pretended to come from a good, dignified family. These women, after several years of working, had been able to save a little bit of money, and that was what the men were after. On their wedding days, the brides wore trendy wedding dresses, put on excessive perfume, and strutted in front of the village girls who wore unfashionable clothes and had mud-stained feet and calloused heels.

However, these former bar girls with blemished skin were not the most admired group in the village.

The most admired ones were those who had been born under a lucky star and had an American, European, or Taiwanese husband. Right below them were those who were married to Chinese or Korean men. Whenever their families opened huge parcels of gifts that their daughters had sent from abroad, the villagers' eyes grew wide as they stared in awe at all the foreign luxuries. They envied the parents who had such fortunate and affluent daughters. When these daughters were allowed to come back for a visit, they were viewed as exemplary women for others to emulate.

Many village girls obsessively wanted to be admired like those ex-pats. They dreamed of going to a big city where opportunities awaited them. They filled out forms at agencies that could help them find foreign husbands. The local authorities stamped the forms to verify these girls' identities, knowing that the girls weren't applying for actual jobs in the city, but for something else.

No jobs remained in the village after the flood, and hunger and poverty reigned. So the authorities didn't question the applicants— everyone needed to feed themselves and survive however they could.

Three girls packed their clothes in duffle bags and left the village.

The address of the agency they were given was located down an alley in a beach city that they had heard much about on TV but never had had a chance to visit. They were excited and anxious. The city's air pollution and traffic noise made them dizzy and nauseated.

They entered a narrow, filthy alley. At the end of the alley, they saw a huge house protected by high red-brick walls. One of the girls reached up and pressed the doorbell. Dogs barked loudly behind the gate and the girls peered in nervously. The heavy iron gate opened a crack, and a skinny man surrounded by several fierce dogs asked in a rude tone, "Who are you looking for?"

The girls handed him their folders, which contained their application forms and ID cards. The man's frigid face showed no emotion. He signaled for the girls to come in and shut the gate immediately behind them. The dogs stopped barking and lay down. Another man led the girls into the living room where they sat on a red couch and looked around, admiring the glamorous furniture and decor. Contrasting images of villagers clinging to trees and crying for help on rooftops entered their minds. They shuddered.

A few minutes later, a woman walked into the room. She was beautiful in her elegant purple dress. When she smiled, her straight, white teeth mesmerized them.

"I'm Mai Lan. Was it difficult to find this place?"

"Not really. By the way, you're so beautiful!" one girl replied.

"Thank you," she said softly and gently. "Now, let me show you the photos and personal information of the men. Then, tell me which one catches your attention the most."

The girls' faces turned red, and they looked at each other shyly.

The woman turned her head around and called loudly, "Hùng, please bring me the folders from the desk in my office." Then, she said to the girls, "Now, let me see your dossiers."

"Hùng, these girls are so cute and pretty," she said after receiving the files from Hùng.

Then, she said to the girls, "Give me a few minutes. We have to sign some paperwork, and then you are welcome to stay for lunch. In the afternoon, when you have decided on the men you want, my company will contact them. No worries! These men want to marry Vietnamese women and they are affluent, so your life will never be the same again. They'll take care of your visa-application fees and plane tickets."

A maid brought in a tray of fruit and apple juice, placed it on the table, and invited the guests to have some.

"You'll have plenty of time this afternoon to look at the files carefully," Mai Lan said.

"Choosing the right husband will secure your future, so be certain to make a wise decision. And now, follow Hùng to the steam room, and then take a shower. I've prepared some new clothes for you to wear."

The girls sat in the steam room for about half an hour. A fresh citrus fragrance aided in relieving their fatigue and headaches. Then, a maid showed them where to take their showers and handed them each an ultra-thin sheer dress but no underwear.

Walking around in the sheer dresses, the girls felt like they were dreaming. They wished everyone in their villages could see how beautiful they looked in the new clothes. They wished that they had discovered their hidden beauty much earlier, but years of working in the rice paddy had covered it with mud. They looked down at the way the fabric accentuated their round, firm breasts and slender thighs and they smiled with satisfaction.

From inside a dark room, a man who must be the owner of the opulent mansion looked out his window and saw the alluring new recruits. He said to himself, I must have my way with the prettiest one first.

A small, squat house stood alone in a dreary forest. A few young women with a dour expression sat on the floor inside.

"Sisters, where am I?" asked the prettiest girl, who earlier had caught the attention of the lascivious man, as soon as she was pushed inside.

"Where do you think you are?" a woman asked and laughed. "Your husband's house? Did your boyfriend sell you off, or did he trick you?"

"I can't remember whom I met the other day," the pretty girl replied. "I was thrown into a room and locked inside. I don't remember anything after that." She looked around, bewildered.

Apprehension filled her at the mysterious disappearance of her two companions.

"Let me tell you then," another woman said in a hoarse voice. "This is a border area. Remote. Only gangsters, criminals, prison escapees, drug addicts, and gamblers live here. If you want to survive, listen to us. And don't ever try to commit suicide. We don't help suicidal cowards."

The young girl got up, exhausted, and walked into the bathroom. She stood staring at the drops of water spilling down from a rusted showerhead onto the cold stone floor. She sobbed as she took a shower.

The house's front door flung open. A trafficker walked in.

She cowered in fear in the shower. She craned her neck to look through the bathroom's tiny window. The ancient woods stretched into the distance endlessly.

"Where's the new girl? Come out here now!" the man shouted. "And all of you! Get ready to cross the border tomorrow to start a new life."

"Oh, God! I'm in hell," the young girl said. She covered her breasts with her hands and walked out of the bathroom, trembling with fear. She looked down at her naked feet. The human trafficker felt her breasts as if he were examining livestock. His hands were those of a headless devil. He was heartless and fearless. She cowered when his calloused, disgusting fingers groped her body.

When the man left, the women discussed among themselves how to escape. They drew a simple map.

"This place is right next to the border," one woman said. "The paths in the woods are very dangerous. If we travel along the creek, we might find a way out."

That night, three women fled. They ran down an empty path in the woods and then sprinted in different directions.

The young girl struggled to find her way out of the dark woods that night. Thorns scratched her face and body. She arrived at a large creek and began to wade across it, remembering that they had crossed it on the way to the isolated house. She felt lucky when she saw the creek, but didn't understand that it was still flood season. While it had stopped raining in the forest, the downpours continued in the higher regions upstream. The water rose rapidly, and the swirling current tugged her to the bottom of the creek where she drowned.

Three men led the two apprehended women. Their trek across fallen leaves and broken tree branches after a rain left everyone exhausted. The men's shoes and the women's slippers were stained with mud.

The men were being paid fairly well to find Vietnamese women who escaped after having been sold and smuggled across the border. The men turned the captured woman over to their boss, who sorted them into social classes and then blackmailed their families. Those who had no family were sold to brothels. The traffickers were the ones who profited the most from these women who were inveigled to cross the border for a better life.

The men were young and rough-looking. Allured by lucre, they didn't mind traipsing through perilous forests. At first, all they wanted was to earn money to ameliorate their lives, believing they were providing an honorable service—finding trafficked women and bringing them back to their families. So they deserved rewards. The police used to recognize and applaud them for their work. Of course, their boss got all the credit and the men received only humble monetary rewards from the victims' families.

Then their work changed. If one could bring back "trafficked goods," one could also export them. Exports brought in huge profits. When a single foreign man across the border was able to find a woman to marry, sometimes both husband and wife were overjoyed. When they had their first child, the couple would inform the men of the good news. Thus, the men thought they were doing humankind a great favor.

Later, everything completely changed, however. The men deceived and tricked women who were even more monetarily rapacious than they were. At first, the men didn't think they should feel guilty for trafficking these vicious, avaricious women. Maybe after they crossed the border, the women indeed would have finer lives. Holding their commissions in hand, they thought about needing no longer to spend their lives in the vast, dangerous, and mysterious forests filled with traps, wild animals, and ghostly human shadows.

Two women were rescued while floating in the flooding creek. As for the pretty girl, nobody knew whether she was lost in the woods or had died someplace where no one would know to burn a stick of incense for her.

Long, the youngest man in the group, hummed a song, *What is left inside me will one day be a curling thread of smoke in the air.*

"Bastard! Shut your filthy mouth!" the oldest man shouted. "Are you singing to the forest ghosts? I'm starving."

The older man's name was Thìn. His face was full of knife scars and whenever he went to the market, people would turn their heads to stare at his horrifying appearance.

"Let's have lunch," the second youngest man, Nhị, suggested.

The three men sat on the wet grass, unwrapped rice balls, and split them equally among themselves.

The forest was wildly beautiful. The rain had washed the dust from the leaves and they now shined bright green. Birds flitted from branch to branch. Every now and then a bee flew past the men's faces leaving a scented trail of nectar. Up above, the wind howled constantly as if a choir of forest ghosts was singing.

Suddenly, they heard a wretched moaning sound being carried on the wind.

"Something's wrong," Long said, his ears perked.

Thin dropped his rice ball when he heard the moans.

The men carried short guns and quietly approached the mouth of a deep cave. The moaning came from the very bottom, where a troop of monkeys was gathered. The monkeys jumped up and down hysterically and uttered heart-rending lamentations as if begging for the humans' help.

At that moment, Thìn could be considered neither virtuous nor evil.

"I don't know if they are humans or monkeys," he said. "Let's go down and see. We might get lucky and find ingredients for monkey bone soup."

The men climbed down along the rugged edge of the cave, grasping the branches of old trees that grew out of rock crevices. They looked like commandos. Their hands almost slipped a few times because the rocks were slick from the rain. But because they had practiced climbing to deal with situations exactly like this, they were able successfully to reach a ledge above a narrow crack in the split rock face. A small monkey was stuck inside, which was why the troop hadn't run away when they saw the men.

The crack was beyond the men's reach, and the little monkey was stuck so far inside that he could no longer squirm or groan. He looked up desperately and cried out for his mother's help. The mother sitting on the edge of the cave was despondent. She didn't hop around frantically like the other monkeys, but instead lowered her head and watched her child attentively. Her eyes were red and teary.

"Let's fix a post in the ground," Thìn suggested. "Then, throw down a rope ladder. I'll climb down, and you guys stay here to make sure the post stays stable. If we can rescue the child monkey, we can easily catch his mother and a few other monkeys."

They sat a post used for professional mountain climbing. Thìn put on a harness and went down the rope ladder.

When he came to the crack where the monkey was stuck inside, Thìn patted the monkey's head, saying, "Stop floundering around or you'll fall in deeper. If you do, I can't do a thing to help."

The monkey recognized Thìn was trying to rescue him, so he wagged his tail cheerfully. Thin stabilized himself by placing his foot on the cliff so that the rope ladder wouldn't swing back and forth. Then, he used a knife to chisel the rock. The sound of him striking the rock made the monkeys stop their groaning. The mother monkey gripped a bush that grew from the rock cavity where the men had fixed the post. She bent forward as if trying to help these strange saviors.

After chiseling for a while, Thìn was able to pull the little monkey carefully out of the narrow crack.

"If we hadn't been here in these old woods, you would've starved to death," he grumbled. "Your mother probably would've jumped down here and died with you. So even if you do end up being thrown into our pot and made into monkey stew, at least you'll be more useful than you were before."

The rope ladder was pulled up, and the troop of monkeys cheered mirthfully. The mother monkey murmured while holding her rescued child against her breast. She hugged the baby not knowing that the men didn't rescue him out of good will.

Thìn and his companions were speechless when seeing how thrilled the monkeys were. The mother monkey wasn't afraid of these ugly, filthy men but jumped toward them and rubbed her naked, stinky feet on the men's feet. She was so thrilled that she emitted a high-pitched squealing noise.

The men were stunned. When Thìn put his hand on the grip of his gun, Long grabbed it and pleaded, "Please don't . . ."

Nhị lowered his head, not wanting to witness the coming tragedy.

A breeze blew in and the men felt cleansed. It was as if they had returned to the untarnished lives they lived before becoming gangsters.

What happened next was etched in the men's memories forever. The troop of monkeys howled with joy and repeatedly bowed to their rescuers.

Long felt a stinging sensation in his nostrils.

Nhị said, regretfully, "Let's go."

When they reached the woods, the two women whom they had captured were still waiting for them. Seeing their pallid faces, Thìn was suddenly moved and asked, "Why didn't they escape? They had their chance."

Long sang, *A yellow leaf is falling on the roof of someone's house while there's no wind.*

The weird lyrics his companion sang no longer irritated Thìn.

Nhị unzipped his pants and peed on a termite mound. Then he turned back and said, "Why do we have to take these women to our boss? Why don't we take them back to their families? Even the monkey we rescued got to reunite with his mother."

The three men sat down on the grass. It was soft and wet after the rain. The trees in the woods rustled mysteriously.

In the twilight, the old forest was intensely beautiful.

THE SOUND OF A LIP LUTE BEHIND THE STONE FENCE

ĐỖ BÍCH THÚY

With some small pots and pans, rice, salt, oil, and a dog, Chúng moved into a hut he built on a farm lot given to him by a friend. When his wife, Mao, asked why he packed so much stuff, he explained that he would need to make frequent trips to the river to do some trading, which was far from their home, and thus he planned to stay occasionally at the simple structure. This was, in fact, just an excuse.

Staying away from home would mean his house would fall into disrepair and it would be ravaged by pouring rain and wind. Their goats, pigs, and cows had begun disappearing more often. The wooden gate leading to his house had not been replaced since his grandparents' time and now its latches were simply for show, as it could be easily pried open. This was neither because he was unconcerned with doing housework nor because he enjoyed staying out eating and drinking. It was only because he found his home to be suffocating, akin to a gray sky that precedes a storm.

Time seemed to move faster when he sat watching his daughter May slice vegetables for the pigs. And his son Trài was growing up very fast, now towering above the machete lying against the wall at the end of the house. Chúng had to take care of his two children for a few more years until they were fully grown and then he wouldn't need to worry about being alive or dead, rich or poor. Mao might have felt the same way about herself.

With Chúng having moved to the farm, it felt so empty in their home that Mao kept preparing an extra set of bowls and utensils for each meal. Every night, Mao would move about the house, checking the gate, putting out the fire in the stove, and tying the dog up in the horse stall before lying down beside May. May would hold her tightly and Mao always said her body was as hot as the stove.

One night May stayed up later than usual. It was partly because the house was empty—Trài took the horse to breed, her mother went to check in on the neighbor's child—but partly because from behind the stone fence the sound of a lip lute floated in the air. May had heard the instrument being played in the market once in a while. The melody seemed to follow her as she moved about the house—the quicker May walked, the faster the notes followed her. When she slowed her pace, so did the music. Now it was lingering just beyond the fence. Several times May got up and thought about walking to the gate to see who was playing it, but her legs trembled, and she had to sit back down. The melody was so distracting that she pricked her fingers again and again with the needle while embroidering a handkerchief. Eventually, she settled down and was able to ignore the sound of the lip lute, extinguish the fire, and head to her bedroom. The lip lute continued to linger until finally drifting away. The footsteps that accompanied its departure were hesitant, too.

May tossed and turned in bed. On the roof, a cat was carrying her kittens back and forth, again and again, tussling in a pile of corn. The house was desolate and the wind rushed through, irritating her ears. Closing and opening her eyes, May tried not to look at the wooden chest at the corner of the house that held a glamorous, rainbow-like dress that her mother had embroidered for May's wedding day. May had seen her mother open the chest to pull out the dress that morning. For what reason was her mother going to wear the dress? The wedding season had just passed, so nobody would be arranging marriages for their children. Where was her mother going? Was she going to the market on March 20th? If so, what could May do? Was it because her father had left for the farm? Or was it the reverse, and her father left because he knew that Mao would go to the upcoming market? May had forgotten that her father used to take rice and salt to the other side of the Nho Quế River to trade and was suddenly worried that something might have happened to him. He was not like the men in other families who built huts to tend their cattle and protect them against the monkeys that emerged from the woods to attack them. The more she mulled over it, the more confused she became. She was unsettled but couldn't articulate why. In the attic, moisture was falling to the floor, mimicking the sound of rain.

Winter came late that year, arriving with bone-chilling temperatures. The frosty weather would last a long time, until March or April. And even once the sun rose again, it would still be cold. By January, the cherry blossoms had already bloomed, which was an ominous sign. The Duanwu festival this year would be sad. It was still far off and a capricious God could mean that people would suffer if the harvest was less abundant. The soil had become less and less fertile. On some farms, rocks rose to the surface of the dirt that held seeds awaiting germination. Fertilizer soon would nurture that soil.

The dog was moaning outside, thumping his tail against the dirt. Chúng had returned.

Mao had come home a little earlier and scurried to open the gate, greeting him: "Why are you home so early? Why didn't you wait for the sun to rise? It's cold and foggy now."

"Yeah," he said in a husky voice. "That's what I had been planning to do. But some people from Xín Cái asked to share a boat with me, so we went together. Anything new?"

"No. But some bars in the horse stable broke. So if you can stay home a little longer and please fix them."

"Alright. I'll fix them shortly."

Everything in the home and horse stable was old. Long ago, even before his son was born, Chúng's father built the ironwood house. Decades had elapsed, Chúng couldn't remember how many. The house was now in need of renovation. But it was still quite durable, wasn't it?

The sun was bright and Chúng wandered around the house and scrutinized the stable before fetching a saw to fix it. Mao followed him to see if she could lend a hand. Chúng worked while talking with her.

"You know, spring is coming late this year, and people will flock to the market on the 27th. I wonder if you want to brew some corn wine to sell there," he said.

"There is still a lot of corn wine available. Before New Year, Sùng asked me to make several jars for his son's wedding and his relatives also contributed a lot so there is still plenty leftover."

"So, how about packing it on our horse and taking it to the market to sell?"

Mao sensed something strange in his voice. Homemade wine was always the best, and the older the better. And between now and the start of the next year, there would be several occasions that necessitated it, so why did he want her to sell it at the market? Everyone knew that selling wine in the market on the twenty-seventh brought in no profit because people sat around drinking together. The customers often would get so tipsy that they would forget to pay or just offer whatever pennies they had left in their pockets, which sometimes weren't even enough for a bag of salt. The New Year was usually on the twenty-seventh, but by the twenty-first or twenty-second, a few people already were coming to the market with wine. People who toiled on their farms growing corn and beans and tending pigs and chickens had barely any leisure time. Without kids to wrangle, people spent their free time during the New Year drinking together. Men forgot about their knives and bows, women their laundry baskets and kitchens. No one could blame them for drinking out of restlessness. She looked at him for a while, but he was concentrating on his work, paying no attention to her, and she probably hadn't given his comments much thought.

Unspeakable circumstances put a wedge between Chúng and his wife. They all centered on a woman who would soon come and then leave again before the New Year. It would have been fine if she had left forever the last time, but they knew she would be back.

She arrived a month before New Year. May and her mother were making a traditional sticky rice cake when Hoa arrived. May recognized her as soon as she opened the gate. Hoa stood still, staring at May as if she didn't know who May was.

May turned back to run indoors, leaving Hoa to drag her bulky bags in behind her. May was enraged, her knees shivered. It was as if a foul wind had blown into the house that would bring everyone trouble. Nothing would be left unscathed. Why did Hoa come back? Why wouldn't she disappear for good? May and her brother had already forgotten the old days, why did they now have to remember them again?

Hoa entered the house, nodding to Chúng who was sitting at the table drinking tea. He looked at her, saying, "Ah! Home again!"

"Yes," Hoa muttered, lowering her head, her fingers fidgeting with the straps of the bags in front of her.

"Why are you back?" Chúng asked in a way that suggested it wasn't a question.

"I came home to check in on everyone, to see how you are."

"How are we? We are all fine. We adults are getting older and the kids have grown up," Chúng said as if talking to no one. He called for May and Trài.

Only Trài came while May remained outside, pretending not to hear her father.

Mao went out to carry wet logs in from the horse stable to hang over the stove and yelled in May's ear, "You shouldn't behave like that, dear. Hoa is not a stranger. She hasn't been home for a while, but how could you forget her so quickly?"

"I haven't forgotten anything, mom," May said. "Anything. Not even the buffalo she took."

"Well, it is water under the bridge. We remember only what we want to. We need to forget the unpleasant things. When the rain troubles a stream, the water just flows away. So it is with people."

Despite what her mother said, May couldn't force herself to forget. She ran inside then outside, taking all the wet logs from the horse stable into the kitchen and hanging them behind the stove. A log dropped into a boiling washing bucket. Who cares? Sweat streamed down May's face. Her clothes were muddy. On her last trip into the kitchen, Trài stopped her at the door and looked her up and down.

"Are you a four-year-old kid?" he asked.

May pursed her lips. Trài should've outgrown such comments. How dare he talk to her like that! May pushed him away, picked up the log that fell into the washing, and stirred the bucket vigorously, making a mess.

May's mother had been married to her father for more than twenty years. Everyone in the region admired her mother, for her beauty and kindness. Girls up and down this village could never surpass her embroidery and weaving skills. In the entire region, only Chúng could afford the silver, rice, and wine that Mao's family requested as a bridal price, after which Mao followed Chúng to join his family. Before their wedding day, the restless clomping of a horse behind the stone fence disturbed Mao and left her sleepless. When dawn arrived, the horse left, and soon the sound of a lip lute arose from the mountain cliff. Its music resonated across great distances. Mao sat up and stared through her tiny window at the misty, opaque sky. Fog fell on the front yard and garden, blurring the short distance from the house to the pond. The sound of the lip lute from afar seemed to her like approaching arrows penetrating thick layers of fog. The notes were melancholic, whining. Mao sobbed quietly. Ever since then she could never bear to hear a lip lute if alone.

One year, two years, three years after her wedding, Mao still hadn't gotten pregnant. During that time, her in-laws searched everywhere for good doctors who could help her conceive, but after a while, they gave up. They loved their daughter-in-law so much that they couldn't tell their son to seek a new wife, especially because Chúng was the youngest man in their clan. Eventually, one after the other, her parents-in-law passed away.

When alone, Mao tried to persuade Chúng, time and again, to return to her family so that Chúng could marry another woman and have a child. But Chúng declined. Chúng knew that he could easily find another woman to replace her, but he needed to keep Mao the way he kept the gate of his house. Every time he left home to run errands, Chúng would quicken his pace to get back home, fearing that she would be sad if left alone for too long, and with only half a blanket would be too cold to sleep at night.

One year, each family in the hamlet had to send someone to help carry rocks and dirt to build a new road to Thượng Sơn. Everyday Mao would wake up early to make Chúng a fine breakfast of sticky rice and grilled chicken and pack him a lunch. As the road stretched further and further along, Chúng had to stay at the worksite and take rice with him to the construction site for the collective meals they ate. He would return home once in a while and console Mao, encouraging her to wait just a little longer before he could come back to her for good. The road was almost finished.

But he didn't return until the dry season. Without Chúng, the house felt empty. But Chúng didn't return alone. He was joined by a worker from his construction team. She was a young girl, a few years younger than Mao, hailing from the plains.

Mao quietly moved her things to the third bedroom. She had cleaned the room very often, but no one had stayed there for a long time so it was empty.

When Mao lifted her chest and headed to the door, Chúng stopped her. Mao stared straight into his eyes. Chúng couldn't stand that look, so he had to step aside and let Mao go. That night Chúng sat peeling banana trunks by the stove, not going to bed until very late. After cleaning the house, Mao didn't go to bed either but stayed up to slice vegetables for the pigs. They both sat in silence, listening to the sound of the chopping knife. Mao rose to her feet to pour the vegetables into the washing bin before stooping over to add more logs to the stove. Chúng pulled Mao's lapel, asking her to sit down with him, and they just sat there, side by side, saying nothing. Chúng whittled the handle of a knife, cutting into his fingers until they bled and he had to put them into his mouth. He didn't know how to begin the story. Mao was staring at the stove, her face blushed by the light from the fire. Suddenly, Chúng became scared of Mao. If she yelled at him, he would feel much better.

After that, the three of them lived together under one roof. They slept separately on three beds in three different rooms. They barely talked to one another. Mao stayed in the kitchen, Hoa took the living room, and Chúng worked in the garden. They sat together only at meals. Every night, the creak of their beds was the only sound to break the silence. Whether they woke up late or early, their eyes were dark with sadness. What miserable lives they were living! What if they all fell ill one day? One night, Chúng sat up, walked to the second bedroom, and reached for the door handle to find it tightly latched from within. Chúng remained there for a while before coughing lightly, but the door remained shut without any sign of someone waking over to open it. Just then, inside the third bedroom, came a sob. It was the sob of a woman burying her face in the pillow because she knew the door to his room was left ajar.

It was cold that night, but sweat covered Chúng's face.

After May was born, Hoa stayed, which was not what Chúng had told Mao would happen. But Hoa didn't know how to farm, plant beans, or stoke a fire. When May was two months old, Hoa left May to Mao and went into town to start a fabric store, rarely coming home.

May was as frail as a kitten. From early morning to late evening, Mao carried her on her back. Oftentimes, May sucked Mao's nipples, biting them until they bled. When May turned two, still unable to crawl over the doorstep, Hoa gave birth to Trài, who replaced May's place on Mao's back and took the role of biting her nipples.

Hoa came home less and less often, and never for long enough even to have a family dinner. But she always brought May and Trài a huge bag of candies, shoes, and clothes. But after she left, May and Trài would throw all candies into the horse stall, and they never wore the new clothes, preferring the ones Mao wove for them.

When May was about to turn eleven, and Trài nine. Hoa visited for what she said would be her last time, vowing never to return. Chúng and Mao didn't believe that promise, however. That night, she stayed for dinner and slept with the family. Chúng had gone hunting so only Mao, May, and Trài were home. That night May and Trài went to bed early and the next morning when they woke up, Hoa was gone. Mao said only that Hoa woke up early and left. That same night, the family's only buffalo disappeared. Someone untied it and took it. Without that buffalo, the family would have to plow the field by hand. At noon, when Chúng returned from his hunting trip, May gripped his leg and told him that Hoa had come and they lost their buffalo. Neither Chúng nor Mao said anything. Chúng simply spent several sleepless nights drinking on the patio beside the dogs.

To plant that year's crop, and the crop after that, Mao and Chúng had to plow the field by hand. Mao's palms developed calluses as thick as the stable's burnt candlewicks. Every night, she would stroke the backs of May and Trài until they both fell into a deep sleep.

Eventually, Hoa had been gone for so many years that everyone in the family began to wonder if she actually was gone for good. Sometimes Chúng went into town but never saw Hoa selling fabric in the store anymore. And while Hoa was away May and Trài had grown into adults. Then all of a sudden, Hoa returned. Had she traveled the entire world, but unable to find a place to rest, come back?

Hoa brought havoc to their peaceful cocoon. Chúng didn't remember anything Hoa had said, and he refused to even listen to her. Only when she asked to take May and Trài down to the plain to visit their relatives did Chúng yell at her. His house wasn't a deserted guava garden to be used by whoever came and went.

It was difficult to talk to him. After that night, Chúng recognized how old and hollow Mao's eyes had become. Her hands held the stable's manger, trembling. He was waiting for her to say something. But she remained quiet, concentrating on her work without lifting her face.

Mao avoided his gaze while he avoided Hoa's. Hoa was still as pretty as a blooming flower on a balmy day. She was only a few years younger than Mao but looked like her daughter. Hoa looked at Chúng, with impassioned eyes. When she rolled up her pants to wash her feet, she exposed her calves. Suppler than May's, Chúng tried to block the strange ideas that were spilling into his mind. Hoa slept in the second room again without an invitation. Ever since Hoa had left, Chúng had begun sleeping there. Mao was used to sharing a room with the children where she shared the bed with them.

He drank alone again. His back was cold. Behind him, the second room remained ajar. In front of him, the kerosene lamp burned low, its flame smelling like burning wax.

May avoided speaking to her biological mother. May told her father that Hoa was like a stray animal that had lost her family and would leave again whenever the mood struck. Trài was different. He talked with Hoa, which led to May becoming hostile with him. The siblings stopped speaking to each other. When looking at Mao's hands, May pictured dry tree branches and thought her calluses resembled burnt logs.

Only when Hoa lifted her bag in preparation to leave did May look straight into her eyes. It was the first time she had done so since Hoa arrived, and it sent a shiver down her spine, a jolt to her heart. Those eyes, the ones Mao always said looked like May's, were swollen and blood red, and her cheeks were deathly pale. But May stayed silent as if her lips had been glued shut.

May couldn't look at those eyes any longer. Then Hoa left, disappearing into the dry cornfield that awaited harvesting. May sprinted out of the house toward the stream that flowed deep into the woods. Mao was doing laundry there, hanging wet clothes on the huge rocks on the bank. May rushed to her, crying, "Left. . . . She left, mom! Hoa . . ."

Mao held May's shoulders. The cold stream slapped onto the rocky shore, splashing their dresses. Mao sighed softly.

May had already met her future husband. One night when she was sitting inside, the sound of the lip lute kept calling and calling. It took all her courage to walk to the gate. The man who played it, Chử, came from Thượng Sơn. He was very young, only one or two years older than May but she was only as tall as his shoulders. Under the moonlight, May couldn't see his face clearly, but could still sense his fiery eyes that made her body burn. That very first night, May lingered only for a moment before rushing back inside the house. May feared that she would fall if she lingered any longer. Gradually as her fear subsided, May stayed longer and longer. Some nights she stayed until her shawl was soaked with dew. Now May had accepted to go with him to the market on the 27th.

The next morning, Chử would be waiting for her at the intersection a ways from the entrance to the market. It would still be dark when he got there. May couldn't sleep the entire night. She went to bed late and lay waiting, but the roosters never seemed to start their crowing. She lied to Mao and said that Ly had asked her to go to her house to bake cakes. Mao didn't say anything, telling May not to forget to greet the elders properly and go to bed before them as she did at home.

When morning arrived, May took the horse out of the stable. The horse seemed to understand May, gently letting her put a saddle on its back. May shivered, fearing that some acquaintance in the village would see her and tell her parents and then May would be scolded. But what should she be afraid of? She wouldn't be alone after all.

At the market May saw three or four friends, each with a young man whom May didn't know. When they saw one another, they said nothing, walking past each other with quiet smiles. When night fell, a group of young men made a campfire in the center of the market where young people gathered, bringing with them whatever food they had prepared to share. May and her friends tethered their horses and joined the group. No one seemed to be shy anymore because everyone was equal and thus had no reason to be reserved. The glowing fire made it seem as if the girls were blushing.

The next day, March 27th, the sun rose behind the scarlet woods. Chử took May's hand and led her toward the long line of elders. Most young men stopped briefly by the line and then left for other, less crowded areas. They sat down at a liquor shop but hadn't even said anything to the seller when May blurted out: "Go, please go to another place. Hurry up!"

She pulled Chử up to run as if they were being chased. May had seen, without question, her mother wearing that splendid rainbow dress. Mao was sitting behind the jar of wine. Her face was red. And that unknown person standing next to her? Was he a friend of hers? Was he the one who stopped playing the lip lute once she got married? May dragged Chử away as he stared at her speechless. Chử lived alone with his father once his mother had passed away when he was only a toddler. When he turned six, Chử learned how to play the lip lute from him. He followed his father to a farm when he turned ten. When May's friends learned of Chử, they said that May was fortunate because if she married him, she could enjoy the sound of Chử's lip lute, which was even more beautiful than his father's. And even better, May wouldn't have to flatter or praise Chử's mother.

May went home very late that night. When she arrived, Mao was drying her hands over the stove and told May to wash her hands and feet in the cold water. Mao was wearing her simple home clothing but had forgotten to change her shawl, which shared a bright rainbow pattern with the dress. May sat beside her. Mao had asked May's father to go downtown with Hoa and hadn't returned yet. Hoa had, apparently, arrived the day before. Yes, Hoa had come back. Was that something to be stressed about? Why hadn't Mao said anything more?

"Mom, what is your plan?" May asked reluctantly.

"So what do you think I should do?" Mao said, looking at May before turning away, her chin on her knees, her hand stoking the stove, increasing the flames. "My dear, being the mother of someone else's kids is like being a rock under the pillar of the house."

When Mao said this, tears welled up in May's eyes. So, for the past twenty-odd years, her old mother thought of herself only as a rock and didn't consider May and Trài to be her true children? Did she want to give them back to Hoa the way people returned horses to someone they had borrowed them from? Did she still want to be, at her age, a rock under someone else's house? May pulled up a chair and sat closer to her mother, struggling to say something appropriate despite her broken heart.

It was late but her father wasn't home yet. The region's streets had been much improved so it took only half a day to make a round trip to the market. Why was he so late? Without saying anything to each other, both May and Mao stayed awake waiting until the fire died down, and then finally went to bed. As soon as they closed their eyes, May heard the sound of the lip lute floating in the air, just behind the gate, not near the edge of the house as before. May intended to ignore it. She had just seen Chử after all and the smell of his hair still lingered. She was tired too. But the music kept calling and calling. It sounded strange, longer, darker, and more hesitant when flowing over the stone edge like a running stream. Although May had listened to the lip lute countless times, her heart was still pounding. Suddenly, Mao moved from beneath the blanket. Perhaps she forgot to tie the dogs to the horse stable. When she opened the door, May followed her. She should go ask Chử to go home. Go home to rest for tomorrow's work.

May ran to the front yard, her head hitting the hanging string where beans were being dried. She only wanted to zip out and back so her mother wouldn't notice. But when she walked to the yard, May came to a dead stop. In front of May, only two steps from her, her mother was standing with her back turned, her head lowered, her shawl slipping off her shoulders, her hands gripping the wooden gate as she spoke to someone. Who?

May grasped the trunk of a nearby pear tree, holding her breath. The weekend moonlight was so soft. A cold wind blew in from the mountain, the old pear leaves were falling with a soft rustling noise as they landed on the stone fence.

UNDER THE BLOOMING GẠO TREE

TỊNH BẢO

S ince the day Mrs. Ba received the news that her daughter would be released from prison early on account of good behavior, she had to walk faster in public to avoid people's inquisitive eyes. She didn't blame them, as country people were simple and sincere, caring and nosy by nature. They tended to exaggerate things to an extreme, though they meant to do her no harm and didn't realize their words cut deeper than knives.

For the last two weeks, the news had become a hot topic of conversation in the village. Housewives holding their babies in their arms chattered about it in coffee shops. Middle-aged men brought it up while drinking and chewing on a guava after a day of hard labor at one of the village's many construction sites. Female merchants in the marketplace gossiped about it when they weren't busy with customers. Even schoolchildren talked about it while playing marbles under the old *gạo* tree. Discussing the news was part of the villagers' daily routines. Some people talked about it derisively, some showed sympathy, some were skeptical, and some made up stories about Mrs. Ba's daughter, even though her life had nothing to do with them.

Mrs. Ba slowly wiped the dust from the altar with a cloth. Crow's feet circled her eyes, caused by her love for her daughter and all the emotional pains she had endured. Every now and then she gazed at the large yellow streaks and stains on the ceiling. She put gladioli in vases, looked at the photo of a man in his fifties on the altar, and sighed.

"It has been eight years. I'm not sure if our daughter is ready to accept all the changes out here when she sees me again, and if she'll be able to deal with all our neighbors' vitriolic words and society's vicious discrimination. I'm very worried. Whenever I visited her in the prison, my heart ached. She was skinny and kept a vacant look hung on her face. The warden once told me that she had nightmares almost every night and lost her appetite. She was genuinely contrite for what she had done but still had to pay such a hard price!" the old woman said to the man in the photo, her voice quivering.

She quietly looked at the spotless altar and the burning incense and continued, "Life is never fair. Loan sharks and murderers are not punished for their crimes, while my kind, good-natured daughter had to spend her most beautiful years in jail for an act of self-defense. It's ironic."

Mrs. Ba sat down on a chair, picked up a cloth, and cleaned the table. She rearranged the cups and saucers, and then placed a hot teapot into a coconut shell to keep it warm. She looked at her wrinkled hands covered in age spots and recalled the first time she visited her daughter in jail. She had begged her husband to go with her but he refused, saying that he had no such daughter who would dare disgrace the family. She was furious, but when she looked at him, she realized that even she, his wife, and their daughter meant nothing to him. To him, acknowledging his own mistakes would equate with a loss of authority and manhood, and he expected his wife and daughter to dutifully assume their roles. She was reminded of the fact that he never wanted a daughter. Before that first visit, she stopped at the market to buy some mangosteens and took the bus to the prison. Mrs. Ba held her daughter's tiny hands in the visiting room and sobbed. Her daughter choked out the words, "Mom, I'm so sorry," when Mrs. Ba was about to stand up and leave.

The chickens in the yard squawked and clucked endlessly and the cacophony interrupted her thinking. The chickens gathered around a bunch of vegetables she had left outside. She quickly stood up and waved a broom to shoo them away.

Mrs. Ba then walked out to the veranda and sat down to pick dead leaves from the bunch of vegetables and put the ripe ones into an old basket. A mother hen cooed to call her chicks after she had found some grain left from their breakfast by a hedge of hibiscus. The old woman looked at the chickens and her eyes became blurry. All she had ever wished for was a harmonious family, a humble life, a kind and hardworking husband, and a simple house. To her, that was felicity. Unfortunately, her married life had drowned her in tears. She smiled bitterly and blamed herself for being gullible—for believing her husband's ingratiating words when they were in love. After their wedding, her dreams were shattered and everything turned upside down. She became responsible for her husband's debts, even though she had no idea where, exactly, he spent his nights gambling.

She went into labor on a stormy, wind-filled day. The torrential rain made the roads treacherous, green leaves fluttered everywhere, and dead trees fell across streets. While she was taking her struggling steps to the clinic, he was busy playing cards. Not once had he visited her in her maternity room, but she hoped that seeing their firstborn would change his way of life. Three days later she was discharged and walked to their house holding their newborn in her arms. He was sitting in the living room with a bottle of wine in hand. Upon seeing her, he pointed his finger at her and scolded, "Worthless woman! Don't you know how to give birth to a boy? I told you I wanted a son. Don't you understand? Your daughter will end up miserable like you."

"It's your child, no matter if it's a boy or a girl," she blurted out.

Before she finished her sentence, he slammed the bottle of wine on the floor. Pieces of shattered glass scattered all over the floor. From the kitchen, Mrs. Ba's mother heard the quarrel and rushed into the living room. He glared at and berated his mother-in-law, "It's none of your business. You don't need to tell me how to *teach* my wife."

The scene was not unfamiliar to Mrs. Ba's mother, a traditional country woman who dared not challenge patriarchy and always put her own husband above all else. She said nothing and quietly took the baby into the kitchen. The insolent son-in-law was so inebriated that he soon fell asleep on the floor and snored like a freight train.

Mrs. Ba joined her mother in the kitchen, looked at her newborn in her mother's arms, and realized that her feelings for her husband were dead.

She remained patient until the day her daughter received a college acceptance letter. On that same day, two tattooed gangsters smashed open the gate of their home and stormed inside. They pinned her husband down on the floor, beat him, and broke everything in their home. The turmoil was terrifying. She was powerless, and out of desperation, she knelt down to beg them to forgive her husband. She wasn't paying attention to her daughter who had snuck away and returned carrying an iron bar.

Mrs. Ba's outdated cell phone, which could only make and receive calls, rang in her pocket. The repetitive ringtone snapped her attention to the present. She quickly wiped away her tears and answered.

"You forgot the chicken you bought here. I've de-feathered and cleaned it for you. I looked around for you but you were gone," a middle-aged woman from the market said cheerfully over the phone.

"My gosh! I forgot. I saw some gladioli in Mrs. Như's shop next to yours and went to buy them, and completely forgot the chicken. Let me run there and get it," Mrs. Ba said in a hurry.

"Okay! Hurry up because I'm about to go home."

"Definitely, definitely. I'll be there shortly. My daughter loves boiled chicken, and I must cook it for her."

"How could you forget it, then? How about this? Let me ask my son to take the chicken to you."

"No need to. I have to go back to the market to buy some herbs, anyway. I am old and I forget things easily."

"OK, then. See you soon."

Mrs. Ba stood up quickly, used her conical hat to fan the chickens away from the gate, and locked it behind her as she left. She vanished behind the thick, green hibiscus hedge.

The motorbike repair shop at the entrance to the village was quiet. Its owner and sole mechanic was bending over to tighten screws on an old electric bicycle. He held a cigarette that had been smoked down to the butt in his lips. He grabbed it with his fingers, flicked off the ashes, inhaled one last time, and threw it into the street.

Two dark-skinned boys around nine or ten years old were walking by and jumped out of the path of the flicked cigarette butt. "Hey, don't litter!" one of them looked at the man and shouted.

He glared at the boys. Intimidated, they ran. "Forget him," one of them said. They went to the kapok tree to hear what Biên had to say about Mrs. Ba's daughter's early release from jail.

The man exhaled the smoke from his mouth and turned back and forth, looking for a tool from among the piles of stained metal items strewn across the ground. The two little boys had irritated him. He sat on the floor with his elbows on his knees and he looked outside. He lit another cigarette and took a long drag.

He recalled vague images of a skinny girl with pigtails swinging over her shoulders like fried Chinese breadsticks. The girl was shy and cowered when her peers picked on her while walking home from school. He often stood up for her, because otherwise, what would have happened to her? The girl had an oval face and often-puckered lips. She threw him a guava or a piece of candy and then ran away whenever he told her that when she grew up she would have to pay him back for his protection. Unlike other kids in the village, the girl never called him a fatherless bastard. She was fearful, like a scared hare.

The day the police stormed into her house, he was at its gate. He had been on his way to the vocational school and saw the gathered crowd. He, out of curiosity, elbowed his way through the villagers and craned his neck to see what was going on. A police officer stopped him there. About thirty minutes later, an ambulance arrived and soon drove away with a big, tall, tattooed man lying on a stretcher inside. Then, he saw Mrs. Ba's handcuffed daughter being escorted to a police car, followed by her father. Mrs. Ba insisted that she accompany her daughter but her request was denied. The crowd started to gossip noisily:

"She must be sleeping around. That's why her jealous boyfriend came to teach her a lesson."

"Such a disgrace for a girl to be beaten by her boyfriend right in her own home. She looks like a good girl, but who knows . . ."

"Don't judge her so harshly," asserted an elderly woman, in defense of the girl, but her words were drowned out immediately by slanderous remarks.

He was unable to approach her to ask what happened. When she walked by him, she looked at him as if she was pleading or trying to explain something. He desperately wanted to run toward her and defend her, as he had often done. He was five years older than her, and thanks to her untiring encouragement, he finally finished high school, at the age of twenty-three. She had given him her used textbooks and tutored him on the difficult subjects. It was she who had helped him keep from falling into a life of crime. Without her assistance, he probably would have joined a gang and become just another cursed bastard.

The cigarette he held between his fingers had burnt all the way down and nearly seared his skin. The sensation brought him back to the present. He shuddered, stood up, and wiped his oil-stained hands on his dirty pants. The waistband was so loose that it slid down his hips, revealing his underwear. He tugged the pants up while looking at the disassembled electric bicycle and frowned.

"Obsolete model. What's the use of keeping it? Fixing it all the time is costly. If Mrs. Ba had let me marry her daughter, I would've bought her a new bicycle a long time ago," the man mumbled to himself.

He reached into his cigarette pack for another smoke and was about to flick the lighter when the owner of the shop next-door stomped in. The mild stink of sweat always wafted off her fat body.

"Hey, your future wife is back now. Has your mother-in-law said anything to you yet?" the woman asked with a sneer.

The man spat onto the ground and snickered.

"Do you really think it's easy to marry Mrs. Ba's daughter? She is not a bunch of vegetables that you can buy at the market."

"Why not easy?" the woman pouted her lips, asking. "She was beautiful when she was a high school student wearing her white áo *dài* to class. Now, she is just an ex-convict; it shouldn't be difficult for you to have her. She and her mother might be overjoyed, and you might gain a real jewel."

"You're right," the man glanced at the chubby woman and scoffed. "She is an ex-convict, but she's far better than a lot of people out there who want to judge others while they themselves have all kinds of vices."

The woman pouted her lips again and plodded toward him.

"Hey, do you have money? Lend me some. If I win the lottery this afternoon, I'll pay you back."

The man remained indifferent, rubbed the grime off his hands, and put a cap on his head.

"I have no money to lend you. I'm just a mechanic trying to make ends meet. No extra money to lend you."

The woman elbowed him in his hip.

"Such a devil! Are you afraid that I won't pay you back? If I can't pay you back with cash, I'll pay with something else," she said with a wink.

"Only your husband, a drug addict, would want that. No other man would want to touch you," he deadpanned as he led his Honda 67 through the door.

"Hey, so you won't lend me money? Seriously?" the woman yelled histrionically.

"I don't even have enough money to feed myself. No money to lend you."

"Hey, we're talking. Why are you leaving?"

"I'm going to buy some supplies. Do I have to ask your permission?" the man replied before revving his engine and speeding away.

"Bastard!" mumbled the woman as she walked out in a huff.

The noon sunlight danced across the young woman's shoulders. Some of her shiny black hair had freed itself from a rubber band and was fluttering in the breeze.

She was wearing a discolored white T-shirt and held the straps of a duffle bag slung across her shoulder as she walked down the dirt road. Each footstep tossed up tiny plumes of dust.

The engine of an old Honda 67 coughed and sputtered as it sped toward her. The driver was thin, his skin dark and glistening. He was bare-chested, wearing only a pair of old, grease-stained jeans. He bent over the handlebars as he passed her.

She moved to the side of the road to wait for him to pass her before she continued ahead and covered her nose and mouth with her hand to avoid the dirt flying up in his wake.

Her shadow shrunk in front of her as she continued on a road that led between two fields filled with yellow rice plants.

The young woman stood in front of the shoulder-high hibiscus hedge and craned her neck to look for something inside the hedge.

The gate was locked. The house was quiet. Two plastic baskets, a bunch of vegetables, and a pot of uncooked rice sat on the veranda.

She inspected the house carefully, conjuring images from the past. One rainy night when she was a little girl, she and her mother had fled into a storm to escape her father's beatings. And the loan sharks of the times came to her house and humiliated her mother because her father had borrowed money from them for gambling but failed to pay them back. Or when she and her mother had to share a single boiled sweet potato because they ran out of rice. Or when she suddenly awoke at midnight and saw her mother facing the wall weeping.

Her hands gripped the duffle bag. She walked toward the *gạo* tree growing beside the iron gate.

She stared up at its flower-laden branches. The foliage and the flying clouds reflected in her eyes.

On this same date eight years ago, the sky was blue, the breeze was cool, and the *gạo* tree was blossoming. She was giddy like a child as she ran home to show her mother the acceptance letter the post office had just delivered. She shouted with excitement, "Mom, Mom!" while she was still on the dirt road. Everything was ruined when the two usurious mobsters came into their house. She could have remained quiet, cowered in fear, and let things go. She could have studied hard and eventually freed her mother from her present life and her degenerate father. If the two mobsters had only slapped him in the face as a warning and kicked him in the back. But when they attacked her mother—the woman who tried to hold onto life just for her sake, the woman who had suffered miserably at the hands of her wicked father and who had embraced her multiple times in her arms and wept long into the night—she had to defend her. The scrawny girl had no option other than to pick up an iron bar and swing it at the thugs as hard as she could.

"You're an unfilial daughter! You want to kill me, don't you? Everybody, neighbors, come and see my wicked daughter," her father bellowed in rage.

The siren of a police car that soon blared outside their home announced the death of her youth. Her eight years in jail were ones of constant psychological torment. She detested her father, although her mother advised her not to. Forgiving her father's abuse was unthinkable. It was he who robbed her of an education and ruined her future. It was he who soiled her reputation. It was he who had made her mother miserable.

In the eyes of the public, she would always be an ex-convict, a sinner, a murderer. She hated herself. Behind bars, daily nightmares ravaged her. When she looked at her hands, she saw them covered in blood. She perpetually trembled and sweat in a constant state of panic. She questioned if God was punishing her for failing to maintain filial piety.

Mrs. Ba kept reminding her daughter that she shouldn't hate her father, but the logic of that plea made no sense to her. How could her mother be so forgiving and placid although her love for him was long gone? During Mrs. Ba's last visit, she had said, "It's the way things are. Women always have stood below men. But your generation is more educated. You'll have to live for yourself. Marriage is not the only path to happiness." Looking at her dejected, emaciated mother, she told herself that nobody but she herself would determine her fate.

She heard a motorbike stop next to the gạo tree and the engine shut off.

The young woman recognized the driver of the Honda 67 as the man who had passed her on the dirt road earlier. He grinned at the middle-aged woman sitting behind him.

Mrs. Ba got off the motorbike, took out a 20,000 đồng note from the small wallet in her pocket, and handed it to him.

He waved his hand in protestation, "No, no. You don't have to pay me, Mom." The man often called Mrs. Ba "Mom." "I just happened to see you on my way home and gave you a ride."

"Let me chip in some gas money. If I hadn't met you, I would've had to take a motorbike taxi home."

The man grinned again and used his foot to ignite the motorbike.

"I'm not a motorcycle taxi driver. I'm your neighbor, Mom."

"Come back and have lunch with me today, then."

"Of course! I can't say no to your delicious food. I'd come even if you didn't invite me."

The man started the engine and zoomed away, leaving behind columns of dust. Mrs. Ba smiled and turned toward the iron gate.

"Mom, I'm home," her daughter cried out.

Mrs. Ba whipped her body around and tears immediately poured down her face. She stared at her daughter for a second and embraced her in a long, tight hug.

Mrs. Ba placed greens in a plastic basin of saltwater to soak and pulled a chicken out from a black plastic bag before washing it in the sink. She filled a pot with water and put it on a stove. Then Mrs. Ba walked outside.

The daughter held incense sticks in her hands and slowly placed them in each bowl on the altar. She bowed to each photo of the dead. When she placed an incense stick into the last bowl in front of the photo of a man in his fifties, her father, she stood motionless, staring at the photo. Her face froze.

Mrs. Ba moved closer to her daughter and gently tapped her on the shoulder.

"It's all in the past now. Let it go. Dad is no longer with us. His debts are paid."

The daughter relaxed her face, looked at her mother, and smiled.

"Listen to me, dear," Mrs. Ba continued. "Forgive him. From now on, this house will no longer be home to a degenerate gambler, and you won't ever accidentally kill another villainous loan shark. Only you and I will live here now."

Mrs. Ba caressed her daughter's hair and smiled.

"Do you remember Tuân—the guy who used to ask me if he could become my son-in-law?"

"Is he the guy that gave you a ride earlier?" The daughter smiled wistfully. "Mom, he asked you that when I was just a little girl."

"True. You were a child back then but he was not. And ever since then he's been asking me to let him marry you. He helps me a lot around the house. I'm too old to do much maintenance, after all."

"But I just got out of jail and I can't dream of getting married."

Mrs. Ba sighed and stroked her daughter's hair.

"I'm just letting you know. It's true, when we rely on good people, they may turn out to be wicked, and then we have to put up with them. I believe that Tuấn is a good man, but I respect your decision."

The daughter looked at Mrs. Ba and nodded.

A fat black cat sauntered into the kitchen and burrowed its head between her ankles. Mrs. Ba bent down, picked it up, and held it in her arms. She caressed the cat and brought it closer to her daughter, saying, "Black cat, your sister is back to play with you."

The daughter petted the cat's head and took it from her mother's arms. She looked at Mrs. Ba and both of them smiled.

Suddenly, they heard the sound of the Honda 67 at the gate and Tuân's voice: "Mom, I'm coming to help you prepare lunch."

ACKNOWLEDGMENTS

I n the pursuit of bringing the constellation of Vietnamese women literary voices to a broader audience, we stand on the shoulders of many whose unwavering support and collaboration have made this book possible. To each and every individual who has contributed to this literary endeavor, we wish to extend our deepest gratitude.

Our heartfelt appreciation goes to the authors whose stories grace the pages of this anthology. Your trust in us and the generous granting of permissions to translate your narratives have been the anchor of this project. Your stories are not just words on paper; they are bridges connecting cultures, fostering understanding, and celebrating the diversity of human experiences.

We are deeply indebted to Travis Snyder, Isabelle Thuy Pelaud, and the Diasporic Vietnamese Artists Network (DVAN) for their invaluable insights, generous guidance, and unwavering commitment to the vision of this anthology. Your passion for literature and dedication to promoting cross-cultural understanding have been instrumental in shaping this collection.

Special thanks to Paul Christiansen and Professor Huỳnh Như Phương for their aesthetic and scholarly contributions, which have added depth and context to the translated works. Your expertise has enriched the anthology and provided readers with a more profound understanding of the cultural nuances embedded in each story.

The success of this project would not have been possible without the hard work and dedication of the entire Texas Tech University Press team and the anonymous reviewers. Your generosity, talent, and professionalism have transformed this book from a vision into reality.

A special nod of appreciation to our copy editor Hubbard Savage, whose meticulous attention to detail has polished the anthology to perfection. Your dedication to linguistic precision has ensured that the essence of each story remains intact, while scintillating leaps of the imagination.

To our friends Trần Ngọc Cầm, Kiều Bích Hậu, Võ Thị Lệ Thủy, and Võ Thị Xuân Hà, who facilitated connections with the authors, your generosity and support have been invaluable.

As always, we wish to thank our beloved family members. Your love, compassion, and endless support have inspired our creative endeavors and made this book a labor of love.

CONTRIBUTORS

An Thư is the penname of Nguyễn Thị Minh Thúy. She was born in 1987 in Thanh Hóa, northern Việt Nam. Growing up in an indigent farming family, An Thư had a humble but peaceful childhood. After finishing her undergraduate studies in journalism, she took a job at the Thanh Hóa Television Station. Not a professional writer, An Thư considers literature a hobby. Thus, she writes sporadically when inspiration strikes or special circumstances demand it. She didn't know she had a talent for short fiction until 2012, when she turned twenty-five and was tasked with writing a historical article that required research. The research inspired her to write her first story, which was published in a local journal of arts and literature. Within the following year, she penned ten more stories; they were published in *Arts and Letters Magazine*, *Journal of Military Literature*, and *Tuổi Trẻ Sunday News*. The ancient grave referred to in "The Red Cushion" is the tomb of a descendent of national hero Lê Lai, located in Hoằng Hải commune, Hoằng Hóa district, Thanh Hóa province. The body is buried in an upright position in this type of grave in accordance with a traditional belief intended to bless the dead's subsequent generations.

Dạ Ngân is among Việt Nam's most famous authors writing about the American War and its aftermath. She was born as Lê Hồng Nga in 1952 in Hậu Giang, southern Việt Nam, and currently lives in Hồ Chí Minh City. Although she is technically retired, she remains an active contributor of articles and short stories to newspapers and literary magazines. Dạ Ngân is a prolific author, having published nine short-story collections, four novels, and six books of non-fiction.

Her story "Above the Woman's House" appears in *The Other Side of Heaven* (Curbstone, 1995), and "The House without a Man" in *Love after War* (Curbstone, 2003). The English version of her novel *An Insignificant Family* was published in the US in 2009. When she was a child, Dạ Ngân excelled at literature in school and found literary inspiration from the simple, natural beauty in her home garden. At the age of fourteen, she joined the Việt Minh, and when she was a soldier in the Trường Sơn Mountains, she read books by French, American, British, Chinese, and Russian authors. She started writing after the war ended, realizing how the war continues to cause severe damage to the Vietnamese people and their homeland. Thus, her fiction depicts the tragedy of the Vietnamese during and after the war. She asks herself this: Can the Vietnamese, both at home and in exile, reconcile, and why does hatred still dominate the hearts and minds of many people? The story "White Pillows" depicts the tragedy of one family caused by the cruelty of war.

Born in 1975 and raised in a mountainous area in northern Việt Nam, Đỗ Bích Thuý has emerged as a well-known writer of ethnic narratives in Việt Nam. Her first story was published in the *Tiền Phong News* in 1994. During her twenty-year career, Đỗ has published twenty books of short stories, novels, and essays. She writes compassionately about ethnic minority communities, traditional cultural values, and women and young girls in mountainous areas. The English translation of her short story "Sage on the Mountain" appears in *Wild Mustard* (Curbstone, 2017). Besides writing short fiction, Đỗ pens plays, as well as movie and television screenplays. The short story "The Sound of a Lip Lute Behind the Stone Fence" has been made into a celebrated film, *Story of Pao*, in Việt Nam; it won the Golden Kite Award at the National Film Festival in 2005.

Born in 1972, **Kiều Bích Hậu** studied at the Hà Nội University of Foreign Languages, where she won a literary award for her short story "The Legendary Beauty." She published her first short story,

"That Haunted Hill," in a newspaper for teenagers in 1984. Her works fall into the genre of magical realism and are often described as romantic, sarcastic, witty, and clever. Her style and themes have evolved over the years, due partly to her itinerant lifestyle and connections in international literary circles. Her stories span environments, regions, and borders, and the settings' vastness inspires characters who collide comfortably with contemporary life's challenges and landscapes. She has garnered several national literary awards and published fourteen collections of short stories, novels, and poetry. The English translation of her story "Waiting for the Ferry" appears in *Wild Mustard* (Curbstone, 2017), and her bilingual poetry collection, *The Unknown*, is published in Itaty (IQdB, 2020).

Nguyễn Hương Duyên is a full-time writer in Quảng Bình, a province in central Việt Nam. Born in 1977, she writes fiction that records the emotions, perspectives, and events she witnesses in her quotidian life. Nguyễn is interested in depicting female experiences and obstacles, as well as women's ability to overcome life's challenges. She believes that rural women in Việt Nam rarely have the opportunity to educate themselves about individualistic advancement and gender equality. They generally live for their husbands rather than for themselves and accept prescribed gender roles while blindly complying with social expectations. In response, her stories aim to change the disadvantaged groups' perspectives and allow them to discover their self-worth.

Nguyễn Thị Châu Giang is nationally and internationally known as an oil painter. Born in 1975 in Hà Nội, she moved to Hồ Chí Minh City with her family when she was eight years old. She graduated from the Hồ Chí Minh University of Fine Arts, and her paintings have been exhibited in the United States, the United Kingdom, Germany, Holland, Hong Kong, and Thailand. Prior to 2001, she was a prolific writer and contributed short stories to numerous magazines and newspapers in Việt Nam, and some of her stories have been translated into English and French. Since 2001, she has been devoted her time entirely to painting. Her story "Late Moon" was written while she was a sophomore in college, and has been made into a short film. Nguyễn said that she, an introvert, finds it difficult to share her emotions vocally with others. Thus, she wrote fiction to express her innermost feelings. In both her fiction and painting, she is interested in the human psychological conflicts that trouble today's society, especially the experience of women across generations. "Late Moon" and most of her art exhibitions honor the Vietnamese women around her. Regardless of their backgrounds, personalities, physical appearances, accomplishments, or failures, they are beautiful flowers that emit sweet fragrances.

Born in 1984 in the coastal city Phan Rang, **Nguyễn Thị Kim Hoà** grew up in a family of grape farmers. She graduated from the College of Foreign Trade and is currently working as a "village teacher," teaching elementary and middle school English to students at her home. She started writing in 2019, and her first story was published in the popular student magazine Áo *Trắng*. Nguyễn's audience is primarily women and children. Her writing for children is praised for its themes of innocence and imagination, while her adult fiction expresses sophisticated and fierce perspectives. She was awarded two First Prizes in two prestigious national literary contests. Her short story "The Straw Prince," awarded the First Prize in a 2013-2015 contest hosted by the Embassy of Denmark and Junior Press, has been translated into English. "The Smoke Cloud" is one of three award-winning stories set in her hometown, Phan Rang. The story chronicles a woman drifting through the nation's war-torn years. Presently, the author is exploring the fates of women in history, while continuing to create works involving children.

One of the most celebrated and prolific authors in Việt Nam, **Nguyễn Ngọc Tư** was born in 1976 in Cà Mau, Việt Nam's southernmost province. Possessing a uniquely passionate writing style,

Nguyễn describes her southern region with a mellow but fierce voice. She pays attention to the turbulent and miserable lives of people whose hearts are filled with love for their homeland. Her collection of short stories *The Endless Field* has been highly lauded, winning several awards before being made into a film. Nguyễn publishes prodigiously, and her works have been translated into Korean, English, Swedish, and German. In the United States, her story "The End of a Season of Beauty" is anthologized in *Love after War* (Curbstone 2003), and "Birds in Formation" in *Other Moons* (Columbia UP, 2020). In "The Island," she imagines the solitary, windy Trống (or Emptiness) Island where a blind man named Sáng (which ironically translates to "Bright") lives a challenged life. Even without vision to observe storms or sunshine, he can still see what seethes beneath the still surface of ocean and sky, and all sailors thus rely on his magical intuition. Yet, Sáng can never decipher the tempest in his soul as he meets "the Gift"—a prostitute sent to him as a reward for his weather forecast, which had saved a person's life.

Nguyễn Phan Quế Mai was born in 1973 in northern Việt Nam and moved to the Mekong Delta in the south at the age of six. She completed her undergraduate studies in Australia and later earned a Ph.D. in Creative Writing at Lancaster University. She is the author of the best-selling English-language novel *The Mountains Sing*, recipient of the 2020 Lannan Literary Awards Fellowship for a work of exceptional quality and for its contribution to peace and reconciliation. The novel received the Bookbrowse Best Debut Award of 2020 and was named a best book of 2020 by more than 10 media establishments, including NPR Book Concierge. Most recently, her second English novel, *Dust Child*, came out in 2023. Her eight books of poetry, fiction, and non-fiction in Vietnamese have received some of the top literary awards of Việt Nam. "Spring Buds" is the first short story she ever wrote.

Niê Thanh Mai was born in 1980 in the central highlands province of Đắk Lắk. She belongs to the Êđê ethnic minority, and her culture and homeland feature prominently in her works. "The Bitter Honey" was published in the *Arts and Letters Newspaper* in 2020, and it became popular when posted on the Sài Gòn Literature website. Niê's writing focuses on the resilience and bravery of Êđê women in spite of significant cultural and economic hardships. She has published three collections of short stories: *A Stream of the Woods, Going to the Other Side of the Mountain,* and *Tomorrow Is Shining.* The English translation of her short story "In the White Rain" is included in *Wild Mustard* (Curbstone, 2017).

Phạm Thị Ngọc Liên, born in 1952 in Hà Nội, is a well-known Vietnamese poet and short-fiction writer. In the 1980s, she worked as a singer, actress, tour guide, and piano teacher before becoming a professional writer and journalist in 1987. Phạm has published four books of poetry and four short-story collections. She has won many literary prizes; her stories and articles often appear in anthologies of contemporary Vietnamese literature, literary magazines, and newspapers in Việt Nam and abroad, including *Cosmopolitan, Esquire,* and *Shape.* The female protagonists in her short-story collection *Mysterious Women* are often unfortunate individuals with failed marriages. They love their men zealously and make sacrifices so that their husbands can be happy. The women, however, are not meek and submissive. Rather, they are dominant and often jealous. Their male lovers take advantage of their dedication to make them suffer emotionally. Pham believes that, in any dysfunctional relationship or marriage, women bear more severe consequences, and women tend to prioritize their family's happiness above everything else.

Phạm Thị Phong Điệp published her first story when she was only twelve years old and won her first literary award at age fifteen. Born in 1976 in Nam Định, she began writing when still in grade school, but her family discouraged her from writing, because they imagined a harrowing journey ahead. Yet, she demonstrated her talent and justified her choice via numerous accolades. She has published across various genres, including novels, short stories, and essays. Phạm has earned numerous prestigious literary awards, such as the Second Prize (without a First Prize awarded) in a 1996-1997 literary contest for the story "Ghost Cat," which has been translated into English and anthologized in *Wild Mustard* (Curbstone, 2017), and "Mother and Son" was named the best short story about postwar women in a literary contest organized by *Journal of Military Literature* in 2015. She has an unrivaled writing style that is terse, original, and pithy, but also rich with suppressed emotions. She is considered a feminist writer as exemplified by her acclaimed novels *Blogger* and *Station of Memories*.

Tịnh Bảo is a young, emerging author. She was born in 1983, in Kiên Giang, southern Việt Nam, and works as a full-time writer and a scriptwriter in Hồ Chí Minh City. She started her writing career rather late although her mother, an elementary school teacher, introduced her to literature at a very young age. Her fiction frequently depicts individuals trapped in unfortunate situations, surrounded by social prejudices, and vices, but it tends to have optimistic endings with attempts at healing broken relationships or bridging the gaps between social classes. "Under the Blooming *Gạo* Tree" won Fourth Prize in the 2019 fiction contest "The Other Half of the World" in Việt Nam.

Tống Ngọc Hân is best known for her fiction focusing on ethnic minority communities living in northwest Việt Nam. She was born in 1976 in the northern province of Phú Thọ, where she runs a small business today. Việt Nam has fifty-four ethnic groups, but the majority of the stories in this anthology are written by Việt (Kinh) people, a group that accounts for 87 percent of the total population. Việt Nam's ethnic minority groups typically reside in remote mountainous areas, and each has its own unique culture, customs, traditions, and spiritual practices. Tống's expertise lies in her close observations of the ethnic groups' daily lives and vernacular language, and her writing records their cultural practices and histories. Women belonging to these ethnic groups are far less privileged than their Kinh counterparts, and they are often victims of antiquated customs that deprive them of their freedoms, voices, and agency. Tống writes about them with the hope that these ethnic women will be able to pursue their happiness free of imposed constraints. In her fiction, she frequently depicts how the under-privileged minority women are often illiterate and get married at a very young age. Many are victims of domestic violence, broken marriages, human trafficking, and poverty. Her story "Raindrops on His Shoulders" exposes the outdated cultural practices of the Dao and Hmong ethnic groups, and it emphasizes the need of education to foster progressive thinking and economic development.

Trầm Hương is the pseudonym of Bùi Thị Thuỷ. Born in 1963 and growing up in Bến Tre, she worked in the Southern Women Museum for thirty years and is currently working at the Việt Nam Writers' Association in Hồ Chí Minh City. A poet, novelist, and screenwriter, she is a prolific and resilient writer. She entered the literary world only after working as an agricultural engineer. Her first story, which depicts the contradictory lives of women before and after the American War, has won a top award for short fiction. Some of her widely read works are *The Unlit Town*, *The Woman in Violet Autumn*, *The Beauty of Tây Đô*, *Mother*, *The Fairy Tales for My Kids*, and *The Sleepless Night in Sài Gòn*. Many of her novels have won prestigious national awards. Her works often embrace women who suffer misfortunes and disconsolate lives while enduring brutalities during war and in peace, but who still thrive thanks to their strengths and virtues. A few short stories she wrote have been translated into French and Japanese. The Vietnamese original of "The Haunted Garden" was printed in the collection of short stories titled *The Private Dreams* in 1998.

Trần Thanh Hà was born in 1971 in Quảng Trị and currently works as an editor in Hồ Chí Minh City. She is the author of six books and several short stories, published in such prestigious literary magazines in Việt Nam as *Journal of Military Literature* and *Cửa Việt*. Some of her stories have been translated into English. She graduated from the Huế University of Education in 1992 and started writing while teaching in Quảng Trị. Trần is a pioneer of Western-style detective fiction in Việt Nam, and her works are typically set in the nation's central region, where nature is hostile, living conditions are harsh, and lives continue to be severely affected by the American War. Her fiction often portrays postwar human tragedies, the beauty found in daily life, adolescent confusion, and aspirations for change. The story "Desolate Grassy Hill" is set in central Việt Nam of the 1980s, a few years after the end of the American War, when the country was struggling with a slowly developing economy and prevailing poverty.

Trần Thị Thắng was born in 1948 in the northern province of Phú Thọ and studied literature at Hà Nội University in the late 1960s. When she was a child, her father introduced her to French literature, while her mother ignited in her a love for Vietnamese literature, especially works by Thạch Lam, Vũ Trọng Phụng, and Ngô Tất Tố. Trần fought in the war against the Americans and almost lost her life while hospitalized for malaria when the Americans bombed her hospital in 1971. She is both a poet and a fiction writer. In 2016, she was invited to participate in a creative writing workshop at the William Joiner Institute at the University of Massachusetts in Boston. Trần's fiction often depicts the Vietnamese people's diligence and morality. "After the Storm" is based on a true-life story and narrated in a journalistic style.

Trần Thuỳ Mai was born in 1954 in Hội An and is one of her generation's most prominent feminist writers. She taught Vietnamese folklore at Huế College of Education for ten years before devoting herself to creative writing. Trần has published fourteen collections of short stories, one anthology of Vietnamese proverbs, one novel, and one long story for children. Some of her stories have been made into films and translated into English, French, Japanese, Chinese, and Swedish. In the United States, her story "The Ylang-Ylang Flower" is anthologized in *Love after War* (Curbstone, 2003). The story "Green Plum" portrays prostitution in central Việt Nam. Like many of her stories, "Green Plum" examines the emotions and aspirations of women living in a patriarchal society who frequently suffer poverty and social prejudices. Trần currently divides her time between San Francisco and Huế. Her literary work is set primarily in Việt Nam. In 2020, her historical novel, *Queen Từ Dũ*, was awarded Best Novel by the Việt Nam Writers' Association and Best Book by the Institute for Research and Education Development. "Green Plum" was first printed in a collection of short stories titled *Rain of the Afterlife* in 2005.

Trịnh Bích Ngân was born in 1960 in Cà Mau, the southernmost point in Việt Nam, and studied literature and creative writing at the Hồ Chí Minh National University of Social Sciences & Humanities and the Nguyễn Du School of Creative Writing, respectively. Her award-winning novel, *A Distorted World* (2009), focuses on a disabled veteran who lost his legs in a border war and struggles with notions of the self. Trịnh believes that authors must embark on psychological journeys to understand their characters. She cites Pavlovich Chekhov as her greatest literary influence. Regarding marital issues, Trịnh believes that Vietnamese women of her own and previous generations often accept the status quo and refuse change in their lives. Men take advantage of women's submissive, stoic, and sacrificial tendencies, which causes inequality in marriages.

Trịnh Thị Phương Trà, born in 1976 in Tuy Hòa City, inherited her appreciation for literature from her parents. Her father is a farmer whose life is attached to the fields, but he maintains a love of prewar poetry. Her first story was printed in a small journal when she was a college student. Her second story was published in *Phú* Yên's Arts and Letters Magazine when she started her career as a journalist. She has published two collections of essays, one collection of short stories, and one book of unstructured writing. She writes about women's dreams and destinies. In 2019, her short story "In the Light of Heaven," which portrays cardiologists who help resuscitate the hearts of the dying, was awarded First Prize in the short-story contest "The Worker of Today," hosted by the *Lao Động News*. "On the Rạng Riverbank" was inspired by a true love story that occurred in the aftermath of American War in Việt Nam.

Võ Diệu Thanh, an elementary art schoolteacher, began writing while still in school. Her first story won First Prize in a literary contest. Yet, she was dubious about her literary talent, gave it up to focus on teaching, and didn't write again for ten years. Võ has since published fifteen books across various genres, for both adults and children. She is currently planning to release numerous graphic novels: two written and illustrated by herself, five written by her and illustrated by another artist. She is also working on a narrative about the tumultuous life of a young Vietnamese traditional stringed-instrument virtuoso. "Boozing with a Khmer Rouge" was written while she was doing research on war and the devastating psychological effects of the fears of invasion. It portrays the bravery of women who are able to confront those fears. In the story, a warrior is not only a strong, weapon-wielding man in a uniform but also a brave and compassionate woman with a frail body.

Võ Thị Xuân Hà was a middle school math teacher before becoming a professional writer. She was born in 1959 in Thừa Thiên Huế, central Việt Nam, and now lives in Hà Nội, where she currently holds a full-time administrative position with the Việt Nam Writers' Association. Her passion for writing led her to pursue an undergraduate degree in Creative Writing at the Nguyễn Du School of Creative Writing in the early 1990s. Võ has published numerous short-story collections and four novels. "Rice and Salt" is her first story to be translated into English and anthologized in *Love after War* (Curbstone, 2003). In her writing, Võ often coveys her belief in love, but goes beyond romantic notions, stating that she is interested in Buddha's noble teachings about universal love and kindness, including the need to harm no sentient being. She also wants to ignite a passion for reading quality literature in today's society, which is plagued by a narrow-minded education system. She views literature as a way to preserve Vietnamese culture. When asked about her writing for and about women, Võ said that because she is a woman, her narrative tone tends to be feminine and that a female author must fight for women's equal rights and happiness. She does not want people to pity women for their weakness or submissiveness.

PERMISSIONS

Dạ Ngân, "White Pillows" ("Nỗi niềm gối trắng"), from *Báo Nông Nghiệp Việt Nam*, số Tết Đinh Dậu. Reprinted in Văn *mới, 2016-2017*.

An Thư, "The Red Cushion" ("Bồ đoàn đỏ"), from *Văn Nghệ Quân* Đội. Copyright © 2020 by the author.

Trần Thùy Mai, "Green Plum" ("Trái xanh"), from the short-story collection *Mưa* đời *sau*. Copyright © 2005 by the author.

Nguyễn Ngọc Tư, "The Island" ("Đảo"), from *Báo Nhân Dân hằng tháng*. Copyright © 2014 by the author.

Tống Ngọc Hân, "Raindrops on His Shoulders" ("Mưa ướt áo ai"), from *Báo Nhân Dân*, số Xuân Canh Tý. Copyright © 2020 by the author.

Nguyễn Thị Châu Giang, "Late Moon" ("Trăng muộn"), from *Báo Phụ Nữ* and *Văn Nghệ Trẻ*. Reprinted in *100 Truyện ngắn hay Việt Nam thế kỷ 20*, tập 5. Copyright © 2014 by the author.

Trịnh Bích Ngân, "The Eternal Forest" ("Cánh rừng vĩnh cửu"), from *Văn Nghệ Quân* Đội. Reprinted in the short-story collection Đường đến *cây cô* đơn. Copyright © 2014 by the author.

Kiều Bích Hậu, "Selecting a Husband" ("Chọn chồng"), from *Báo Thanh Niên*. Copyright © 2017 by the author.

Trầm Hương, "The Haunted Garden" ("Vườn ma"), from the short-story collection *Những giấc mơ riêng*. Copyright © 1998 by the author.

Trần Thanh Hà, "Desolate Grassy Hill" ("Miền cỏ hoang"), from *Văn Nghệ Quân* Đội. Reprinted in *Tuyển truyện ngắn* đoạt *giải cao, 30 năm* đổi *mới, 1986-2016*. Copyright © 1995 by the author.

Nguyễn Hương Duyên, "Longing in Vain" ("Bến đợi nhọc nhằn"), from

Printed in the USA
CPSIA information can be obtained
at www.ICGtesting.com
JSHW082314250124
55961JS00003B/83